Paperback ISBN: 978-1-0686770-0-7

With many thanks to.

Tanya

Anita

Bev

Sue

Nigel

Andy

Stuart

Andrew

I want to thank the many friends and family who have supported me along this long and winding road.

Preface

It all began with a pub crawl around London, a chance to explore the hidden gems and iconic landmarks that make the capital unique. Little did I know that this seemingly ordinary outing would inspire Timeline.

From the moment we disembarked the train at London Waterloo, our stroll along the South Bank of the Thames became an adventure for the imagination. Tower Bridge stood tall, a testament to London's grandeur and resilience. At the same time, the quaint charm of St Katherine Docks offered a serene departure from the bustling cityscape.

Savouring a delicious burger and a crisp, cold beer, our excitement grew at the thought of exploring more of London's classic pubs and their vibrant atmospheres, especially Ye Olde Cheshire Cheese, a historic inn on Fleet Street famous for its regular literary patrons, such as Charles Dickens, GK Chesterton, and Mark Twain.

We met with Stuart in the ambience of The Old Bank of England. After a few sips of beer, Stuart was enthused about the London Stock Exchange (LSE), and it struck a chord. His words vividly depicted the Exchange's significance at the centre of global commerce, supported by the Greenwich Mean Time (GMT) line. An idea began to take shape.

Reflecting on that day fills me with gratitude for the incredible moments and chance encounters that have shaped my life's journey.

Timeline isn't just a story. It is a celebration of friendship, adventure and the endless possibilities that come from chasing dreams.

May the pages transport you to a place of intrigue, excitement, and discovery. May you find as much joy in reading this book as I have writing it.

Stephen Wilde

Statement of Fictionality

In this book, all characters and events are entirely fictional, and any resemblance to actual individuals, living or deceased, is purely coincidental.

Through the narrative, I delve into the realms of imagination, where creativity knows no bounds. Every character, every twist of fate and every momentous event exists within the confines of this fictional world.

Here, I explore the human experience through the lens of invented personas, allowing you to immerse in a tapestry of fantasy without the constraints of reality.

So, as you journey through these pages, remember that nothing is implied. Every aspect is crafted for storytelling and entertainment.

1: Forwards

In Timeline, one man's audacious idea sets the stage for a seismic shift in the global power balance: moving the Greenwich Mean Timeline from London to New York City. What begins as a flicker of an idea quickly snowballs into a world-changing financial coup. This isn't just about adjusting clocks. It's about redirecting the flow of billions, transforming New York into the heartbeat of world finance and reshaping global geopolitics.

As banks, corporations, and governments scramble to align with the new time standard, the mastermind manoeuvres through a maze of political intrigue, secret deals, and dangerous enemies. But beneath the ruthless ambition lies a world he never predicted, filled with love, risk, and the threat of losing everything.

Timeline is a high-stakes thriller where power, money, and ambition collide, turning time into the ultimate weapon. Will this bold plan catapult New York to undisputed supremacy, or will it bring down everyone?

The history of the London Stock Exchange (LSE) is more than just dates and numbers. It's a saga of power, ambition, and survival. From its 17th-century roots to its modern role as a financial titan, the LSE has shaped the economic landscape of Britain and the world. What began as a modest trading hub became a global powerhouse, financing wars, weathering frauds, and surviving the chaos of markets. With its leap into digitisation, the "Big Bang" of 1986 solidified its dominance, but at its core, the Exchange's heartbeat is one of unrelenting hustle.

For London's traders, being first isn't a strategy. It's survival. Before the city stirs, they are already buried in data, eyes flickering over screens in the eerie glow of pre-dawn. The rest of the world is asleep, but not them. Every second before 8:00 a.m. GMT is a chance to seize an edge to shape markets before anyone else even wakes up. When the clock strikes eight, it's as if a starting gun fires and the LSE explodes into action. Traders are not just reacting; they are controlling the game, moving billions, and setting the tone for the day across continents.

This early window is everything. London stands at the crossroads of global finance, where Asia's day ends and New York's begins. In this brief, high-stakes moment, the decisions made on the LSE trading floor ripple across the globe, shifting currencies, reshaping markets, and influencing economies. It's a delicate dance of power where a single move can make or break fortunes.

But the cost of living on this razor's edge is steep. There's no room for hesitation, no off switch. The pressure is persistent, and the rewards are fleeting. The sacrifices made for a shot at the top are missed dinners and sleepless nights. Yet, the rush is worth every second for those who thrive. Because here, being first doesn't just mean winning. It means rewriting the game's rules.

2: The Roots of Ambition

In the sunbaked city of Lubbock, Texas, where the horizon seemed to stretch forever beneath a boundless blue sky, a young boy named Andy Steven Stuart found his universe expanding far beyond the dusty plains around him. The air in Lubbock was dry, the earth cracked, and the wind blew persistently across a seemingly endless expanse of flat land. But even in this desolate landscape, inspiration thrived. It was a town steeped in the legacy of music legends, where creativity had taken root despite the barren surroundings.

Growing up in a modest home, Andy's world was shaped by the tales of two local heroes who had transcended the borders of their small town to leave an indelible mark on the world: Buddy Holly, the rock 'n' roll pioneer who had revolutionised music in the 1950s, and Waylon Jennings, the country outlaw whose rugged voice had carved out a new path in country music. Their spirits seemed to linger in the hot Texas air as if whispering to Andy that greatness could be found even in the most unlikely places.

He was different from other kids who spent time kicking dust in the streets or chasing tumbleweeds. His curiosity was insatiable. While his friends played with their toy trucks or swung from tree branches, Andy was busy dismantling his, carefully unscrewing the parts, trying to decipher the mystery behind their mechanics. Old radios, broken appliances, and anything he could get his hands on became his playground. By the time he was ten, he could fix things that left adults scratching their heads, his tiny hands deftly navigating circuits and gears with the precision of a surgeon.

In his home, Andy's father, a hard-edged oilfield worker with calloused hands, and his mother, a gentle but no-nonsense schoolteacher, filled his world with two simple values: hard work and grit. His father's harsh, sunburned exterior masked a deep love for his family, a love expressed in long hours under the punishing Texas sun to ensure that his son had opportunities he never did. On the other hand, his mother filled their house with books and knowledge, drilling into his head that no dream was too big if he was willing to fight for it.

As Andy grew older, it became clear that he wasn't just a kid who could fix things. He was a kid with a mind that thrived on solving problems others couldn't. Science and technology became his world, and soon, his academic achievements outpaced his surroundings. While his peers were content with football games and Friday night lights, his mind was already elsewhere, envisioning a future where technology could reshape everything. His teachers marvelled at his talent, and before long, a scholarship from the prestigious Massachusetts Institute of Technology landed in his lap, offering him a one-way ticket out of Texas and into the halls of the most elite scientific institution in the world.

At MIT, surrounded by some of the brightest minds on the planet, Andy truly began to shine. The boy who once took apart radios in his parents' garage was now pushing the boundaries of artificial intelligence. These developing algorithms left even his professors in awe. His research attracted attention from tech companies long before he graduated, and it wasn't just his intellect that drew people to him. Andy had a charm about him, a way of making others believe in the impossible. His peers called him a visionary, but those closest to him could see something else simmering beneath the surface: a hunger, an ambition bordering on obsession.

When Andy finally set foot in Silicon Valley, he entered a world that seemed made for him. The towering glass buildings and the unrelenting pursuit of innovation mirrored his restless energy. He was a young man in his prime, hungry to prove himself, eager to build something lasting. And build he did. One startup after another, each more audacious than the last. He seemed to have an almost supernatural ability to predict the next big trend and investors flocked to him, throwing millions at his ventures. His name became synonymous with success.

His rise was meteoric, but as with all meteors, the question was whether he would burn out. Beneath his brilliance and drive, darker currents swirled. His perfectionism, once a strength, became an all-consuming force. Failure was unacceptable. The people around him, his employees, and his partners, learned quickly that Andy's standards were impossible to meet, and those who couldn't keep up were swiftly cut from his inner circle. He demanded loyalty and pushed his team to heights they hadn't thought possible yet his relentless pursuit of perfection left casualties in its wake.

And there was more. Behind closed doors, his charm often veered into something more predatory. Rumours spread of his treatment of women and his charm in public, masking an arrogance that bordered on cruelty. His romantic entanglements, though mainly kept out of the public eye, were the stuff of whispered conversations in the tech world, where sexism still lurked in dark corners. Those who worked closest to him knew that the brilliance came with a cost, and the people around him often bore that cost.

But for all his flaws, Andy was undeniably brilliant. His ability to foster creativity, to see possibilities where others saw dead ends, was unmatched. He separated the dreamers from the doubters, creating environments where innovation wasn't just possible. It was inevitable. His ventures in artificial intelligence revolutionised the field, and as his influence grew, so did his reputation as the man who could change the world. Yet the question remained: would his insatiable drive lead him to greater heights, or would it be the thing that caused his downfall?

Andy Stuart was a man of contradictions, an enigma wrapped in brilliance and burdened by his dark tendencies. As his empire expanded and his ambition reached even further, it became clear that his story was far from over. He was destined to make a mark on the world. The only question was, would that mark be greatness or destruction?

3: An Idea

The dictionary:

Idea. noun. a thought or suggestion as to a possible course of action.

Near Gilroy, California, the afternoon sun blazed on the perfectly manicured Eagle Ridge Golf Course greens. Heat shimmered off the landscape, casting long shadows across the fairways, where oak trees stood like sentinels against the golden backdrop of rolling hills. Andy, dressed in a crisp white polo and khaki slacks, strode purposefully alongside his business associates, the light crunch of their cleats on the grass punctuating the quiet tension of the game.

Doug Young walked at a pace behind; his usually measured steps were slower today. The ex-Silicon Valley CFO was known for his sharp mind and impeccable attention to financial detail, but now, a frown deepened on his face as his thoughts weighed heavily. He glanced at Andy repeatedly as if trying to decipher the wheels turning in his colleague's head. Despite the serene surroundings, Doug couldn't shake the tension that clung to the air like humidity before a storm. Trailing behind them was Nigel Strutt, who strolled casually, exuding a different kind of expertise one honed in the art of tax manipulation. Nigel's easy-going demeanour belied a mind constantly at work, seeking loopholes and opportunities in a system designed to be tight. He smirked as Doug casually brought up the financial losses, he had just incurred early that morning.

The third tee loomed, a daunting challenge for even the most seasoned golfer. The fairway stretched out before them, framed by hazards on both sides. To the right, a winding creek glistened in the afternoon light, ready to claim any ball that veered off course. On the left, a row of bunkers waited, eager to punish a shot that strayed too far. Beyond them, the boundary line marked the edge of the course and the point of no return for a misplaced drive.

Andy stood over his ball, the pressure of his missed putt on the earlier hole still weighing on him. It was a rare misstep for a man who prided on precision and control. His grip tightened on the driver as he visualised the perfect shot, a drive that would cut through the risks and land squarely in the middle of the fairway. His body moved in one fluid motion, the club slicing through the air with a satisfying crack. The ball arced gracefully, soaring high before landing exactly where he intended. He allowed himself a slight smile. This was the game he knew how to play.

Doug, however, needed to be more focused on the game. As they walked down the fairway, the tension radiating from him was evident. His mind wasn't on golf but on the storm brewing in his financial portfolio, which had taken a brutal hit overnight while sleeping comfortably, unaware of the sudden shift in the London Stock Exchange. His furrowed brow deepened as he spoke in muted tones, recounting the events that had blindsided him.

"I woke up to chaos, Andy," Doug muttered, his voice tight with frustration. "Years of careful investments wiped out in hours. All because of a time zone I can't even control."

Andy, walking in straightforward strides beside him, listened intently. Doug's words carried more than just financial frustration; they were steeped in the realisation that the global system, with its inherent inequalities, had played him like a pawn. For Doug, it wasn't just about the money. It was about London's unfair advantage and the ability to act before the world opened its eyes.

"They're using time against us," Doug continued, his voice rising. "The whole damn system is rigged. London gets the first look and move, and we're left scrambling to catch up."

Andy paused mid-stride, the weight of Doug's words sinking in. He turned to face his friend, his blue eyes narrowing with the sharpness of an idea forming. The concept of time as a weapon, a tool that could be wielded to control markets to dictate the flow of wealth, resonated deeply with him. He had built his empire on being first and predicting trends before anyone else knew they existed, and now, here was Doug, laying bare a system that thrived on the very advantage he had always looked for.

"You're right," Andy said slowly, his voice thoughtful. "This isn't just about the market. It's about control. Time is the ultimate commodity, and whoever controls time controls everything."

Andy's mind was already racing ahead as they reached the third green, mapping out possibilities. Doug was still fuming over the injustice, but his thoughts had shifted. This wasn't a setback, it was an opportunity. If the British financial system could exploit their time zone advantage, why couldn't he? The seed of an idea had been planted and he could already feel it taking root in his mind, its implications stretching far beyond the golf course.

The fourth hole approached, a par five that snaked through a dense oak forest, its 574-yard stretch presenting both challenge and beauty. Doug, usually talkative, fell silent as they entered the shaded corridor, the trees towering above them. The hole's solitary oak tree, positioned like a sentinel halfway down the fairway, cast a long shadow across their path. For most, the tree was a hazard, something to be avoided. But for Andy, it stood for something more than an obstacle to be conquered.

Doug's voice broke the quiet, his frustration turning to disbelief. "It's centuries old, this system. Greenwich Mean Time is the heart of their power. They've been controlling the world's clocks for over a hundred years. It's no wonder they always get the upper hand."

Andy paused on the fairway, the quiet hum of the golf course around him unable to drown out the storm brewing in his mind. The British system, governed by the steadfast Greenwich Mean Time, had dictated the rules of global timekeeping for centuries. But he had not followed the rules, especially those etched into history. He thrived on disruption, on breaking the mould to create something entirely new.

"You know," Andy began, his voice simmering with conviction. This isn't about fighting the system. It's about creating a new one where we control the clock."

Standing beside him, Doug looked over, startled by the intensity in Andy's tone. "What are you saying?" He asked a hint of caution in his voice.

Andy's lips curled into a subtle, knowing smile. "I'm saying it's time to stop playing catch-up. It's time to build something that redefines the game entirely." Then, almost casually, he dropped the bombshell. "I think it's time we moved the timeline from London to New York."

Nigel Strutt, who had been listening quietly to the conversation, scratched his head in confusion. "Surely it doesn't matter where the timeline is, not in today's 24-7 world?" Nigel asked, genuinely curious.

Andy paused, his gaze drifting momentarily to the oak trees swaying in the breeze. Then, with a seriousness that cut through the serene surroundings, he turned to Nigel.

"It matters, Nigel, more than you might think. The timeline dictates the start of the new global financial day. It's the point where the world's most critical financial decisions begin. It affects the flow of billions through banking systems and global tax revenues. Being second or third doesn't count much when you're always playing catch-up. It's all about who controls those first billion dollars."

As they approached the green, the air felt heavier, as if the conversation had shifted the atmosphere around them. The rustling of leaves above seemed to hold its breath as Andy's mind raced ahead, seeing a future only he could fully grasp. His ambition had always driven him to push beyond the ordinary, to look for the cracks in the system where innovation could thrive. And now, with Doug's intrigued stare following him, he knew he had found his next move.

It wasn't just about controlling technology anymore. It was about controlling time itself. And if anyone could do it, with all his brilliance, determination, and flaws, it was Andy Stuart. The man who had already rewritten the rules once and was ready to do it again, this time on a global scale.

4: Setting Things in Order

In the vibrant heart of New York City, amid the din of honking taxis, the ceaseless rush of pedestrians, and the soaring ambition that pulsated through its streets, Andy stood as a figure of both awe and fear. To those who worked under him, he was a magnetic force, a visionary with an uncanny ability to turn ideas into fortunes. Yet there was an undercurrent of fear in the reverence he commanded. Success had made him hungry for more, and his appetite for dominance knew no bounds. He had conquered Wall Street, redefined corporate mergers, and turned small startups into global powerhouses. Still, none of it satisfied the burning drive inside him.

Today, as he stood in his sleek, glass-walled penthouse office overlooking the city, he contemplated his next move. The skyline stretched before him, a glittering tapestry of power and possibility. His thoughts, however, were far from the here and now. He was fixated on a concept that had haunted his mind for months: a bold and audacious plan that would change the game and rewrite the rules entirely. He would shift the global timeline, transferring the world's financial heart from London to New York.

The seed of an idea that had been planted while playing golf grew further in the quiet of a sleepless night, a flash of inspiration from years of watching the world's economy ebb and flow. Despite being the beating heart of global finance, New York still ran on a timeline dictated by London, the old guard. He knew that the real power lay in his city, the city that never slept, where markets moved faster, and fortunes were made instantly. It was time for New York to assert itself as the new global hub, not just in finance but in time itself.

Andy's mind raced as the afternoon sun set, casting a golden glow over the skyscrapers. He could feel the electricity in the air, the energy of possibility. He knew this plan needed to be more complex. It wasn't just about changing time zones. It was about shifting the very axis of global power. He would need to navigate political waters, orchestrate economic shifts, and gain the buy-in of the world's financial elite. It was a chess game of the highest stakes, and every move had to be perfect.

Behind him, his office reflected the life he had built. It was ultramodern and opulent, with walls lined with abstract art from the world's most renowned artists and furniture crafted from the finest materials money could buy. Yet, even in this sanctuary of success, he felt the weight of what he was about to embark on. This was no ordinary deal. This was his legacy, his chance to reshape the world in his image.

But Andy could not do this alone. He needed someone as cunning, ambitious, and fearless as himself. There was only one man for the job, Ravi Jayasekera.

Ravi was a wildcard, a man of contradictions and mystery. Born into a wealthy Sri Lankan family, Ravi had spent his youth in the hallowed halls of the UK's elite educational institutions, where he cultivated not just knowledge but also powerful, far-reaching connections. While Andy was a builder of businesses, Ravi was a master of intrigue. He had amassed a vast fortune through political manoeuvring, secretive deals, and a web of influence across continents. He knew how to manipulate people and systems, bending them to his will with the precision of a chess grandmaster. He sent Ravi a message via Telegram, the secure messaging App. He had not seen or spoken to Ravi in some time, so he had yet to learn where he could be. He thought with a wry smile, probably on the moon, knowing Ravi. His phone pinged an hour later, 'See you in Santorini,' the message read. He rolled his eyes as the sun set on another day.

Twenty-four hours later, Ravi was enjoying the fruits of his success, sailing aboard a gleaming superyacht across the cerulean waters of the Ionian Sea. The yacht, a floating palace of luxury, was not his own. It never was. Ravi lived by a simple philosophy: "If it flies, fucks, or floats, rent it." His wealth was carefully curated, and he always spent on things that depreciated. The sun kissed his bronzed skin as he lounged on the deck, surrounded by an entourage of models, champagne glasses in hand, the very picture of carefree abandon. But despite appearances, Ravi's mind was never indeed at rest. Beneath the playboy façade, he was always thinking, always plotting.

Ravi had set sail from the party island of Ios, leaving behind the raucous nightlife in search of quieter shores and deeper conversations. As he navigated the pristine waters, the wind tousled his hair and the sun kissed his bronzed skin, filling him with a sense of freedom. On the horizon, Santorini beckoned, its iconic cliffs rising like beacons of promise, and Ravi looked forward to the evening ahead.

Eighteen hours earlier, Andy sat in the first-class lounge at JFK Airport, sipping a glass of champagne while waiting for his flight to Santorini via the Greek capital of Athens, as there are no direct flights from the US. The hum of the airport buzzed around him. Still, his mind was elsewhere, lost in the calculations and possibilities of the audacious plan he was about to set in motion. He wasn't one to get rattled, but this was no ordinary business deal. Shifting the world's financial timeline was a move that could either cement his legacy as a visionary or end in catastrophe.

He gathered as the boarding call rang out and went to the gate. Once on the plane, he settled into the plush leather seat, feeling the familiar rush of adrenaline that came with long-haul travel. The soft hum of the engines began, and soon, they were in the air, soaring over the Atlantic. He pulled out his tablet, intending to review some financial reports, but his focus wavered. Several magazines were laid out neatly in the seat pocket before him, and one caught his eye: **New Scientist**. The cover featured a woman of arresting, almost ethereal beauty. Her face, framed by loose waves of chestnut hair, free of makeup, or if there was any, it was so subtle it was invisible. Something was spellbinding about her natural allure, and it unexpectedly pulled at him. As his gaze lingered on her serene expression, he felt a pang of something that startled him with regret.

His thoughts drifted back to a woman he had known not too long ago, a whirlwind affair that had burned too bright, too fast. He had met her at a high-profile gala, another beautiful, ambitious woman drawn to his power like a moth to flame. But it hadn't been love. It had been an obsession, a moment of passion tangled with his insecurities and desires. He had known from the start it would end badly and had been another relationship soured; another woman left hating him. The memory twisted like a knot in his stomach, and he wondered when things had become so transactional. His business success had always come at the expense of something else: friendships, relationships, and trust. The thought weighed heavily on him, though he rarely allowed it to show. "Another one to go on and hate me," he mused bitterly, tossing the magazine aside.

He shifted in his seat, trying to shake off the memory. As he looked down at the magazine, it had landed open, revealing further pictures of the mystery woman. He reached forward, picked up the magazine, and started to read the article.

"Well, hello, Dr Emily Clark," Andy thought...

Waking from a quiet moment, the thought of Ravi stirred a new sense of anticipation or dread. The feeling that swept across Andy. While he was methodical, calculating, and driven by results, Ravi was the opposite, unpredictable and enigmatic, a man whose charm and wit masked a dangerous mind. Together, they were unstoppable, two sides of the same coin. He was the architect, the man with the blueprint, but Ravi was the magician who could make impossible things happen with a well-placed phone call or a sly smile. He felt the familiar tension knotting in his chest as the flight neared its end. There was no turning back now. The stakes were too high, and the reward too great. He had to navigate political waters that would have terrified anyone else. Still, he had one thing going for him: Ravi's calm cunning. With Ravi at his side, they could move mountains, let alone adjust the world's clocks. They had done it before, manipulating markets and bending governments to their will. This was no different, except it was because it was everything.

On landing in Athens, his phone pinged again, and a message from Ravi said, 'The Selene restraint 8 PM'. Andy boarded a smaller plane bound for Santorini. His body ached from the journey, but his mind was excited. Santorini, with its postcard-perfect cliffs and azure waters, seemed an odd backdrop for what would surely be a tense reunion. But Ravi had insisted on meeting there. The billionaire was always unpredictable, always a step ahead, and he had learned long ago to follow Ravi's lead regarding these matters. The plane touched down on the sun-baked tarmac, and he disembarked. The warm Mediterranean breeze hit him, carrying with it the salty scent of the sea. Santorini's iconic whitewashed buildings clung to the cliffs like delicate jewels, shimmering in the late afternoon light. For a moment, he allowed himself to take in the breathtaking beauty of the place. But beauty didn't distract him for long. His mind was already racing ahead to the night that awaited him.

A sleek black sedan awaited him as he stepped outside the small airport, the driver standing at attention. Andy slid into the backseat, loosening his tie as the car began its winding journey up the narrow roads toward Fira. The island was alive with tourists and locals alike, their laughter and chatter rising into the evening air. The streets, flanked by stunning views of the Aegean, twisted and turned as the car climbed higher, and soon, the quiet beauty of the island seemed worlds away from the chaos he knew awaited him. Ravi had made a reservation at Selene, one of Santorini's most exclusive restaurants, perched high on the cliffs overlooking the caldera. As the car approached, he could already imagine the scene that awaited him: lavish dishes, fine wine, and Ravi's smirk as he laid out the pieces of their plan. He had braced himself for a night of heavy drinking, knowing that no evening with Ravi ever ended sober.

But it wasn't the alcohol he was concerned about. It was the man himself. Ravi was a storm, calm on the surface but with an undertow that could pull anyone under. The two had shared many nights like this, over gourmet food and vintage brandy, plotting, scheming, and dreaming of the next great conquest. But this time felt different. The stakes were higher, and he could feel the weight of what was about to unfold pressing down on him. As the car pulled to a stop outside the restaurant, he took a deep breath, steeling himself. He had to be sharp tonight. This was not just another deal, this was history in the making. He stepped out of the car, the sounds of the island's distant music and the hum of conversation filling the air around him. He went inside, his heart pounding with the familiar mix of excitement and tension that always preceded one of Ravi's games.

As the last course was cleared from their table, Selene's dim lighting cast long shadows across the walls, softening the outlines of the room while the warm flicker of candles illuminated the faces of the diners. Outside, the sky had deepened into a velvety black, dotted with stars and the soft hum of the Aegean below. The air carried the faint scent of jasmine from the restaurant's entrance, blending with the aroma of grilled meats and the lingering sweetness of Greek desserts. Andy leaned back in his chair, swirling the amber liquid in his glass before sipping. The brandy was smooth and potent, burning his throat in a comforting and jarring way. It mirrored the fire quietly igniting in his chest, the one that came with every bold idea he allowed himself to entertain. He felt the familiar thrill of risk, the same one that had propelled him to where he was today. But this idea, shifting the world's financial timeline from London to New York, was something even he knew bordered on madness.

Across from him, Ravi Jayasekera reclined casually in his seat, his fingers lightly tapping the rim of his glass, his dark eyes fixed intently on Andy. The soft candlelight reflected off the surface of the brandy, casting a warm glow on his face. Ravi, with his casual air and perpetual half-smile, had a way of making everything seem effortless. But Andy could see the gears turning behind that calm exterior. Ravi's curiosity had been piqued, and now he was fully engaged. Andy began explaining his vision, his low but intense voice, and the ambient noise of the restaurant, provided them with the privacy they needed. He laid out his plan to shift the international financial timeline, moving it away from the traditional Greenwich Mean Time in London to a new hub in New York. The city that never slept would become the epicentre of the global financial system. It would mean redefining the world's relationship with time, giving the United States a renewed economic and symbolic dominance.

As he spoke, Ravi's eyes grew sharper, glinting with a mix of intrigue and calculation. For a moment, he said nothing, simply absorbing the weight of what Andy was proposing. He let the silence stretch, the only sound the occasional clink of glasses and the hum of conversation around them.

Finally, Ravi leaned forward, his lips curling into a small smile which always suggested he knew more than he was letting on. His gaze shifted from Andy to the dark horizon beyond the window as if he were transported elsewhere. His mind drifted back to a moment from earlier that year, during a brief stay in Atlanta, Georgia. It had been a typical warm April afternoon, where the sun seemed to hang lazily in the sky. Ravi had been staying at The Ritz-Carlton, an opulent refuge just a stone's throw from Centennial Olympic Park.

It was during a casual walk through the city that something had caught his attention. At the intersection of Peachtree Street and Baker Street, Ravi stumbled upon a sight that stuck with him like a dark cloud. Towering above the busy street was the US National Debt Clock. The number displayed was almost too large to comprehend, growing steadily with every passing second, like an insatiable beast. Ravi had paused in front of it, mesmerised by the ever-increasing digits. Trillions of dollars in debt. It felt like a ticking time bomb, and in that moment, he had realised just how precarious the United States' financial situation was.

He had pulled out his phone and snapped a picture of the clock, capturing the enormity of the figure but also the weight of its implications. It had gnawed at him ever since. The national debt increased by billions daily and was more than a political talking point. It was a ticking clock that could bring down empires. With that realisation came an idea that became more apparent as he listened to Andy.

"I can still see it," Ravi said softly, breaking the silence.

He set his brandy down gently and leaned back, a thoughtful expression crossing his face. "Earlier this year, I stood and looked at Atlanta's American national debt clock. The US National Debt. It's a monster, growing faster than anyone wants to admit. I stood there, looking at those numbers, and all I could think was this is the kind of chaos that gives birth to opportunity."

Andy nodded, recognising the shift in the conversation. He knew Ravi wasn't one to get philosophical without a reason. He'd been waiting for this, Ravi's moment of insight.

"The thing about chaos," Ravi continued, his voice calm but with an underlying intensity, "is that it creates voids. Voids that need filling. Washington's already panicking. They're grasping at straws, trying to manage the unmanageable. But that's the beauty of it. When the system is on the verge of collapse, you can slip in and take control."

Andy watched as Ravi's mind turned, piecing together the fragments of his earlier thought.

"So, you suggest the debt crisis is our way in?" Andy asked, leaning in, his voice dropping to match Ravi's.

The restaurant around them felt far away like the rest of the world had faded into the background. Ravi's eyes glinted with excitement.

"Exactly. The debt crisis is the leverage point. The US is drowning in its mess, and the public must gain confidence quickly. They're looking for someone, anyone, to fix it. That's where we come in. We take advantage of the instability, shift the timeline to New York, and suddenly we're in control: New York has become the financial centre of the world. The timeline moves, and with it, so does the power."

Andy sat back, absorbing the weight of Ravi's words. It made sense, too much sense. The chaos in Washington, the debt, and the desperation of the American people were all fertile ground for a power shift. And if anyone could orchestrate that kind of seismic change, it was Ravi.

"How do we do it?" Andy asked, his voice steady, though his heart raced with the thrill of what was now within reach.

"We need to start by identifying key players," Ravi replied, his mind fully engaged in the plan's mechanics. "Influential business leaders, policymakers, people who understand what's at stake. We craft a narrative and make them see that shifting the timeline is not about power, it's about survival. We make New York the beacon of stability in an unstable world." Ravi's words were smooth, but there was an edge to them, an unmistakable hunger. This was the kind of play he lived for, a chance to rewrite the rules, to upend the status quo.

Andy drained the last of his brandy, feeling the warmth spread through his chest. The night had taken a turn he hadn't fully anticipated, but now everything seemed more straightforward. They had the pieces; they just needed to move them into place. New York would become the new axis on which the world turned, and they would be the ones to make it happen.

As they sat there with the faint sounds of laughter and clinking glasses around them, the future seemed to unfold as bold, dangerous, and utterly theirs for the taking.

5: Honeytrap

Ravi sat in his chair, listening intently as Andy outlined his vision for shifting the global timeline to New York, his gaze steady but racing far ahead of the conversation. He nodded along, offering the occasional word of agreement. Still, his thoughts were already crafting a different path forward that he knew Andy wouldn't fully appreciate. For Ravi, this wasn't just about the technicalities of changing a financial framework; it was about pure, unbridled power, and to seize it, he needed more than just his plan. He required leverage, which could only come from someone deeply entrenched in the corridors of influence.

He knew exactly who that person was. Tom Dunnagan, the US Secretary of State, was the key to unlocking the political alliances necessary to make Andy's plan a reality. But it wasn't Dunnagan's position alone that made him valuable; it was his vulnerability. Ravi had learned long ago that the most influential people were often the easiest to manipulate because they had the most to lose and Tom Dunnagan, with his impeccable public image and roiling private life, was no exception.

Ravi intended to keep this plan private from Andy. He knew him too well. His vision was broad, but he wasn't one for subtle manipulation. No, Ravi would keep this card close to his chest. After all, he had honed the art of getting what he wanted without showing his whole hand.

As the waiter cleared their plates and refilled their brandy glasses, Ravi's mind wandered back to the web of connections he had spun around Dunnagan. Like Ravi, Tom Dunnagan's biggest weakness was not political missteps or financial blunders. It was the opposite sex. Women had been Dunnagan's Achilles heel since his youth, and Ravi knew this weakness could be exploited with surgical precision.

Dunnagan's first marriage had been a classic tale of young love and recklessness. He had met his first wife in college and swept her off her feet with his southern charm and rising political star, sadly their marriage crumbled when a torrid affair with his wife's younger sister became known. The scandal hadn't just destroyed his personal life; it had nearly ended his political career before it truly began. The press had a field day with it, and Dunnagan barely managed to keep his seat in

Congress through a mix of public apologies and well-placed favours.

The wreckage of that first marriage had cast a long shadow over Dunnagan's life, which lingered even after he remarried. His second wife, Charlotte, was as polished as they came. She was a former model with an Ivy League education and a veneer of perfection that made her the ideal political spouse. Together, they were the picture of stability, smiling for the cameras at every gala, fundraiser, and press event. They played the part of Washington's power coupled with impeccable precision, and the public bought into the illusion.

But Ravi knew better. Beneath the surface, Dunnagan's marriage was little more than a carefully crafted performance for Washington's social elite. Charlotte knew about her husband's infidelities but played the dutiful wife, recognising that the political benefits outweighed the personal toll. Behind closed doors, their relationship was icy at best, vastly different from the warm embraces they displayed for the cameras.

Dunnagan's affairs were no secret in certain circles, and Ravi had made it his business to know precisely where those skeletons were buried. Dunnagan still couldn't resist the thrill of a new conquest, and it was only a matter of time before his indulgence in fleeting affairs would spiral out of control. Ravi had watched him at political events, his wandering eye lingering just a little too long on the younger staffers and interns. It was only a matter of time before Dunnagan's lust led him into another scandal. Ravi intended to be there when it did.

It wasn't just about blackmail. It was about positioning. Ravi knew that if he could entangle Dunnagan in a web of favours and secrets, he could secure his support when the time came. Dunnagan's influence as Secretary of State was invaluable. With his backing, Ravi could make inroads into the deeper political arena that Andy's plan required. Dunnagan would be the Trojan horse, delivering their vision into the heart of Washington's power structure.

The key was subtlety. Dunnagan could only be approached indirectly about the full scope of the plan; it needed to be riskier. No, Ravi was required to play the long game, slowly weaving himself into Dunnagan's personal and professional life until he became indispensable. Ducted by his desires and weaknesses, Dunnagan would be none the wiser, thinking he was in charge all along.

Ravi had already planted the seeds. He had orchestrated a few well-timed meetings and casual introductions that didn't raise any red flags but left an impression. He'd made himself available to Dunnagan, offering advice on international affairs and providing connections that Dunnagan couldn't ignore. Slowly, he was becoming the man Dunnagan turned to when things got tricky, and soon, when the time was right, Ravi would pull the strings.

Back in Santorini, Andy and Ravi's conversation flowed seamlessly from politics to business, with the occasional joke and reminiscence thrown in. But, as Andy laid out the next steps of his grand plan, Ravi's thoughts were elsewhere. He watched Andy talk with enthusiasm, but his mind was already with Dunnagan, envisioning the next move he would make.

Andy was brilliant, and there was no denying that. His ambition was contagious, his ideas bold. But Ravi knew that bold ideas required more than just execution; they required leverage, which came from knowing where to strike. In this case, Dunnagan's weaknesses were the perfect pressure point. The Secretary of State would only realise what was happening once it was too late, and by then, he would be too deep in the game to pull out.

As the evening wound down, Ravi raised his glass to Andy, flashing a knowing smile.

"New York," he toasted, his voice smooth and confident. "and to ensure the world's timeline runs on our schedule."

Andy clinked his glass with Ravi's, his face excitedly lit up. But beneath the surface, Ravi's mind was already working, piecing together the steps leading them to the top. He had a plan that involved more than just shifting the financial timeline. It involved reshaping the power dynamics of the entire world. And with Tom Dunnagan as his unwitting pawn, Ravi knew the game was his to win.

Meticulous as ever, Ravi set his plan in motion with the precision of a chess grandmaster. He understood the subtle art of manipulation, knowing power wasn't seized in one bold stroke but earned through a thousand carefully calculated moves. His strategy revolved around Tom Dunnagan's most exploitable weakness: his wandering eye and insatiable desire for female companionship. Over the weeks, Ravi carefully orchestrated a series of "chance" encounters with Dunnagan, always at exclusive, discreet social events where politics mixed with luxury. He was patient and never rushed through the process. Instead, he let Dunnagan's curiosity and desire take root, slowly guiding him deeper into Ravi's carefully spun web.

At each gathering, Ravi introduced the official to a different circle of captivating women, each more alluring than the last. But one woman in particular captured Dunnagan's attention, and Ravi knew she was the key to his plan: Anna Morocover, a woman whose allure was as powerful as her role in Ravi's plan.

Anna was unlike any woman Dunnagan had encountered before. Born into a family of Russian and

Ukrainian descent, she was a striking blend of Slavic beauty and Western sophistication. Her honey-blonde hair cascaded down her back in soft waves, framing a face that seemed to glow with an otherworldly radiance. Her emerald-green eyes sparkled with intelligence and mischief, drawing attention in any room she entered. Tall and statuesque, Anna carried herself with a grace that hinted at her aristocratic upbringing. Beneath her polished exterior, she harboured layers of complexity forged by her past and the choices that had shaped her into the woman she had become.

Anna's upbringing had been one of privilege and expectation. Her parents, old-money aristocrats who had fled to the West during the turmoil in Eastern Europe, had ensured that she was educated at the best schools, immersed in high culture, and prepared to marry well. Anna had never been content to follow the path laid out for her. From a youthful age, she was fiercely independent, determined to carve out her destiny, and she had done just that, though not in the way her family had anticipated.

Instead of marrying into wealth or becoming a fixture in society, Anna chose a different path that gave her autonomy and control over her life. She became a high-class escort, a decision that shocked those who knew her family's history. Anna embraced the role not as a victim of circumstance but as a deliberate choice, reclaiming power in a world where women were often objectified. To her, escorting was not just about sex or money, it was about playing the game on her terms, turning the transactional nature of her relationships into an advantage. She navigated her profession with the same strategic mind that Ravi admired in himself.

Her career not only afforded her a life of luxury and independence, but it also allowed her to meet men of influence, men like Tom Dunnagan. Anna was not just a pretty face to decorate a politician's arm. She was intelligent, sharp, and always a step ahead. Her ability to read people to anticipate their desires and motivations made her invaluable to Ravi's plan. She had become a master of her craft, knowing when to be demure, when to challenge, and when to offer the kind of intimacy that made powerful men feel invincible.

Ravi knew that Anna's allure would be irresistible to Dunnagan. He had watched how the Secretary of State's eyes followed her every move, and his gaze lingered on her graceful figure at events. It wasn't just her physical beauty that ensnared Dunnagan, it was the air of mystery and sophistication she carried with her. Anna was the kind of woman who made men feel like they were in the presence of something rare and valuable, someone who could elevate them merely by association.

Over time, Ravi positioned himself as Dunnagan's confidante, who always seemed there when the official needed advice or a listening ear. With Anna by his side, Ravi played the long game, allowing Dunnagan to believe he was the one pursuing her. In truth, Ravi and Anna carefully choreographed every step. They knew how to feed Dunnagan's desires without letting him feel too secure.

Anna, for her part, enjoyed the challenge. She liked Dunnagan well enough. He was charming in his way, though predictable, but for her, this game was where she and Ravi were the actual players, orchestrating moves Dunnagan couldn't even begin to see. She admired Ravi's intellect and ability to see the bigger picture and respected his trust in her. For Anna, this wasn't just about money or power. It was about being part of a larger plan that could reshape global politics.

Oblivious to the game's intricacies, Dunnagan became increasingly captivated by Anna. She was unlike the other women who had come and gone in his life, a woman who seemed to understand him on a deeper level. Dunnagan's dependence on her attention grew as their meetings became more frequent. He began confiding in her, sharing details about his work, his frustrations with the political machine, and his ambitions for the future. Anna listened, offering just enough sympathy to make him feel understood, but never so much that he doubted her independence. She was careful not to become too accessible, and keeping

Dunnagan chasing after the idea of her was part of the strategy.

As the weeks passed, Ravi and Anna's plan began to bear fruit. Dunnagan, encouraged by his growing infatuation with Anna, became more malleable and more willing to bend to Ravi's subtle suggestions. Ravi carefully planted ideas in Dunnagan's mind, steering conversations toward policies that would benefit his and Andy's long-term goals. The Secretary of State, eager to impress both Anna and his newfound confidante, began to see Ravi as a valuable ally in navigating the complexities of Washington's political landscape.

Anna, always the consummate professional, kept Dunnagan on edge. She never entirely gave in to his advances but offered just enough to keep him returning for more. She knew exactly when to push and when to pull away, and the tension only heightened Dunnagan's obsession.

Ravi watched it all unfold with quiet satisfaction. The pieces were falling into place, and soon, with Dunnagan's influence at their disposal, he and Andy would have the leverage they needed to shift the global timeline. While Andy dreamed of financial dominance and geopolitical power, Ravi's ambitions stretched even further. He wasn't just interested in moving markets, he wanted to rewrite the rules of the game entirely.

Ravi first encountered Anna at a lavish gala in London, held in one of the city's most prestigious hotels. The ballroom was a grand display of wealth and power, with crystal chandeliers casting a warm, golden glow over the assembled guests. The air was filled with the soft hum of polite conversation, punctuated by the clink of champagne glasses. As the son of a prominent Sri Lankan diplomat, Ravi moved effortlessly through these circles, his charm and confidence making him a natural fit among the elite. Still, on that evening, someone else commanded his attention.

Like a rare jewel, Anna stood out amidst the crowd of diplomats, socialites, and billionaires. She was working as an entertainment hostess, a role that demanded a delicate balance of elegance and allure. She exuded a quiet power, dressed in a sleek black gown that hugged her statuesque figure. Her honey-blonde hair fell in soft waves down her back, and her striking emerald eyes sparkled with intelligence, taking in the room with a keen awareness. Anna wasn't just another pretty face to decorate the event; there was an unmistakable depth to her presence, something that piqued Ravi's curiosity the moment he laid eyes on her.

While Ravi was used to women falling under his spell, Anna didn't seem to play by the same rules. When he approached her with his signature confidence, expecting an easy conversation, he was met with a reserved yet polite demeanour. She had heard whispers about Ravi's reputation. He was known for his sharp mind and ability to manipulate situations and people to his advantage. Having navigated the complexities of power dynamics before, Anna was not eager to be just another pawn in a wealthy man's game.

Their initial exchange was brief but charged. Intrigued by her reluctance, Ravi made it a point to engage her further. They began to talk as they stood by the bar, sipping champagne. At first, the usual pleasantries about the event and the people around them were superficial, but their conversation deepened as the evening wore on. Ravi, sensing Anna's wariness, chose a different approach. Instead of flaunting his status or wealth, he shared stories from his upbringing in a world not dissimilar to hers. Both had been raised in families straddled cultures, immersed in tradition yet exposed to the modern world's demands.

Anna found herself softening as she listened to Ravi speak. There was a vulnerability in his words that surprised her. Despite his calculated exterior, he seemed genuinely interested in her thoughts, background, and experiences. She realised that beneath the carefully constructed image of the mighty son of a diplomat, there was someone who, like her, had to navigate expectations, identity, and the delicate politics of influence.

As the evening progressed, their connection grew. They found themselves lingering in corners of the ballroom, sharing quiet moments away from the crowd. Ravi's wit and sharp intelligence drew Anna in, but he could see beyond her surface beauty that caught her off guard. He wasn't just interested in her as a hostess or an object of desire. He valued her mind, ambitions, and ability to hold her own in a room full of powerful men.

Over the next several months, their relationship evolved into something far more profound than expected. Despite his reputation for using people to further his ambitions, Ravi treated Anna with the respect she hadn't often encountered in her work. He admired her for her beauty and the strength and independence she had cultivated over the years. He saw a partner in her, someone who could match his intellect and navigate the complexities of high society with grace.

For Anna, Ravi became more than just a wealthy connection. He opened doors for her, introducing her to influential figures within his network and giving her access to events that elevated her status. Still, it wasn't just about the material gain or the connections. She appreciated Ravi's sincerity and ability to see her not as an object but as a woman of substance. Over time, she trusted him, realising that he genuinely valued her despite his scheming nature.

Ravi was careful not to push too hard, knowing that Anna's independence was part of what made her so intriguing. He admired her ability to hold her own in a world dominated by powerful men, never letting anyone define her worth. He respected her for her choices, even if they were unconventional, and saw in her a kindred spirit, a strategist, just like him.

Their bond transcended the professional arrangement that had initially brought them together. While Anna continued to work in her world, she found herself leaning on Ravi for advice, and he was on her. They shared a mutual understanding of what it meant to live in a world where power was the ultimate currency, and both were determined to control their narratives.

Ravi, ever the strategist, began to involve Anna in his more extensive plans. He saw her as more than just an asset; she was a partner in his schemes, someone who could help him manipulate the players he needed to get closer to his goals. Anna, for her part, relished the challenge. She enjoyed the thrill of being part of something bigger, of playing the game alongside someone who understood its rules as well as she did.

Together, they became an unstoppable force, two minds working in tandem, precisely navigating the world of influence, seduction, and power. Where Ravi provided the strategy, Anna offered the finesse. She knew how to play her role perfectly, whether charming a billionaire at a high-society event or subtly influencing a political figure behind closed doors.

Their partnership was built on mutual respect and ambition, and the lines between business and personal blurred over time. They understood each other in a way that few others could, bound by a shared desire to rise above the limitations of their circumstances. For Ravi, Anna was no longer just a tool in his plans. She was his equal, someone who could help him achieve greatness. For Anna, Ravi represented an opportunity not just for advancement but for something more, a sense of belonging, of being indeed seen.

In their glittering world, where alliances were fleeting, and trust was rare, Ravi and Anna had found something unique: a bond forged not by love or lust but by mutual ambition and respect. They would rewrite the game's rules together, and no one would see them coming.

With each passing encounter, the entanglement between Anna and Tom Dunnagan deepened. What had started as a calculated introduction evolved into something far more complex. Anna found herself playing a dangerous game that blurred the line between manipulation and genuine connection. Dunnagan, a man who had spent decades wielding political power, was no easy target. Beneath his composed exterior, Anna saw the cracks in his vulnerabilities, desires, and hunger for something beyond the carefully constructed image he presented to the world.

Anna was skilled in reading people she had to be, having spent years navigating the delicate balance of seduction and influence. She quickly learned Dunnagan's motivations, his need for validation, his fear of failure, and the loneliness of his position. He was drawn to her not just for her beauty but because she represented an escape from the crushing weight of his public life. Anna knew how to make herself indispensable, offering him a sanctuary where he could be vulnerable without fear of judgment.

Ravi, orchestrating everything from the shadows, watched with calculated satisfaction. He had set this plan in motion, knowing that Anna's allure would be impossible for Dunnagan to resist. But as the weeks passed, Ravi began to sense a shift. Anna was getting closer to Dunnagan than even he had anticipated. What had once been a transactional relationship was now a tangled web of attraction, ambition, and power. While this played into Ravi's hands, it also unsettled him in ways he hadn't expected.

There were moments when Ravi would observe Anna with Dunnagan, noting how Dunnagan's eyes lingered on her and how his posture relaxed in her presence. Anna was weaving her magic, and Dunnagan fell deeper under her spell. Yet, Ravi couldn't shake a growing unease. Was Anna still playing her part, or had she begun to lose herself? He needed her to stay focused on manipulating Dunnagan to make decisions that would benefit them. Anna, with her ambitions and desires, was not so easily controlled.

Anna, too, felt the tension. The more time she spent with Dunnagan, the more she saw the power he wielded. It wasn't just the political influence or the connections. It was the ability to shape the world around him and bend reality to his will. While she stayed loyal to Ravi's plan, the temptation to use Dunnagan's affection for her gain grew stronger by the day. She was walking a razor's edge, balancing her duty to Ravi with the seductive lure of the power Dunnagan offered.

Their meetings became more frequent and more intimate. Dunnagan would confide in her in the quiet confines of his office or the discreet corners of upscale restaurants, sharing secrets he wouldn't dare utter to anyone else. He told her about the pressures of his position, the political games that never seemed to end, the alliances he was forced to maintain. Anna listened carefully, offering comfort where needed but always with an ear for information that might serve Ravi's agenda.

But it wasn't just the information that drew her in. Dunnagan, for all his flaws, was a man who craved real connection. Anna, who had spent so much of her life playing roles for others, was drawn to that vulnerability. She hadn't expected to care for him, but as their relationship deepened, she realised she was no longer just playing a part. There was something real here, something she hadn't anticipated.

As her feelings for Dunnagan grew, so did the conflict within her. Ravi had given her a purpose, a path to power that she had never imagined possible. However, with his position and influence, Dunnagan represented a distinct way to rewrite the rules entirely. Anna was caught between two powerful men, each offering her a different future. The more she thought about it, the more she realised that whatever choice she made would ripple out, affecting not just her but everyone involved.

Ravi, ever the strategist, noticed the subtle changes in Anna. She was more guarded in their conversations and less willing to share details of her time with Dunnagan. He sensed her growing attachment to the man they were supposed to be manipulating, which infuriated and intrigued him. On one hand, Anna's closeness to Dunnagan was precisely what he had hoped for, it gave them unprecedented access to one of the most influential figures in Washington. On the other hand, it threatened to upend everything they had worked for.

Jealousy gnawed at Ravi, though he would never admit it. He had always seen Anna as his equal, someone who understood the game as well as he did. But now, watching her with Dunnagan, Ravi felt a pang of something unfamiliar fear. Fear that Anna might betray him, she might choose Dunnagan's power over their carefully crafted partnership. He couldn't afford to lose her, not when they were close to achieving their goals.

The tension came to a head one evening as Ravi and Anna sat in a quiet restaurant, the air thick with unspoken words. Ravi sipped his whiskey, his eyes never leaving Anna's face.

"You're getting too close," he said, his voice low and measured. "Don't forget why we started this."

Anna met his gaze, her expression unreadable.

"I haven't forgotten," she replied, but there was a hint of something in her voice: defiance, perhaps, or a flicker of doubt.

"Things are changing. Dunnagan… he trusts me. More than I expected."

Ravi leaned forward, his eyes narrowing.

"and that's exactly why we need to be careful. One wrong move, and everything we've built falls apart. Don't let your feelings cloud your judgment."

Anna smiled, though it didn't reach her eyes.

"You think I'm in love with him?" She asked, her tone almost mocking.

Ravi didn't answer, but the silence between them spoke volumes. Sensing the power shift, Anna leaned back in her chair, a quiet confidence settling over her. She knew she held all the cards now: Dunnagan's trust, Ravi's ambition, and her growing sense of control.

As the stakes grew higher, Ravi realised he was no longer the only one pulling the strings. Anna was a player in her own right, and the game they had started together was far from over.

Back in the empty hotel room, the vase of fresh flowers, delicate orchids interspersed with roses, sat innocuously on the table. Its elegant arrangement belied the sophisticated technology hidden within an HD camera, its microscopic lens discreetly nestled among the petals. From this vantage point, Ravi watched intently on his laptop screen, his face bathed in the soft blue glow of the monitor. Every detail, every whisper, every touch would be recorded, giving him all the leverage he needed to push Dunnagan over the edge. The setup was immaculate; Tom Dunnagan would not escape once the final play was set in motion.

Hours earlier, the atmosphere had been different, more measured, even innocent, at least on the surface. Dunnagan and Anna had sat through a lavish six-course tasting menu at one of the city's finest restaurants, each course more decadent than the last, with the soft clink of silverware on porcelain, the delicate flavours of truffle-infused risotto, seared scallops, and aged wagyu beef, the evening had been a sensory symphony. But through it all, there had been an unspoken undercurrent, a tension that simmered beneath the polished conversation.

Anna had played her role masterfully, as always. Her laughter had been light and effortless, her emerald eyes sparkling in the candlelight as she listened to Dunnagan recount tales of his youth and current frustrations in Washington's political minefield. Every tilt of her head, every subtle touch of her hand to his arm, had been calculated. She knew exactly how to keep him on edge and fan the flames of his desire without letting him get too close.

But as the hours stretched on, the anticipation grew. Even Dunnagan, usually so controlled and composed, had begun to unravel, his gaze lingering on her for a moment too long, his words slurring slightly as the wine worked its magic. By the time dessert arrived, a delicate plate of chocolate soufflé with a molten centre, Dunnagan was already lost in her, his focus narrowing to the curve of her lips, the way she licked the spoon clean after each bite.

The moment they left the restaurant and stepped into the sleek elevator, the change in the air was noticeable. The ride to the suite was silent, thick with the weight of what was to come. Anna stood beside him, calm and composed, though her heart raced beneath the surface. She had done this many times before, but something about tonight felt different. Dunnagan wasn't just another mark; he was the key to something much bigger that could change the course of power in ways she couldn't fully comprehend.

When the doors to the suite slid open, the room's luxury hit them. Gold and cream tones adorned the walls, a plush king-sized bed at the centre, its crisp white sheets beckoning. Anna moved with practised ease, slipping off her heels when they crossed the threshold. Dunnagan followed her with a sense of hunger barely concealed, his breath shallow, his hands already reaching for her as she moved toward the bed.

Anna's fingers played at the strap of her dress, teasing it down over her shoulder just enough to let her skin catch the soft glow of the bedside lamp. She could feel Dunnagan's eyes on her, the intensity of his gaze like a physical force, and then, as if some silent signal had passed between them, the dam broke. Dunnagan lunged toward her, his hands rougher than she had anticipated, pulling her close, his lips crashing into hers with an urgency that had been building for weeks. His desire had been carefully stoked, cultivated by Ravi's plan, and now it consumed him.

The camera, hidden so cleverly among the flowers, captured every moment with perfect clarity: the flush on Anna's cheeks, Dunnagan's hands roaming greedily over her body, the subtle way her posture shifted, guiding him just enough to keep control without him ever realising it. And all the while, Ravi watched from his private vantage point, his fingers steepled in satisfaction as the scene unfolded precisely as he had planned.

In that moment, Ravi felt a surge of triumph. This was the final piece, the leverage he needed to bend Dunnagan to his will. With this footage, Dunnagan's political career, already teetering on the edge of scandal, would be in Ravi's hands. One misstep, one word of defiance, and the video would get into the wrong hands. Dunnagan wouldn't dare risk it. Ravi had him now, completely and utterly.

But there was more at play here than just the video. Ravi's thoughts drifted to Andy, the man whose timeline they were trying to shift, whose future hinged on Dunnagan's compliance. Andy had always been the idealist, dreaming of ways to alter the political landscape between London and New York. Ravi, ever the pragmatist, knew it would take more than dreams to make that a reality. It would take power, which could only be won by those willing to get their hands dirty, and that is precisely what Ravi had done.

As the scene in the suite heated up, Ravi leaned back in his chair, a slow smile spreading. He did not doubt that

Dunnagan would be entirely under their control once the night ended. With Dunnagan's influence at their disposal, Andy's path to shifting the timeline and reshaping the world as they knew it would become apparent.

Yet, as victory drew near, a flicker of something else stirred in Ravi's chest. Watching Anna now, so skilled in her manipulation, so ideally in control, Ravi couldn't help but feel a pang of something darker. Was it jealousy? It was strange, almost absurd, but undeniable. For all his careful planning and manipulation of Dunnagan, Anna held the real power at this moment, and Ravi couldn't help but wonder if, in the end, she would use that power for herself.

As Dunnagan and Anna finally collapsed onto the bed, Ravi closed his laptop, his mind racing ahead to the next move. The pieces were in place, but the game was far from over and, as always, the most dangerous players were the ones you least expected.

For now, though, Ravi allowed himself a moment of satisfaction. The night had gone exactly as he had hoped. The evidence was secured, the leverage undeniable. Dunnagan's submission was guaranteed, and the path to power lay wide open with it, but as he rose from his chair and poured himself a drink, Ravi couldn't shake the feeling that Anna had her own game to play. He might even be just another piece on the board in that game.

6: Compromised

As Tom Dunnagan stepped into the room, the gravity of the situation seemed to hit him all at once. Dimly lit and devoid of distractions, the suite felt suddenly suffocating. Across from him sat Ravi, composed and sharp-eyed, with the unmistakable air of someone who held all the cards. The Secretary of State shifted uneasily in his chair, his fingers twitching as he struggled to maintain his usual veneer of control.

Without a word, Ravi reached into the sleek leather briefcase beside him and carefully laid out the photographs. One by one, they slid across the table like damning evidence in a courtroom. Dunnagan's gaze locked onto the images, his breath catching as the reality sank in. There, he was captured in excruciatingly intimate detail, wrapped around Anna in moments that should have been private, moments he had thought would never resurface. His chest tightened. Silence reigned in the room for a moment, punctuated only by the quiet hum of the city outside. Then, Ravi spoke, his voice steady, cutting through Dunnagan's rising panic.

"You know what's at stake, Tom," Ravi said, his words measured and precise. "These photos, should they fall into the wrong hands, will do more than just ruin you. They'll destroy the President's chances for re-election. They'll dismantle the administration, and you… well, you'll be nothing more than a footnote in history. Another scandal to wash away."

Dunnagan's stomach churned as Ravi's words settled over him like a heavy fog. He wanted to protest, to deny the truth staring back at him from the photos, but he knew there was no escape. The weight of his actions, the affair with Anna, and his reckless indulgence were now in Ravi's hands. A weapon wielded with clinical precision. But Ravi wasn't done. With a slow, deliberate motion, he leaned back in his chair, the faintest hint of a smile playing on his lips as he let the silence stretch out.

"But I'm not here to destroy you, Tom," Ravi continued, his voice softening with a deceptive warmth. "I'm here to offer you a way out. A solution. A path forward that saves you guarantees the President's re-election and secures America's future. It's about shifting the timeline."

Dunnagan's brow furrowed in confusion. Shifting the timeline? What was Ravi getting at? But before he could ask, Ravi pressed on, painting a vivid picture of the grand plan he and Andy had been formulating in the shadows for months.

"It's simple, really," Ravi explained, his hands gesturing smoothly as he spoke. "The world economy is in disarray. The US national debt is a ticking time bomb, threatening not just the future of your administration but the stability of the entire nation. What we propose isn't just a political manoeuvre; it's a solution. A power shift, a recalibration of global alliances that will alleviate the debt and secure certainty for the future, and all it requires is your cooperation."

Dunnagan sat frozen, his mind racing to keep up with Ravi's words. He had heard whispers of such plans before, murmurings among the elite about restructuring the global order, but this… this was far more calculated and dangerous. And yet, as Ravi spoke, Dunnagan couldn't deny the appeal. The promise of redemption, of being part of something bigger than himself, was tantalising. But it came with a price: his complicity in whatever game Ravi played.

Ravi leaned forward, his smile widening as he sensed Dunnagan's internal struggle. "You deliver the message to the President, Tom. You make him understand what's at stake. The re-election, the debt, everything hangs in the balance. We can shift the timeline and reset the future in America's favour. All you need to do is ensure he listens."

Dunnagan's throat felt dry as Ravi's words settled in, each syllable carrying the weight of shared ambition and looming catastrophe. He couldn't deny the power Ravi held over him. Now, one wrong move and his entire career would come crashing down, and his life would be reduced to a cautionary tale of lust and ruin. As Ravi finished, a silence descended upon the room again, heavier this time. The Secretary of State's mind drifted back to the night with Anna. What a night it had been. The adrenaline, the passion he had been intoxicated, consumed by the heat of it all. But now, as the consequences stared him in the face, that night felt like a distant memory, darkened by the cold reality of blackmail.

Was it worth it? The question gnawed at him. The ecstasy of that night, the thrill of Anna's touch, had been fleeting. Now, in its wake, lay the wreckage of his political career, the threat of scandal hovering like a sword above his head. If those photos got out, it wouldn't just be his undoing. It would be the President's too. The entire administration would implode in scandal, impeachment, and disgrace. A shiver ran down Dunnagan's spine, the nightmare scenario playing out in his mind. The press hounding him, the whispers in Washington's corridors, the shame his family would endure. It was almost too much to bear. Ravi's voice, smooth and confident, cut through his thoughts once more.

"Think about it, Tom. What we're offering is not just a lifeline. It's an opportunity. You'll be part of something that changes history. But you need to act and act soon."

Dunnagan swallowed hard, his eyes darting back to the photos on the table. The evidence of his indiscretions and weakness lay there, threatening to tear everything apart. He could feel the walls closing in. There was no way out except through Ravi. With a slow, reluctant nod, Dunnagan met Ravi's gaze.

"All right," he said, his voice hoarse with defeat. "I'll do it. I'll deliver the message."

Ravi's smile broadened, satisfaction gleaming in his eyes. He had Dunnagan exactly where he wanted him.

"Good," Ravi said, standing up and smoothing his jacket. "I knew you'd see reason. Now, let's make history."

As Ravi walked toward the door, leaving Dunnagan alone with the damning photos, a chill settled in the Secretary's bones. He had just made a deal with the devil, and deep down, he knew there was no going back.

As Dunnagan stormed out of the room, his composure crumbled with each step. The polished mask of a seasoned politician was stripped away and replaced by raw fury. His eyes blazed, his fists clenched, and the calculated calm he had worn like armour dissolved into something primal, something untamed. The photos, those wretched photos, that had laid out before him on that table like a vile taunt. Without thinking, Dunnagan seized the incriminating images. His hands moved savagely, tearing the glossy prints into jagged fragments, his breath ragged and heavy. Each rip of the paper was like a release of the anger bubbling inside him, each shred of the photo a scream of defiance. His mind spiralled into a storm of rage and regret. The sound of the tearing echoed through the room, violent and unforgiving.

But it wasn't enough. Dunnagan's fury surged like a wave that could not be contained. With a swift motion, he kicked the nearby table, flipping it over with a loud crash. The vase on top shattered into a thousand shards, water and flowers spilling onto the floor in a chaotic, dripping mess. The corridor shook with the force of his outburst, reverberating through the walls and down the rooms on each side, where startled heads turned toward the sound. His outrage was clear, like a force of nature ripping through everything in its path. He stood there, panting, surveying the wreckage he had caused. His chest heaved with a mix of adrenaline and something darker, something colder. It wasn't just rage that consumed him. The creeping realisation was that his life was on the precipice of ruin. A thread dangled his career, reputation, and entire identity. The weight of it pressed down on him like a vice, but beneath the storm of emotions, something else flickered determination.

A glimmer of defiance flared in his eyes, cutting through the haze of his anger. No, he wouldn't be broken by this. He wouldn't be another puppet dangling on Ravi's strings, no matter what evidence they had against him. Dunnagan had survived worse scandals, betrayals, and the darkest corners of Washington's political underbelly. He wasn't a man who backed down quickly and wasn't about to start now.

"Never!" He spat out, the word tasting like venom. Once silenced by fear and manipulation, his voice boomed through the room with newfound resolve.

"Never will I do anything for you!" The words rang out, bold and defiant, even though he was alone. He felt the venom in his voice, each syllable punctuated by the disdain coursing through his veins.

He stared at the pile of torn photographs scattered like confetti on the floor. Each fragment represented a piece of his past, a fleeting moment of lust, a betrayal of his principles. He had been weak, but that weakness would not control him. He wasn't the man who would grovel at the feet of blackmailers. If Ravi thought he could twist him into submission with these sordid images, he was gravely mistaken.

"I'll get these back," Dunnagan muttered, the whisper of determination becoming a fierce promise. His pulse raced, but his mind was sharpening.

"Ravi will be sorry."

His jaw clenched as he plotted his next move. He would not only stop Ravi but also destroy him. This wasn't just about survival anymore; it was about revenge.

With one final glance at the destruction he had wrought, Dunnagan stormed toward the lift door, his steps heavy with purpose. His mind was no longer clouded by fear. Now, it was focused, honed into a weapon. He was no longer a man cowering under the weight of blackmail; he was a warrior, ready to battle the forces of darkness that threatened to consume him, and as he stepped into the lift, leaving the wreckage behind, Dunnagan knew one thing for sure: he would fight. He would reclaim control of his life, career, and dignity, and anyone who tried to stand in his way, Ravi included, would regret it.

Dunnagan's mind raced, but beneath the surface chaos, his instincts were laser-sharp, honed from years of military discipline and the cutthroat world of politics. He couldn't let Ravi's treachery stand, not after all he had sacrificed to reach the pinnacle of power. He had fought too hard, outsmarted many opponents, and navigated through scandals that would have sunk a lesser man. This time would be no different. His hand instinctively reached for his phone, fingers hurrying as he dialled the one person he knew could help him out of this mess, Kowalski. Dunnagan didn't need to think twice. If anyone had the skills and the network to dismantle Ravi's scheme, it was him.

Kowalski was more than an old friend; he was a fellow Marine, a man forged in the same crucible of battle. They met years ago during training when the Marine Raiders Regiment tested their physical and mental limits. The exercises were brutal, gruelling endurance marches, hand-to-hand combat drills, and sleepless nights navigating hostile terrain. Dunnagan and Kowalski's friendship was born in the fire of shared hardship. Kowalski was tough, and his no-nonsense approach was matched only by his sharp, tactical mind. A natural strategist, he had an uncanny ability to think three steps ahead of the enemy. Even back then, Kowalski had been a force to be reckoned with, catching the eye of their superiors for his ability to adapt to any situation, no matter how dire. He was the guy who got things done, no matter the cost.

On the other hand, Dunnagan was a charismatic leader who could rally his unit even in the most harrowing circumstances. His calm under pressure and his ability to make decisions with life or death hanging in the balance were the qualities that set him apart. They had made an unstoppable team in training and later during their deployments. In the chaotic war zones of the Middle East and beyond, they had learned to trust one another implicitly. Kowalski's cool-headed strategy saved them countless times, and Dunnagan's unwavering dedication kept their unit grounded when the violence threatened to tear them apart. Their bond had been cemented in the crucible of war, and even as they drifted into different spheres, Dunnagan into the political arena and Kowalski into the covert world of intelligence, their trust in one another remained unshakable. The phone rang twice before Kowalski picked up. His voice was gruff but familiar, an anchor in the storm Dunnagan was battling.

"Tom, it's been a while," Kowalski said, pointing out that the sound of movement in the background was likely the man multitasking.

"Kowalski," Dunnagan replied, his voice carrying the weight of the situation. "I need your help. It's urgent."

There was a pause on the other end, followed by a shift in tone. Kowalski had always been quick to assess a situation, and he could hear the strain in Dunnagan's voice.

"Talk to me," Kowalski said, his words now clipped and businesslike. "What's going on?"

Dunnagan didn't waste time with pleasantries. He laid out the blackmail, the photos, and the dangerous game Ravi played. He spoke quickly but clearly, knowing Kowalski would catch every word and start formulating a plan the second the information hit his ears.

On the other end of the line, Kowalski listened silently, his mind likely already calculating the next steps. There was a brief pause when Dunnagan finished, and then Kowalski spoke.

"I'll take care of it," Kowalski said, his voice as steady as ever.

"but Tom, you must understand this: Ravi's no small-time player. If he's involved, this is bigger than just some cheap blackmail scheme."

"I know," Dunnagan replied, his jaw tight. "but I won't let him win. Not this time."

There was a beat of silence before Kowalski responded, his voice laced with the grim determination Dunnagan had come to rely on during their tours.

"Good. Because if you're going to fight, we need to strike him. No room for mistakes."

The call ended, but Dunnagan felt the weight lift slightly off his shoulders. He had set the wheels in motion. Kowalski wasn't just a fixer; he was a man who could dismantle entire operations with a single phone call, and right now, that's precisely what Dunnagan needed. As he pocketed his phone, Dunnagan's thoughts wandered back to the battlefield, where he and Kowalski had once been soldiers, not pawns in a twisted political game. In the dusty heat of Iraq or the freezing mountains of Afghanistan, they had fought for survival with nothing more than grit and the iron-clad trust they had in each other.

But this? This was a different kind of war. It wasn't fought with guns and bombs but with secrets, manipulation, and power, yet the stakes were just as high. For Dunnagan, this wasn't just about survival. It was about reclaiming his honour, career, and life from the hands of a man who thought he could manipulate him into submission. Dunnagan wasn't going to back down. He had Kowalski at his side, and together, they would rip apart Ravi's plans piece by piece.

As he stood amid the wreckage of his rage in the darkened room, Dunnagan felt something unfamiliar creeping into his chest hope. He knew the fight wasn't over, but now, he was ready for it. The soldier in him had been reawakened, and if Ravi thought he could win this battle with a few compromising photos and a dirty scheme, he had no idea who he was up against.

Dunnagan picked up his phone and dialled Ravi. The call was answered after five rings.

"I've been thinking about our deal." Dunagan spat out. "I've decided to change it."

"Change it?" Ravi spluttered.

"Yes, you'll give me all the pictures back and move on," Dunnagan said.

"What?" Said Ravi, even more confused now.

"I've got the CIA hunting you down. Give the picture and files up."

Ravi's world flipped on its head. Was this Anna? Was this a nightmare, and would he wake soon? Ravi thought quickly that he would disappear and protect the files.

"May the best man win," Ravi said, then ended the call.

Game on.

7: Unravelling the Threads

Kowalski moved swiftly, driven by the urgency of the task. There was no room for hesitation. The video files needed to be destroyed and Jayasekera, slippery as he was, couldn't be allowed to vanish. Failure wasn't an option. He had been in tighter spots before, both in war zones and on covert missions, but this situation felt different. The stakes weren't just geopolitical; they were personal. Tom Dunnagan had been there for him when it mattered most, and Kowalski wouldn't let him down now.

Pulling up Jayasekera's last reported location, a bustling spot on the volcanic island of Santorini, Kowalski smirked. It wasn't exactly a fortress, but Jayasekera was far too connected to underestimate. Santorini's maze of cliffside streets, high-end resorts, and discreet villas could serve as a perfect hideout. With the right contacts, Jayasekera could disappear into the luxurious anonymity of the island and slip away unnoticed, and if he made it to London, he would be untouchable and well-protected within his network of corrupt officials and wealthy patrons.

But Kowalski had his web of connections. As a former Marine turned CIA operative, he had access to resources that reached everywhere. After making a few calls, he tapped into the local traffic cameras and city surveillance systems. His contacts on the ground in Greece owed him a few favours. It wasn't long before the footage came through a grainy image of Jayasekera slipping into a black luxury sedan at a port-side cafe. Kowalski's eyes narrowed as he watched the live feed. He could feel the adrenaline kick in, the familiar rush of being on a hunt. Jayasekera was moving, heading towards the island's airport. The playboy was making a run for it, and London was his destination. If Jayasekera made it there, the odds would shift drastically in his favour. Kowalski couldn't let that happen. The clock was ticking.

"Gotcha," Kowalski muttered, fingers flying across his laptop as he initiated a data trace on the would-be plane to London. He wouldn't intercept him on Greek soil, which would attract too much attention, but if he could delay Jayasekera's departure, even for a few hours, it would buy him the time he needed to make his move. The next step was to scramble Jayasekera's flight plans. Kowalski called an air traffic controller contact in Athens who had once been stationed in Afghanistan during a NATO operation. It took a bit of convincing, but the controller owed him big time for a favour that had saved his career.

"I need you to ground BA653 (Jayasekera's plane)," Kowalski instructed, his voice firm and measured. "Do whatever you have to make up a weather delay, mechanical fault, whatever. Just buy me three hours."

"You're asking for a lot," the controller muttered. "But I owe you. Consider it done."

With that in place, Kowalski pivoted, pulling up a secure comm link to Dunnagan. He needed to be informed of the plan and coordinate their next steps. Time was of the essence, and every second mattered. Dunnagan's low and tense voice came through as the secure connection buzzed to life.

"What's the update, Kowalski?" Dunnagan asked, impatience barely masked. He knew his fate hinged on Kowalski's success.

"We've got a window. Jayasekera's on his way to London, but I've grounded his plane at the airport in Santorini for a few hours. It's not much, but it's enough for me to intercept. I'll ensure the video files and copies never see the light of day."

Kowalski could hear the exhale of relief on the other end.

"Good. Because if Ravi gets those files back to London, we're screwed. This must end now," Dunnagan replied, his voice steely and determined.

Kowalski was confident in the gravity of the situation. This wasn't just about blackmail. It was about dismantling an empire of corruption that Ravi Jayasekera had built on manipulation and deceit. It was about protecting Dunnagan's career and, in turn, safeguarding national security. Ravi wasn't playing small games. If he gained the upper hand, it wouldn't be long before he twisted the political landscape to his will. As Kowalski closed the call, he returned to the task at hand. Santorini was known for its winding roads, and he needed to act fast if he was going to catch Jayasekera before he disappeared. Fortunately, Kowalski had found a local agent with experience in terrain far worse than this. Kowalski had quickly arranged for a high-speed boat from a nearby marina, knowing it would be the fastest way to intercept Jayasekera at the airport. The sea was calm, glittering under the afternoon sun, but Kowalski barely noticed, though his video link from the agent's camera on the front of his tactical vest. His mind was already running through scenarios, planning his approach, preparing for contingencies.

The boat sliced through the water, the agent's hands steady on the controls. In the distance, he could see the coastline, the luxury resorts perched on cliffs, and the whitewashed buildings gleaming in the sunlight. It was beautiful, almost serene, but they weren't here for the views. His eyes were locked on the airstrip where British Airways ' plane sat idle, its pilot undoubtedly wondering why their departure had been delayed. As the agent approached the dock, he spotted the black sedan parked near the airstrip's private entrance. His pulse quickened, and a grim smile tugged at the corner of his mouth. Jayasekera was still here, and it was time to finish the job.

He docked the boat and moved with purpose toward the airstrip, his hand resting on the holster concealed beneath his jacket. The agent wasn't one for unnecessary violence, but if it came to it, he wasn't afraid to use force to get what he needed. Years of CIA training had taught him to read a situation and anticipate his target's moves before they knew they'd been compromised.

Ravi stood in the gleaming, modern terminal of Santorini Airport, his phone clenched tightly in one hand, his mind preoccupied with plans and a sense of impending danger. He had been thinking about his upcoming rendezvous with Andy in London. He was no ordinary friend and impressing him required more than picking a trendy spot in the city. Ravi needed something unique to solidify their partnership and set the tone for what would come. He mulled over luxurious private clubs, opulent hotels, and restaurants known for their exclusivity, but the unease in his gut kept distracting him.

His eyes wandered to the departure monitors, a flicker of irritation surfacing as he saw his flight to London had been delayed. The sense of control he always prided himself on was slipping away, replaced by an unsettling feeling that things were shifting against him. He knew better than to ignore that instinct. Something was off. Ravi paced for a moment, trying to assess the situation. London wasn't safe for him right now. He'd sensed ripples in the atmosphere ever since he made his play with Dunnagan. The compromised video might have been enough to secure his advantage for a time, but Ravi grew suspicious that his enemies were closing in faster than anticipated. He wasn't about to sit idly by while they got the upper hand.

Glancing around the bustling airport, he scanned the departure board, searching for alternatives. Athens, then onto Amsterdam; a flight left in just forty minutes. Perfect. He didn't need to be in London immediately, and Amsterdam offered the anonymity he craved. Plus, it was a city where Ravi had long cultivated relationships with influential, shadowy figures who owed him favours. Without a second thought, he went to the airline's ticket counter, flashing his passport and purchasing a seat on the Athens flight. As he moved through security, he mentally mapped out his next steps. In Amsterdam, he could regroup, evaluate the situation, and, most importantly, stay out of sight. Whoever tried to delay his plans wouldn't anticipate him making such an abrupt change. By the time they figured it out, Ravi would already be back in control of the game.

Once past security, Ravi slipped into the VIP lounge, the dim lighting and plush chairs offering a temporary respite from the chaos brewing outside. He sat down, ordering an espresso, his mind still ticking through possibilities. Where would he meet Andy now? A part of him relished the uncertainty, the thrill of being one step ahead. He knew Andy well enough to understand that their meeting didn't need a specific place. It needed to be strategic. The click of his phone snapped him out of his thoughts. A message from Andy flashed on the screen:

*Any update on our meeting spot? I'll be in London soon. *

Ravi's fingers hovered over the keyboard. He started typing.

*Change of plans. Amsterdam via Athens first, then London. *

He hit send and took a sip of his espresso, a slight smirk playing at the corners of his lips. This wasn't a setback;

it was a pivot, and if there was one thing Ravi excelled at, it was turning complications into opportunities.

As he sat there, Ravi's thoughts returned to his unfinished business with Dunnagan. The man was dangerous and had unpredictable qualities Ravi admired to some degree, but now, Dunnagan was a loose end, and Ravi had no intention of leaving loose ends. The Secretary of State had been trapped by his desires, and Ravi had the evidence to bring him down. Still, the problem with power was that people like Dunnagan fought tooth and nail to keep it. Ravi needed to stay ahead, or he could be exposed.

The loudspeaker chimed, announcing 'final boarding' for the Athens flight. Ravi rose, smoothing his suit jacket, his sharp gaze sweeping over the other passengers, none of whom paid him any mind. That was precisely how he liked it, moving among people without them ever noticing his presence, it gave him an edge. He was always there, always watching, but never the one being watched. Walking toward the gate, he felt the familiar thrill of manoeuvring through the chaos. This wasn't just about survival. It was about winning. Everything was a calculation, every decision an opportunity. He was on his way to Amsterdam; from there, London would come next. By the time Andy caught up, Ravi would have everything in place.

Stepping onto the plane, he settled into his seat, anticipating the next move.

After losing himself for 36 hours in Amsterdam's narrow canals and hazy streets, Ravi's plane finally touched down at London Heathrow. The landing was smooth, but his mind was anything but settled. He stared out the window as the aircraft taxied slowly toward Terminal 5. The grey London skyline, bathed in a rare shimmer of sunshine, was both a welcome sight and a reminder of the ticking clock. Then, like a bolt of clarity through the fog of exhaustion, it came to him a meeting spot that would set the perfect tone for what needed to be done. Pulling out his phone, Ravi opened Telegram, the encrypted messaging app he and Andy preferred for sensitive discussions. It was only fitting, given their current circumstances. He typed quickly:

"Madison's rooftop bar, 18:00. St Paul's Cathedral view. Perfect for a drink in this rare London heat."

He hit send, already picturing the scene. The uncharacteristically warm weather would loosen people up, ease tension, and blur the lines between business and pleasure. It was just the kind of environment he needed to keep things under control. Ravi knew navigating the labyrinth of London's streets and the endless public transport delays would take him at least an hour and a half. He was prepared for it, and the city's hustle was something he thrived on. The late afternoon sun promised the ideal backdrop: golden light casting long shadows over the bustling financial district as workers spilt out the gleaming skyscrapers for their evening respite. Madison's rooftop, with its panoramic view of St Paul's, was the perfect stage. It was ironic, meeting in the heart of the city's financial power while discussing their own more covert power plays.

Sitting back in the taxi that ferried him from the airport, Ravi felt the familiar rhythm of London pulse beneath him. The glass towers rising on the horizon, the clatter of buses, and the distant hum of conversation all buzzed around him, but Ravi remained in his world, strategising. Every street they passed, every landmark they zipped by, reminded him of the high-stakes game they were playing. London was a city of fortunes made and lost, of people rising and falling spectacularly. As he approached the city centre, Ravi found his mind wandering to Andy. How would he find Andy after all these months? Their friendship had always been one of necessity rather than sentiment, built on mutual benefit and a shared hunger for success. With his calm demeanour and razor-sharp mind, Andy had always been the man to execute the plans Ravi devised. But now, with so much on the line, Ravi wondered if the dynamics between them had shifted. The timeline was getting tighter, and with it, the stakes. Could Andy still be trusted to follow through or had London's brutal machine chewed him up and spat him out since their last meeting?

He looked back at his phone, but there was yet to be a response. He wasn't worried though. Andy always had a flair for the dramatic and never missed an opportunity to make an entrance. The plan was simple: meet at the bar, chat over drinks, and map out their next moves. But behind the casual façade, Ravi knew they were treading a tightrope. The blackmail on Dunnagan had given them leverage, but it had also made them enemies, and in London, enemies were never far behind. The cab finally crawled through the thick evening traffic, dropping him near St Paul's. Ravi stepped out, feeling the warm breeze on his face. The cathedral's dome loomed above him, majestic and imposing against the cloudless sky. He walked toward Madison's, seeing the city workers flooding the streets in a wave of loosened ties and laughter. To anyone else, it was just another warm evening in the capital, a rare, joyful occasion when the weather allowed Londoners to linger outside, sipping drinks in the golden hour, but to Ravi, this was a battlefield disguised as a playground.

Inside the elevator to the rooftop, Ravi caught a glimpse of himself in the mirror. His suit, though slightly crumpled from the journey, still exuded power. His eyes, dark and calculating, reflected the resolve that had carried him through far riskier ventures than this. Ravi's confidence returned as the elevator dinged open, revealing the open-air terrace with its expansive skyline view. The rooftop bar was already teeming with life. Laughter and chatter filled the air, the sound of glasses clinking in celebration mingling with the soft beats of music playing over the speakers. Ravi spotted the perfect table with a prime view of the cathedral and far enough from the crowd to ensure some privacy. He made his way over, ordering a whisky neat as he settled in, scanning the crowd for Andy's familiar face.

The city sparkled under the late afternoon sun, and Ravi felt a momentary thrill. This was his domain, where power flowed as freely as the drinks. As he sipped his whisky, he could feel the tension building. Andy would arrive soon, and the actual game would begin when he did. But for now, Ravi let himself enjoy the view, the warmth, and the quiet knowledge that London's undercurrent of ambition and deception was precisely where he thrived.

The late-summer evening buzzed with life as Andy stepped onto Madison's rooftop. The air was warm, carrying the scent of fresh cocktails and the unmistakable energy of the crowd winding down after a long day. Laughter rippled across the terrace, blending with the clinking of ice against the glass and the soft hum of conversation. Against the skyline, St. Paul's Cathedral stood proudly, its dome bathed in the golden glow of the setting sun, a perfect contrast to the vibrant scene unfolding beneath it. He scanned the terrace and, sure enough, spotted Ravi holding court at a corner table, surrounded by a group of lively young women. Ravi's animated gestures and sparkling grin were unmistakable, even from across the bar. He was the centre of attention, charming his audience with ease. The women were laughing, draped in chic dresses and sipping champagne, clearly entranced by Ravi's charisma. Andy, however, felt a familiar pang of irritation rise in his chest. Ravi's penchant for blurring the line between business and pleasure was nothing new, but it grated on him more than usual tonight.

Andy walked through the crowd with a slight roll of his eyes, weaving between tables and groups of city workers enjoying the evening. He approached the table, forcing a smile as Ravi caught his eye and raised his glass in a toast, calling out his name with exaggerated enthusiasm.

"Andy, my friend!" Ravi's voice was loud enough to turn heads. "Ladies, this is the man I've been telling you about. Come, sit, have a drink!"

Andy nodded politely, exchanging pleasantries with the women who smiled at him, their eyes flickering with curiosity. He could tell they were intrigued, sensing the tension in the air despite Ravi's carefree demeanour.

One of them slid a glass of champagne toward him, but Andy waved it away, his mind elsewhere.

As the evening wore on, the champagne continued to flow, and the conversations became more animated. Ravi, ever the entertainer, entertained his companions with stories, gesturing broadly, his laughter cutting through the hum of the crowd, but Andy wasn't in the mood. He felt the weight of their unfinished business pressing down on him, and Ravi's playful act only made it worse. They had important matters to discuss, and every minute wasted felt like a luxury they couldn't afford.

Finally, unable to tolerate it any longer, Andy leaned over to Ravi, his voice low but firm. "We need to talk," he said, his eyes narrowing as he caught Ravi's attention. Ravi's smile faltered briefly, but he quickly recovered, flashing a grin at the woman before excusing himself with a charming, "Ladies, I'll be right back. Don't go anywhere."

He followed Andy to a quieter corner of the terrace, away from the crowd's noise and prying eyes. The change in atmosphere was immediate. Gone was the playful, carefree Ravi who had been the life of the party just moments before. In his place stood the sharp, calculating man Andy knew all too well.

Andy crossed his arms, frustration simmering beneath the surface. "What the hell was that?" He asked, his voice taut with exasperation. "We were supposed to meet and strategies, not throw a party."

Ravi, unbothered by the confrontation, leaned against the railing and shrugged. "Relax, Andy. We've got time—no need to rush into things. Besides," He added with a smirk, "a little charm never hurts in our line of work. You know that."

Andy shook his head, his jaw clenched. "This isn't a game, Ravi. Dunnagan's breathing down our necks and probably already piecing together a plan to take us down. We don't have the luxury of wasting time with your distractions."

Ravi's smirk faded, his eyes hardening as he straightened up. "I know exactly what's at stake, Andy. But panicking won't get us anywhere. We're on the verge of something huge that could change everything. We need to play this right."

Andy sighed, rubbing the back of his neck. "Play it right?" He repeated, his voice tinged with disbelief. "We've been playing a dangerous game from the start, and now, Dunnagan's on edge. We must be ahead of him, Ravi, not wasting time on rooftop bars."

Andy hesitated, a flicker of doubt in his mind. He wanted to believe Ravi had everything under control, but something felt off. The stakes were high, and it seemed like Ravi was playing with fire.

"Just trust me," Ravi said quietly, sensing Andy's unease. "I've got this."

Andy met his gaze, the weight of their precarious situation hanging between them. After a moment, he nodded slowly. "Fine," he muttered. "but we need to stay sharp. No more distractions."

Ravi clapped him on the shoulder, the playful grin returning to his face. "You worry too much, Andy. We'll get through this."

As they returned to the table, the sun had dipped below the horizon, casting a soft, dusky glow over the city. The women were still there, laughing and chatting, oblivious to the serious conversation that had just taken place. Andy, however, couldn't shake the feeling that time was running out, and with every passing moment, the walls were closing in.

Ravi leaned over to Andy, "I suggest you take the evidence."

Andy looked at Ravi. It was going to be like putting a grenade in your pocket.

"OK," said Andy.

Ravi slipped the small micro-SD card from his pocket and handed it to Andy, feeling the weight of their shared choices settle heavily between them. At that moment, a deep sense of trust passed silently as their eyes locked. Each understood their precarious position as two friends navigating a storm of intrigue and danger, where every decision could lead to ruin or redemption.

"Just be careful," Ravi said, his voice low and earnest, hinting at the gravity of the situation.

He had decided to lay low for a while to remove himself from the line of fire and let the dust settle. Andy nodded solemnly, the acceptance of this plan weighing on him. Discretion was paramount; they knew any misstep could expose them to unimaginable risks.

They embraced, a quick firm hug that spoke volumes of their camaraderie and shared resolve. As Ravi shrugged effortlessly into his tailored suit jacket, the fabric draped over him like armour, ready to face the unpredictable world outside. There was a strength in him, a determination that Andy admired, even if it masked the uncertainty brewing beneath the surface. Watching Ravi's figure melt into the thrumming pulse of the city, Andy felt a pang of gratitude wash over him. He was thankful for his friend's unwavering support, especially in these tumultuous times, but a flicker of guilt crept in at his earlier impatience. He had been frustrated and worried about the stakes, but as he saw Ravi disappear into the crowd, a sobering realisation settled upon him: the responsibility was now his alone.

With a heavy sigh, Andy turned his gaze toward the sprawling cityscape. The high-rises loomed above him like sentinels, their glass and steel facades reflecting the dying light of the day. Long shadows over London's labyrinthine streets hinted at the complexities hidden within the city, each alley and corner concealing secrets waiting to be unearthed. His mind raced with the enormity of what lay ahead. The micro-SD card, now a tangible symbol of their entwined fates, had to be safeguarded at all costs. It held the key to their futures, a delicate thread connecting them to their plan and hope for salvation. As tenacity coursed through his veins, a fire ignited within him. He had to ensure that Ravi's intricate designs were not unravelled.

Andy set out for Heathrow, the bustling streets alive with the sounds of the evening, the honking of cars, the distant chatter of commuters, the intoxicating scent of street food wafting through the air. Each step he took felt deliberate, a reminder of the importance of his undertaking. With its rich tapestry of lives and stories, the city became a labyrinth he needed to navigate with cunning and clarity. He dodged pedestrians, weaving through crowds of people, unaware of the storm brewing beneath the surface of his calm exterior.

Thoughts swirled in his mind like autumn leaves caught in a whirlwind. How could he protect the SD card? Who could he trust? As the underground tunnel led him closer to the airport, he felt the pulse of London beneath his feet, a reminder that even in chaos, opportunity lay waiting. With every footfall, Andy fortified his resolve. He had to be strategic and think several steps ahead. The stakes were higher than ever, and he could not afford to falter. This was not just about the micro-SD card; it was about loyalty, friendship, and the lengths they would go to safeguard their ambitions.

8: Closing the Net

Kowalski sat in the dimly lit surveillance room, glued to the screens displaying real-time footage of Ravi and Andy. His fingers tapped rhythmically on the edge of his desk, the tension in the air tangible. He still hadn't forgiven himself for letting Ravi slip away in Santorini. That debacle had turned his professional mission into something far more personal. Ravi was now a mark, and Kowalski's obsession with catching him had become a vendetta that would not rest until he held the upper hand. When Kowalski learned that Ravi and Andy had met at Madison's rooftop bar, a spark ignited in his chest. The pieces were falling into place, and the nagging feeling that these two were working together had just been confirmed. Watching them on the grainy footage, laughing and mingling under the London skyline, made Kowalski's stomach turn. He had seen this before, individuals enjoying a fleeting moment of freedom, unaware they were already in his crosshairs.

He leaned back, arms crossed over his broad chest, considering his options. Kowalski was no rookie he knew from years of field experience that confrontation was often a fast track to disaster. A clash now would only force Ravi and Andy to retreat further underground, and they'd become even more challenging to trace. No, a more subtle, covert approach was needed. A web of control, delicate but unbreakable. Without hesitation, Kowalski launched into action, harnessing his extensive resources. His team began to check Ravi and Andy's every move. Calls, texts, emails, everything was on his radar now. As the data streams poured in, Kowalski's analytical mind got to work, sifting through layers of encrypted messages and digital breadcrumbs. His face remained impassive as the puzzle slowly came together, a man utterly in his element.

Kowalski chuckled darkly, remembering a lesson from his early days in the Marines: "In an investigation, the smallest details are often the most critical." He lived by those words. Patience was his most significant asset, serving him well over the years. He was a hunter, and every good hunter knew the value of stalking prey, waiting for the perfect moment to strike. So, as the hours stretched, he stayed focused, intent on unravelling the tangled threads that connected Ravi and Andy. With meticulousness bordering on obsession, Kowalski began orchestrating a multi-pronged strategy to disrupt their movements. He knew they had something incriminating enough to be worth all this trouble. The missing video file still hung over his mission like a ghost, and Kowalski's need to recover it became paramount. That file wasn't just a personal vendetta; it was tied to national security. Losing it could jeopardise everything, including people, reputations, and even the president himself.

Every decision Kowalski made was deliberate. First, he worked to isolate them, using his contacts to subtly inconvenience Andy's travel arrangements, forcing delays and last-minute flight cancellations. Meanwhile, he placed a watch on all of Ravi's potential hideouts. By manipulating their environment, Kowalski aimed to rattle them and make them question every move they made. A wry smile played on his lips as he watched a live feed of Andy pacing at Heathrow Airport, clearly frustrated by the sudden delay in his flight schedule.

"Good," Kowalski muttered, "keep them on edge."

It was a classic tactic that would wear down even the most composed operative.

As the hours dragged on, Kowalski felt the weight of the game pressing down on him. It wasn't just about the video anymore it was about control. The longer Ravi and Andy remained in play, the more risks they posed. His eyes flicked to another monitor, where Ravi's last known location was tracked through traffic cameras. London was a sprawling metropolis, but Kowalski had eyes everywhere. His covert approach allowed him to stay in the shadows, ever watchful, ever patient. In this chess game, he knew that the next move had to be his and decisive. One wrong step and one overlooked detail would all come crashing down.

Kowalski's instincts sharpened with every passing hour. His experience told him that Andy Stuart, with his clean-cut tech background, would be too nervous to hold onto something as volatile as the incriminating video file for long. He knew Stuart would eventually pass it off to someone else, someone more practised at handling this kind of heat, and Kowalski's gut rarely steered him wrong. With that hunch guiding him, Kowalski dived headfirst into the investigation, tirelessly pouring over hours of CCTV footage from multiple angles across London. His eyes scanned the screens for anything out of place, such as furtive glances, handoffs, or fleeting moments that could hint at a covert exchange. As days blurred into nights, his patience was rewarded when he caught sight of Stuart in what seemed like an unusually intimate conversation with a man he hadn't seen before.

Kowalski's fingers flew across the keys, running the face through his databases. A match came up: Chris Langrish, an unfamiliar name who was effectively a nobody and was the perfect candidate for holding onto the SD card. Kowalski's pulse quickened. The trail had heated up. From there, it was all about the details, and Kowalski thrived on them. He uncovered a communication pattern between Stuart and Langrish, subtle and unremarkable to the untrained eye but clear to someone like Kowalski. Texts were encrypted, locations were deliberately chosen to avoid detection, and data transfers appeared routine at first glance but held a more profound significance. A digital trail had been laid, and Kowalski was happy to follow it.

What cemented his suspicions were his trusted informants who lived in the city's underbelly, invisible to the public but invaluable to operatives like Kowalski. He called in favours, cashing in on years of cultivated relationships with informers in the tech and security industries. A word here, a slip of information there, and it became clear: Andy Stuart had indeed passed the video file to Chris Langrish.

As Kowalski pieced together the final details, his next move became clear. He traced Langrish's recent movements and confirmed that the man had retreated to his home, a quiet apartment in Athens, Georgia. Langrish was smart enough to stay off the radar, but even the cleverest players could be found with the right resources.

Kowalski smiled as he pulled up the file on two of his top operatives, conveniently located within a four-hour radius of Langrish's apartment. Both men were highly trained, with decades of experience in covert retrieval operations. They had handled far more dangerous situations than a simple SD card extraction, and Kowalski trusted them implicitly. Without hesitation, he sent out the order.

"Retrieve the SD card. No collateral damage." His message was concise but loaded with the weight of the operation. This wasn't just about recovering sensitive material anymore; it was about safeguarding national security, maintaining control over the narrative, and ensuring that Ravi and Stuart's attempts to manipulate those in power would crumble before they had the chance to take root.

Kowalski imagined the operatives moving swiftly through the night like phantoms, their footsteps soundless, their actions precise. Langrish wouldn't see them coming, nor would he ever understand the full extent of the forces aligned against him. Kowalski relished the thought, knowing that the SD card would be in his possession when the sun rose. It culminated weeks of patient observation, tactical brilliance, and unwavering focus.

With the order given, Kowalski leaned back in his chair, his eyes never leaving the monitors. Every minute mattered now, and every second brought him closer to securing the victory he had so painstakingly pursued. He had Ravi, Andy, and now Langrish all in his web. The game was nearing its end, and Kowalski intended to be the one standing when the pieces finally fell into place.

9: A Serendipitous Encounter

Chris Langrish had always been captivated by drama, the raw emotions, the tension, and the transformation. Born in the heart of Athens Georgia, Chris's childhood was a tapestry woven with the rich cultural threads of the southern United States. Athens was a town that breathed art with its indie music scene and eclectic blend of creative minds. Growing up in this fertile environment, Chris found himself naturally drawn to performance, as if the town's creative pulse had become his heartbeat. From an early age, Chris felt most alive on stage. It didn't matter whether it was in front of a crowd of hundreds or a small group of passersby on a street corner, acting was his escape. The stage became his sanctuary, a place where he could not only channel his emotions but also step into the shoes of others, immersing himself in lives far removed from his own. He thrived on the power of transformation, relishing the applause that followed each performance as if it were a validation of his very existence.

In school, Chris became something of a local legend. Teachers admired his natural talent, and peers envied his ability to captivate an audience with only a few lines of dialogue and an expressive glance. Every role he inhabited, from the tragic hero to the comic fool, fuelled his dreams of one day making it big. It wasn't just about fame for Chris; it was about the power to move people, to make them laugh, cry, and think. But as much as Chris dreamed of a future filled with lights and applause, life had other plans for him, as it often does. At fourteen, his family was uprooted, and the streets of Athens, Georgia, were swapped for the rolling green hills of England. The move came without warning. His father had accepted a lucrative position in the UK, and there was no room for debate. Chris was devastated.

The transition from the sun-soaked South to England's misty, cool climes was like stepping into an entirely different world. Gone were the familiar sights and sounds of his childhood, the bustling creative energy of Athens replaced by a small English town's quiet, conservative atmosphere. Chris lost his vibrant personality dulled by the weight of dislocation. His thick Georgian drawl stood out like a sore thumb among his British peers' clipped accents; though he had always been confident, the sudden change left him feeling adrift. At first, Chris resented the move. He resented his parents for tearing him away from everything he knew and loved, and he resented England for being so unlike the home he had left behind. But as time passed, he began to realise that this new chapter, while painful, presented new opportunities.

Theatres in England carried centuries of tradition, and though his first performances in school plays had felt like a dull echo of what he'd known in Georgia, Chris soon found his stride. There was a different kind of power to be found here, a subtle, more restrained form of acting that challenged him to refine his craft. As he grew older, Chris discovered that his passion for performance could be applied in ways he hadn't previously considered. Despite the setbacks that had peppered his journey, Chris Langrish's resilience was undeniable. He owned an irreverent charm that lit up every role he inhabited, pulling audiences and fellow actors into the orbit of his vibrant energy. His presence filled a room, whether on stage or off, making him as unforgettable as any of the characters he played. This magnetic quality would lead to a chance encounter that would forever alter the course of his life.

One crisp London evening, Chris performed in a lively production at the Palace Theatre, nestled in the heart of the city's vibrant theatre district. The air was buzzing with anticipation that night, and the audience's energy was evident from behind the curtain. Chris gave one of his most spirited performances, constantly feeding off the crowd's energy. The spotlight danced on his features as he delivered each line with the same passion and irreverence that had become his signature. And when the final curtain bow came, the thunderous applause was as much for him as for the show itself. Afterwards, as was his routine, Chris made his way to The Cambridge, a cosy, historical pub just around the corner from the theatre. The pub, with its low ceilings, well-worn leather booths, and dark wood-panelled walls, was a favourite haunt of actors and artists alike. It was the kind of place where the warmth of conversation mingled with the clinking of pint glasses, where stories of failed auditions and unexpected triumphs flowed as freely as the beer.

Chris wasn't expecting more than the usual post-show pint this evening and perhaps a chat with familiar faces from the London theatre scene, but as he sipped his drink, he noticed a man sitting at the end of the bar with a pint in hand and a thoughtful look. Their eyes met briefly, and before long, the man started a conversation. His name was Andy Stuart. Tall, with easy confidence, Andy seemed like someone who knew how to command a room without needing the spotlight. What started as small talk quickly grew into something more. A shared passion for the stage drew Chris and Andy together, but it was more than that. Their conversation was fluid and easy as if they had known each other for far longer than the few hours they had been talking. Chris regaled Andy with stories from his Southern upbringing in Athens, Georgia, and the strange journey that had brought him from the American South to the cobbled streets of London. Andy, in turn, shared his experiences, his love of theatre, his work in the world of high-stakes politics, and his tales of personal reinvention.

When the pub's last call sounded, the two were no longer just acquaintances. They were fast friends. Chris felt a rare kinship as they raised their glasses for one last toast. There was something in Andy that resonated with him, a camaraderie he hadn't felt since leaving his childhood home behind. In Andy, Chris found a friend and a kindred spirit who understood the highs and lows of life's unpredictable twists, but it wasn't just the theatre that bonded them. Throughout many evenings spent at The Cambridge or wandering the streets of Soho, they discovered a mutual appreciation for music, especially the pulsating sounds of the UK's 1980s new wave scene. For Chris, this music had always been a lifeline, a way to channel his rebellious spirit and defy convention. The quirky rhythms and bold lyrics of bands like The B-52s, The Stranglers, and Blondie had been the soundtrack to his adolescence in Athens, and now they found new resonance in the streets of London. Chris and Andy would lose hours in conversation about their favourite tracks, swapping stories of concerts they'd been to or albums they'd worn out from overplaying. In Andy, Chris found a rare kind of support. When auditions ended in rejection, Andy was there with a word of encouragement. When Chris triumphed, landing a coveted role, Andy cheered him on, raising a glass in celebration. For Chris, this friendship became a grounding force, a steady presence amidst the turbulence of his life as an actor. The camaraderie they built over pints and shared passions was a rare gift in a world that often felt isolating.

Little did they know, however, that their friendship would eventually transcend the safe confines of theatre and music, thrusting them into a much darker and more dangerous world. The seemingly serendipitous bond they had formed would soon be tested by forces far beyond their control, forces that neither of them could have predicted when they first met in the dim, warm light of The Cambridge pub. As they stood on the precipice of a new chapter, with the innocence of their bond still intact, Chris felt a strange gratitude for the twist of fate that had brought Andy into his life. Still, the shadows of secrets were already beginning to gather on the horizon.

10: The Alliance

Arriving at Heathrow, Andy's frustration spiked when the digital display flashed the dreaded word "Delayed." As the bustling airport hummed around him, he approached the counter, trying to rein in his impatience.

"Are there any other flights going out?" he asked, his voice betraying the tension in his chest. The attendant tapped at her screen, glancing up at him with a smile that felt all too calm, given the urgency swirling in Andy's mind.

"There's a Delta flight to New York that leaves in about an hour," she offered.

New York? Andy thought. It wasn't his planned destination, but the city could serve as a temporary escape. And besides, he needed a change of clothes, as his current attire was wrinkled from days of tension and impromptu meetings. After a moment of contemplation, he nodded. "I'll take it."

With his boarding pass in hand, Andy made his way through security, his thoughts racing faster than the crowds of passengers moving through the airport. By the time he settled into his first-class seat, the weight of the situation pressed heavily on him. The plane began its ascent, the roar of the engines muffling the world outside as London's skyline became a distant, fading memory below. The aircraft climbed to 39,000 feet, the clouds parting beneath like cotton wool scattered across the horizon. Despite the comfort of the leather seat, the ambient hum of the Dreamliner, and the attentive steward offering champagne, Andy couldn't relax. His hand brushed against the inside pocket of his jacket, where the SD card lay concealed. It was small, almost insignificant, but it seemed to pulse with a gravity that threatened to consume him. Every time his fingers grazed its edges, a wave of responsibility surged through him.

Ravi's words echoed in his head as if they were woven into the very fabric of the card.

"Make sure it doesn't fall into the wrong hands," Ravi had said, his eyes dark and serious, the weight of their predicament clear. "I've had the nod, and we're both in the crosshairs."

Andy had tried to shake off the creeping paranoia, but it clung to him like a second skin. The SD card held more than just their plans for manipulating the political timeline. It had their salvation or their downfall. If the contents were exposed, it wouldn't just ruin careers. It could unravel entire governments. The scandal and treachery were blackmail at the highest level, and Andy was carrying it with him halfway across the world. Andy's mind spun through potential strategies for safeguarding the card as the plane cruised. He knew handing it over to anyone in his immediate circle would be a grave mistake. Sarah, his PA, was intelligent, efficient, and loyal, though she was too deeply entrenched in his professional life. The risk was too significant.

No, Andy needed someone trustworthy but distant from the chaos around him. Someone with enough separation from his inner circle to avoid suspicion. His thoughts ran like a catalogue of faces and names until one stood out above the rest **Chris Langrish**. Chris was more than a friend; he was a constant. Chris had been there over the years, no matter the highs and lows. Loyal, steady, with an integrity that was rare in this world of shifting alliances. While Andy's world had become increasingly dangerous, Chris had still been far removed from the political machinations, the intrigue, and the power plays. That's exactly what Andy needed right now: distance but trust. Fortunately, Chris had long since moved back to Athens, Georgia.

Chris might not have known the details of Andy's current situation, but that was precisely why he was perfect. The fewer details he knew, the safer they both would be. Chris had always been a man who understood discretion and this time, it would be no different. Andy could almost picture him now, leaning back with that easy grin, shrugging off the situation's complexity with a wry comment and a reassuring clap. The thought of Chris brought a brief sense of relief. Andy let himself breathe for a moment, his grip on the SD card loosening slightly. He stared out the window, the darkening sky stretching endlessly before him, and resolved to make contact as soon as the plane touched down.

The city lights of New York were a long way off, but as Andy closed his eyes, he imagined the handover. With his extraordinary characteristics, Chris would take the SD card without questioning it, safeguarding it until Andy had figured out the next move. It wasn't just a plan; it was a lifeline.

Arranging to meet Chris in a quiet, tucked-away café on the outskirts of Athens, Andy knew the significance of this handover. The city's vibrant pulse seemed distant here, replaced by the soft murmur of voices and the occasional clink of glasses. The café was chosen for its anonymity, where tourists never ventured, and locals kept to themselves. Andy scanned the tables one last time, ensuring no suspicious eyes lingered, before sliding into the seat across from Chris. Ever the picture of calm with his sun-weathered face and laid-back charm, Chris greeted Andy with a firm handshake and an easy smile, but as soon as their eyes met, both men understood the gravity of the situation. Andy had been a friend for years, but this was a different trust. He was asking for a burden, not just a favour.

With a final glance around, Andy reached into his jacket pocket, feeling the cool, metallic edge of the SD card. It was so small, yet it felt heavier than anything he'd ever carried. He placed it gently into Chris's hand, his fingers lingering longer than usual as though reluctant to relinquish the burden entirely.

"Keep this safe," Andy's voice was low, firm, and unwavering. "No matter what happens, don't let it fall into the wrong hands."

Chris nodded, the gravity of the situation settling over him. His usual light-hearted demeanour shifted into one of solemn focus.

"I get it," he said quietly. "You don't need to say anything else.

He patted the SD card inside his worn leather jacket pocket for reassurance. His eyes met Andy's again and with a small, knowing smile, he added, "Winston Churchill once said, 'You can always count on

Americans to do the right thing after they've tried everything else.'"

Andy couldn't help but chuckle at the quote, though his gratitude for his friend ran more profound than his laughter. The warmth of Chris's words and the firm promise they carried gave him a glimmer of hope. Andy felt a sense of relief for the first time in days as though a weight had shifted, even if only slightly. As Chris stood up to leave, the two exchanged a brief embrace.

"You're a lifesaver, mate," Andy said, his voice quieter now, the tension of the past weeks still rippling under his tone.

Chris gave a wink and turned, disappearing into the winding streets of Athens with the SD card safely tucked away. Andy watched him go, a knot in his chest slowly loosening. He felt he was back in control for a fleeting moment, edging closer to rewriting the history he desperately needed to escape.

But neither man realised that **Kowalski** was already two steps ahead.

Still seething from his most recent slip-up, Kowalski had meticulously tracked their every move. His deep connections in the CIA gave him an unparalleled advantage. Every call, every meeting, every flight, Kowalski was there, lurking just beneath the surface, gathering intelligence like a predator stalking its prey.

It didn't take long for him to piece together that Andy wasn't the sole player in this game. His surveillance of Andy and Ravi had painted a clear picture: Andy was the key, but **Chris Langrish** now holds the most valuable evidence.

In his years as an operative, Kowalski had learned that success came from patience, and this time was no different. With each bit of intel, his determination to bring down Andy Stuart intensified. This wasn't just another mission. For Kowalski, this was personal. He owed Dunnagan. The fallout from the honeytrap scandal would have been catastrophic for the Secretary of State, and Kowalski had vowed to settle the score with those who dared to play such a dangerous game. To him, Andy and Ravi weren't just criminals, they were traitors, and traitors needed to be dealt with swiftly before the rot spread further.

Even as Chris and Andy parted ways, Kowalski's fingers danced over his laptop, his sharp eyes glued to a live feed of Athens. His jaw clenched as he focused on his next move, his mind running through many possibilities. With the information he'd gathered, it wouldn't be long before he closed in. He had alerted two top agents stationed in Greece, giving them strict instructions to recover the SD card with surgical precision. This time, there would be no mistakes, no loose ends.

Andy felt the fragile comfort of hope as the sun dipped lower over Athens, casting the city in a golden glow. But little did he know Kowalski was tightening the noose. As darkness descended over the ancient city, a new game of shadows was about to begin.

11: The Safe House

With the CIA sparing no expense to track Andy's every move, Kowalski was closing in, inch by inch. Each passing moment it brought him closer to his target. His eyes were glued to multiple feeds, satellite images, digital intercepts, and live updates from agents on the ground. Every move was scrutinised, every interaction analysed. He could feel the tightening of the net. This wasn't just business anymore. It was personal. Meanwhile, miles away, **Chris Langrish** knew his window of time was shrinking. The air in his Athens apartment felt tense, the weight of responsibility pressing down on him like never before. He stood in the middle of his living room, the SD card in his hand feeling more like a ticking time bomb than a simple piece of plastic. The stakes had never felt so natural.

Chris's mind raced. He needed to protect the incriminating footage Ravi had passed to him. His fingers hovered over his laptop as he worked quickly, encrypting the SD card with an obscure password. Even he had to chuckle at his ingenuity. "Good luck unlocking that," he muttered, a smirk pulling at the corners of his lips. But there was little time for self-satisfaction. His thoughts snapped to the next challenge: hiding it. He scanned his apartment with a growing sense of urgency. The adrenaline pumping through his veins made everything seem sharper, including the creaks of the old floorboards, the faint hum of traffic below his window, and the clock ticking on the wall. His eyes darted from the bookshelf to the sofa cushions before finally landing on the kitchen cupboard. It was unassuming, rarely opened, and cluttered enough to keep any casual intruder from snooping too profoundly.

"That's it," Chris whispered to himself, almost like performing a line from one of his old plays. With the precision of an actor stepping into character, he moved swiftly, opening the cupboard and tucking the tiny card behind a tin of Earl Grey tea. His heart was pounding, each beat echoing in his ears as he closed the cupboard door with a soft *click*. He took a deep breath as if sealing the act with his quiet flourish. But just as Chris began to steady his nerves, the piercing chime of his **Ring doorbell** shattered the silence in the apartment. The sound sliced through the air, causing him to freeze in place, his hand still on the cupboard door. His heart, which had only moments before started to calm, leapt back into his throat. Every muscle tensed. His phone buzzed on the countertop and with a trembling hand, Chris picked it up to check the live feed from the doorbell camera.

His stomach dropped.

Standing ominously on his doorstep were two figures dressed in black from head to toe, their faces obscured by balaclavas. They stood unnervingly still, like spectres, their bodies dark silhouettes against the backdrop of a dimly lit street. One raised a gloved hand to knock again, but Chris had already seen enough.

His worst fears were confirmed. They had found him.

His mind raced with possibilities. How had they tracked him down so quickly? Had he been sloppy? No, he had been careful. But this was Kowalski. Of course, it was Kowalski. He would leave no stone unturned. A sweat trickled down Chris's neck as he tried to gather his thoughts. He couldn't let them inside. The SD card was too valuable and too dangerous in the wrong hands. Yet, there they were, just inches away from blowing everything wide open. Time seemed to slow as Chris's options flashed before him. Should he run? Hide? He glanced at the fire escape outside the kitchen window but knew it would be risky. Every instinct told him to play it cool, to stall for time. He cleared his throat, forcing his voice into something that resembled calm.

"Who is it?" Chris called out, his voice echoing through the stillness of the apartment.

No response.

His pulse quickened again. He needed to think fast. Glancing once more at the live feed, he saw the two figures exchange a glance before one of them stepped closer to the door. Chris held his breath.

"We know you're in there," came the muffled voice through the door, low and menacing. "Open up. We're not here to hurt you."

The lie hung heavy in the air. Chris had heard lines like that too often in the movies to believe it now. His hands clenched into fists, his nails digging into his palms. He had to stall.

"I don't know who you are," Chris called back, stalling for time. "but you'd better have a warrant if you're knocking at this time of night."

The silence stretched for a moment, heavy with tension, before the second figure spoke up, his voice sharper.

"We don't need a warrant, Langrish. Open the door, or we're coming in."

Chris's blood ran cold. They were serious, and they weren't about to leave empty-handed. He glanced back at the cupboard where the SD card was hidden, the weight of his next decision pressing down on him. Outside, the two operatives exchanged another glance, nodding in unison. They moved with eerie precision, one stepping forward, ready to force entry. Chris knew he had seconds, maybe less. He could feel his heart hammering in his chest. There was no room for error now. If they got in, it was game over. With the SD card, everything would be lost. But if he could buy enough time, there might still be a way out. Gripping the counter with white-knuckled hands, Chris whispered to himself,

"Showtime."

Adrenaline surged through Chris Langrish's body, his pulse racing as he weighed his options. His mind was a chaotic blur, but one thought was clear: he had to move now. Grabbing his car keys from the kitchen counter, Chris looked back at the apartment, the encrypted SD card tucked safely away in the cupboard and prayed it would remain hidden. The people after him wouldn't stop until they had it, but he knew staying was no longer an option.

The chilly air hit his face as he scrambled out the fire escape at the back of his building, moving swiftly but carefully down the metal stairs. Each clang of his footfall echoed in the stillness of the night, amplifying his fear. He could almost feel eyes on him, as if Kowalski's reach stretched across the city, grasping at Chris's every move.

Inside the apartment, the two operatives Kowalski had sent were experts in their field, seasoned in black ops and covert missions. Both men had nerves of steel and were chosen for their efficiency and ability to leave no loose ends. They climbed the stairs to the fourth floor with calculated precision, their senses on high alert. Yet, as they neared the door, a sliver of dread began to creep into their minds. The Ring doorbell attached to the entrance was a glaring oversight, its red light a silent witness to their arrival.

"Damn it," muttering one of the operatives, shooting his partner a look of frustration. The mistake was amateur; now, anyone accessing the doorbell's feed could see them coming. They had to move fast.

The first choice was to knock and ask nicely; plan B was implemented after a few brief words. The first operative kicked the door in with a forceful crack, the sound ricocheting through the narrow hallway. They stormed into the apartment, weapons drawn, senses heightened. The space that had once been a sanctuary of calm, a minimalist apartment adorned with clean lines, framed playbills from Chris's acting days, and scattered remnants of a life lived between performances, was about to become ground zero.

It was clear that Chris had fled. "Did he have the card with him?" the taller operative asked. The second man in the matching balaclava checked his phone; it was linked to a portable scanner they had set up at the rear of Chris's apartment. After a moment, the operative said, "Negative, the card was not on him."

"Then it's in here; let's find it," came the reply.

With grim determination, they began tearing the place apart. Furniture was tossed aside, drawers ripped open, cushions shredded, and every nook and cranny were scoured. They worked methodically, leaving no surface unturned. Papers fluttered to the floor, glass shattered from an overturned table, and the apartment was a war zone of chaos within minutes. As they combed through the space, their frustration grew. Every second without the SD card brought them closer to failure and failure was not an option. Hours they stretched on, each moment dragging painfully as they scoured for the precious piece of tech that had eluded them. The walls seemed to close in on them as the operatives' confidence waned. The more they searched, the more obvious it became they had come up short.

The SD card was nowhere to be found.

One of them, a tall, stocky man with years of field experience etched into the hard lines of his face, clenched his fists in anger. "This doesn't make sense," he muttered. "It's here. It must be."

His shorter and more wiry but equally dangerous partner growled under his breath as he tossed another stack of papers aside.

"We've missed something," he said, his voice tight with frustration, but deep down, both men knew they had come in too late. Chris had gotten away, and the card was still out of reach.

Kowalski watched the situation closely in his safe house, expecting a swift conclusion. The SD card was critical. Its contents were too volatile to fall into the wrong hands. He had warned his men not to fail, but a bitter realisation set in as the hours ticked. They had failed. The repercussions of this were not just professional. For Kowalski, the stakes were personal. This was not just about recovering a sensitive video file but about loyalty to Dunnagan and settling more profound debts than most knew. His men had come up short, and now the clock was ticking on their next move.

Meanwhile, Chris drove through the quiet streets of Athens, his heart still racing, trying to calm his nerves. He'd left the apartment just in time but knew the danger wasn't over. He was on borrowed time now, and every decision moving forward had to be perfect. The SD card was still safely hidden, at least for now, but he couldn't let his guard down. He thought of Andy and the trust his old friend had placed in him, which gave him a renewed sense of determination. Protecting that card wasn't just about the mission anymore; it was about loyalty and doing the right thing in a world where the lines of right and wrong had blurred.

As Chris's car disappeared into the dark streets, the operatives in his apartment stood amongst the wreckage they had created. They had missed their mark, but their mission was far from over. They reported back to Kowalski with grim resolve, who knew the chase had begun.

Chris had slipped away this time, but they were closer than ever. The SD card and its secrets would not remain hidden for long.

Hours later, after gaining miles of distance, Chris finally found a moment to pull over, catch his breath and find a payphone. With quivering hands, it took Chris three attempts to feed the coin into the slot. When he managed to dial Andy's number, the other end rang five times before Andy answered. As Chris spoke, realisation dawned that the curtain had fallen on his role in this clandestine production. He would now be forced to watch as the drama played beyond his control. With a heavy heart, he prepared to disappear into the shadows.

12: Rock Lobster

Andy had barely wrapped up gruelling back-to-back meetings when his phone buzzed urgently on the desk. Distracted, he grabbed it, glancing at the screen to see an unfamiliar number. The sight sent a ripple of unease through him and calls like this rarely came with good news. He hesitated, then answered.

"Andy," Chris's breathless and frantic voice came on the other end, barely above a whisper. My work here is done. The dark forces are rising, and, as the bishop said to the actress, I'm out of here."

A chill ran through Andy as he gripped the phone tighter. Chris's usual flippant tone did little to mask the anxiety underneath, and the cryptic message hit him like a punch in the gut. Dark forces. The phrase echoed ominously in Andy's mind. He knew exactly what Chris was referring to. Kowalski's men had found him. The SD card was now in danger, and so was Chris.

"Chris, wait! Are you safe?" Andy's voice broke through, urgent, desperate to get more from him.

But the line went dead.

Panic rose inside him. His instincts kicked in. Chris was on the run and the SD card, a tiny piece of tech holding career-ending, life-altering evidence, was now a ticking time bomb. He couldn't let it fall into the wrong hands. More than that, he couldn't let his friend end up as collateral in this twisted game. Andy grabbed his bag and shoved his phone into his pocket, cramming in essentials in a frantic rush. Time was running out. He threw on his jacket and bolted out of the office, navigating through the building's narrow corridors, his mind swirling with a thousand what-ifs.

As he sped toward the airport, his nerves stretched taut. He booked the next flight, bound for Athens, where Chris was based. The trip across the city felt like an eternity, each moment adding to the suffocating pressure in Andy's chest. When the cab finally pulled up outside Chris's apartment building, a sense of dread washed over him. Something was off. Andy threw cash at the driver, barely waiting for his change, and raced toward the building. The typically bustling streets of Athens felt eerily quiet as he ascended the narrow staircase. Each footfall seemed louder than it should have been, echoing in the dim stairwell.

As he rounded the final corner, Andy's heart sank. Chris's door was ajar, hanging awkwardly on its hinges, the frame splintered from the force of an intrusion. He approached cautiously, his every step now filled with trepidation. The sight of the Ring doorbell smashed to pieces and discarded near the entrance confirmed his worst fears. They had gotten here first.

Gritting his teeth, Andy pushed the door open slowly, his senses on high alert. The once cosy apartment that Chris had called home was now in ruins. His heart pounded as he stepped inside. Papers were scattered across the floor like confetti after a parade, books had been thrown from shelves, and the sleek furniture Chris had meticulously chosen was overturned. This wasn't just a break-in. It was a hunt. The apartment reeked of chaos, but no sign of Chris. Andy's eyes scanned the room with practised efficiency. He knew what the operatives were after. His pulse quickened as he made his way through the mess, searching for any sign of where the SD card could be.

Suddenly, a faint sound caught his attention. From somewhere within the room, a muffled buzz, the unmistakable vibration of a phone. Andy moved quickly toward it, finding Chris's phone half-buried under the cushions. He picked it up, his heart sinking further. Chris wouldn't have left without it unless he was in serious trouble. Looking around the destroyed space, Andy's mind raced. He needed to think like Chris, quick, resourceful, and dramatic. Where would Chris hide something as crucial as the SD card?

Disheartened, Andy sank into a nearby chair, his predicament bearing down on him. His mind raced, sifting through the chaos of Chris's ransacked apartment. For a moment, his thoughts drifted, and then, out of nowhere, a seemingly trivial memory surfaced. During one of their late-night drinking sessions, Chris once commented offhand about ordinary-looking cans concealing extraordinary secrets. They'd even debated, somewhat drunkenly, the hidden meanings in Warhol's Campbell's soup paintings, arguing whether the pop artist had intended to play with the idea of disguising value within the mundane.

The memory flickered like a dim light in the darkness, a glimmer of hope in Andy's weary mind.

He jumped up, his heart pounding with renewed purpose. If Chris had hidden the SD card anywhere, it had to be somewhere clever, somewhere unexpected, just like in their conversation. Andy made his way to the kitchen, his steps growing faster and more urgent. His hands shook with adrenaline as he began methodically opening each cupboard door, rummaging through its contents. First, he found crockery, rows of glasses, an assortment of jars and bottles, but nothing unusual. His frustration grew as each opened door revealed only more everyday items. The minutes dragged on, and doubt began creeping into his mind. Was this a wild goose chase?

But just as his hope began to flicker and fade, his eyes landed on the pantry. A neat row of tinned tomatoes, kidney beans, chickpeas, and pears sat in the far corner. They seemed unremarkable, except… a small detail made him pause. The cans had plastic lids rather than the typical aluminium seals. His pulse quickened. With trembling hands, Andy grabbed them, one by one, gently lifting each can from the shelf, inspecting them with a mix of dread and anticipation. Could Chris have done it?

On the fifth can, he hesitated, feeling the weight of possibility in his grip. Taking a breath, he popped the lid off, peering inside. His heart surged with triumph. There, nestled in the hollow interior, was the SD card, tucked away like a secret treasure, as unassuming as dangerous. Andy let out a breath he didn't realise he'd been holding. He clutched the SD card like it was the key to salvation because, in a way, it was. This tiny piece of tech had the potential to bring down influential people and protect him from the threats closing in.

Without wasting another moment, he rushed to Chris's desk, where a laptop sat amidst the debris. He inserted the SD card into the adaptor and the USB port. The device hummed to life, the screen flickering as it recognised the card. Andy's excitement built as the digital files began populating the screen. All the videos, documents, and correspondence were the evidence that would set everything in motion.

But then, just as his fingertips hovered over the touchpad, a message appeared on the screen:

'Password required. Seven characters/numbers. Three attempts only.'

Andy's stomach dropped. Of course, Chris had encrypted the files. Typical Chris, always theatrical, always dramatic, even when safeguarding something this important. Andy clenched his jaw. The task now wasn't just retrieving the card; it was unlocking its contents, and with only three attempts, the stakes couldn't be higher.

The room felt smaller, the air thicker. His mind scrambled for a solution. He knew Chris well after years of friendship, inside jokes, and shared passions. Seven characters. That was his first clue. Andy remembered everything they'd ever discussed: plays, music, films, their love for theatre and 1980s new wave bands. But what would Chris have used?

His first instinct was something from the world they both loved. Maybe a song lyric? Something obscure but personal. The B-52s were one of Chris's favourite bands, and they had often joked about the band's quirky lyrics.

Andy typed **'Rocklob'**, the short form they'd used for the track "Rock Lobster." He paused **no**.

Andy's pulse quickened as he wiped a hand across his brow. He couldn't afford a mistake. He needed to get this right.

Think, Andy, he told himself. Chris's theatrical nature meant the password would likely be something dramatic. Maybe a famous quote? His mind raced, recalling their countless nights spent quoting lines from plays and films, and then it hit him **Winston Churchill's famous quote**. Chris had tossed it out the last time they spoke; it was something about Americans always doing the right thing.

Andy hesitated; could it be: **'Winston**.

no

Typical Chris, Andy thought, shaking his head with a gentle sigh. There was a certain inevitability about this moment. Chris's flair for drama and attention to detail had always been part of who he was. A regular security measure wouldn't do. No, Chris had to add his twist, yet Andy felt a flicker of reassurance. If anyone could crack this code, it would be him. They had shared too many moments and too much history for this to be a mystery for so long.

But the situation was hardly ideal. **Seven characters** and **only three chances**. The stakes couldn't be higher.

Leaning back slightly, Andy let his mind wander through the fragments of memories he had with Chris. **Seven numbers**… The passcode had to be numbers. Andy knew it. It couldn't be that complicated, right? His first thought was Chris's birthday **October 1st, 1982**. Seven numbers, easy enough to remember. Andy typed in the digits quickly, his heartbeat keeping pace with the speed of his fingers.

10-1-1982.

The moment he pressed **enter**, the device emitted a harsh vibration, shaking in his hand. The screen flashed red: **'Attempt failed'**.

Andy cursed under his breath, his nerves flaring. **One down, two attempts left**. It wasn't just the password at stake. It was everything: Ravi's plan, Chris's safety, and ensuring the power of persuasion remained in Andy's corner.

He took a deep breath, his fingers hovering anxiously over the keys. What other numbers would Chris use? He dug deeper into their shared history to find significance in a sea of forgotten details. Was there a date or number that meant more to Chris than his birthday? Andy's mind drew a frustrating blank, and then, just when doubt threatened to creep in, an idea flickered to life.

Of course, he thought, his mind suddenly clear. **Chris grew up in England before moving back to Georgia. The UK's date format differed from that used in the U.S. While Americans write

October 1st as 10/1

The British format would list it as **1/10**.

Could it be that simple? Just two numbers in the wrong order?

Andy punched in **1-10-1982**, his heart pounding. As his finger hit the final key, the laptop screen flickered and shook violently again. The same **red error message** appeared: **'Attempt failed'**.

Two down. **One attempt left**. Andy thought.

His frustration mounted, the pressure of time and danger breathing down his neck. Sweat began pooling in his palms, making the keys slick beneath his fingers. One more failed attempt and the SD card could lock permanently, its secrets lost forever. Andy forced himself to breathe. Think, he commanded, his thoughts tumbling over themselves as he tried to steady his mind. Chris wouldn't have made this easy, but it wouldn't be random. The password was buried somewhere in their shared history. It had to be.

His gaze fell back on the screen, and suddenly, a thought occurred to him: their shared love of theatre. They'd spent countless nights quoting lines from plays, films, and TV shows. Chris loved a bit of Shakespearean drama or something from the classics. Could the password be one of those lines? Or a character from one of their favourite plays? No, too obvious, Andy thought. Chris wouldn't go for something that easy, so there had to be a twist. His mind landed on a memory, a moment from their last conversation. Chris had parted with a quote, one they'd joked about for years:

"You can always count on Americans to do the right thing after they've tried everything else."

Andy slumped against the wall, the cool surface pressing his back as his mind raced. Seven characters. Or numbers? He needed them desperately, but the answer kept eluding him. His thoughts swirled in circles, grasping at anything that might connect the numbers to Chris's life, their shared history, or some obscure joke Chris might have thrown in for extra drama. Andy scanned the chaotic room for inspiration. There had to be something he was missing.

Then, out of the corner of his eye, something familiar caught his attention: a framed poster on the wall. One of Chris's favourites was the cover of The B-52's debut album, a visual feast that encapsulated the band's playful, retro style. The vibrant yellow backdrop practically hummed with energy while the band members Kate Pierson, with her towering bob, and Fred Schneider in his quirky stance, were illustrated in all their '60s-inspired glory. **Bold red letters** spelt out "The B-52's," and beneath it in smaller type, the words "High Fidelity" offered a subtle nod to the sonic creativity hidden within.

Andy's gaze lingered on the poster, and a memory began to shape. Chris loved this band, and they had shared countless nights talking about their quirky lyrics, absurdist humour, and deep connection to Athens, Georgia, where both Chris and the band had come of age. The band's iconic song "Rock Lobster" drifted through Andy's mind, bringing a smile to his face even amidst the tension, but then another track surfaced in his memory, something more significant. **Track eight on the album**. The one with a phone number.

6060-something-something-something?

The song's title had always amused Chris and Andy. It was a telephone number connected to a rental property in Athens where the band had spent time rehearsing. Chris had once joked that he could never forget it. Athens was their place, after all, the birthplace of their shared love for music and theatre.

Could it be?

Andy's heart raced as he scanned the CD collection strewn across the floor. His eyes locked onto a bright yellow CD case, unmistakable amid the clutter. He grabbed it. It was The B-52's album, with the same cover as the poster. He flipped it over, scanning the track list until his eyes landed on the familiar digits: 6060-842. Seven numbers.

His hands trembled as he typed the numbers into the laptop. His pulse thudded in his ears, and each keyboard click reverberated in the silent room. With the final digit entered, Andy held his breath and pressed **Enter**.

A tense silence filled the air. The laptop screen flickered. For a heartbeat, Andy feared he had failed again. But then, with a soft chime, the screen unlocked, revealing a cascade of **MP4 video files** and **documents**.

Andy exhaled sharply, a mix of relief and triumph washing over him. Chris had done it and left behind a clue only Andy could decipher, wrapped in their shared love for music and safeguarded by layers of personal history.

He clicked on one of the video files, and as it began to play, the significance of what he had in his possession hit him like a freight train. This was the evidence Ravi had been so desperate to protect, footage of high-level officials caught in compromising situations, emails that revealed backdoor deals, and financial transactions that could implicate entire governments. It was a ticking time bomb, one that had the potential to topple power structures if it ever saw the light of day.

As the contents of the SD card unfurled before him, Andy felt a surge of gratitude toward Chris. His friend had safeguarded their mission with his trademark creative flair, turning what could have been a simple transfer into a puzzle, a challenge, one that only those who truly knew him could unlock.

But even as Andy felt the thrill of success, a deeper worry gnawed at him. Where was Chris now? The last he'd heard, Chris had sounded frantic, his voice a cryptic blend of humour and fear. Andy couldn't shake the feeling that his friend was still in danger. His phone buzzed in his pocket, jolting him from his thoughts. He pulled it out, half-expecting to see Chris's name, hoping his old friend had found safety. Instead, the screen showed a text from an unknown number.

"We know you have it. Time's running out."

The message sent a chill down Andy's spine. Whoever had sent it was closing in and fast. Andy glanced around the apartment, now thoroughly ransacked, as though expecting someone to appear at any moment. The stakes had risen dramatically, and time was no longer on his side.

He needed to move and fast, but a new resolve settled over him as he stood pocketing the SD card and shutting the laptop. They might be coming for him, but now he had leverage. Now, he was the one holding all the cards. With one last look around Chris's apartment, Andy made his way to the door, the weight of the SD card heavy in his pocket. He only hoped Chris had found a way to stay safe because the dark forces they had been running from were closing in.

13: The President's Ticking Bomb

The Oval Office was quiet in the early hours, but Jeff Johnson, the 48th President of the United States, felt anything but calm. Seated at his desk, JJ's gaze fixed on the numbers flashing across the screen of his tablet, the U.S. national debt clock. It was relentless, an unyielding march of digits inching closer to an impossible sum. In less than a year, the debt had surged past $36 trillion, an incredible 109% of GDP, and projections suggested it would cross $38 trillion by next January. He knew every dollar added to that clock was another weight on his shoulders and, more worryingly, on the shoulders of millions of Americans. The responsibility was crushing, the weight of the nation's future resting heavily on his shoulders.

JJ hadn't anticipated the sheer scale of the economic chaos that lay in wait when he took office. During his campaign, his message of unity, social justice, and economic reform had captivated the public, a public tired of partisan gridlock and empty promises. He genuinely desires to lead with integrity, so he accepted the call to serve. But now, staring into the void of a national debt crisis, he wondered if he had underestimated the scale of this battle. The weight of the crisis was blatant, the tension in the air thick with uncertainty.

In the screen's glow, his mind wandered back to his younger days in the small-town Midwest. It was not long before his talent caught the eye of talent scouts, leading to his breakthrough role in a hit television series. With a charismatic portrayal of a struggling everyman, he captured the hearts of audiences nationwide. Over the years, he flourished with notable roles in blockbuster films and acclaimed stage productions. His versatility as a performer allowed him to tackle various characters, from dashing leading men to complex antiheroes, earning him industry accolades. It was a life of make-believe, a stark contrast to the harsh realities of his current role as President.

Among the sparkle of Hollywood, his love life blossomed. After a series of high-profile relationships, he found his way into the arms of Tanya, also a talented actor. Their connection was instantaneous, fuelled by a shared passion for their craft and a deep mutual respect. He and Tanya welcomed two sons into their lives in time, and joy and warmth filled their homes. Despite their hectic schedules, they cherished family time. As his career reached new heights, he stayed grounded by the love and support of his wife and children. Tanya was his rock through the highs and lows of his career.

Soon enough, driven by a desire to effect real change, he began to explore avenues beyond entertainment. His natural charm and ability to connect with people from all occupations helped his transition from the silver screen to the political stage. His advocacy for social justice, healthcare reform, and economic equality resonated with voters nationwide, earning him widespread support. Buoyed by his popularity and a groundswell of grassroots enthusiasm, he boldly decided to run for public office. He embarked on a whirlwind campaign trail, crisscrossing the nation to share his vision for a brighter future. His message of hope and unity struck a chord with Americans weary of political divisiveness, propelling him to victory in a close-run election.

In January 2028, Jeff Johnson was sworn in as the 48th President of the United States of America. He brought a new era of leadership defined by compassion, integrity, and a steadfast commitment to serving the people. Now 62, he shouldered the immense responsibility of leading a nation on the brink of economic collapse.

How distant those days seemed now. He had traded the life of characters for a role with no script, where the stakes were painfully honest, and every choice carried consequences he could feel in his bones.

He looked around at his closest advisors, each seated silently, awaiting his following words. Max Mitchell, his chief economic advisor, had been a respected economist for years. Tall and lean with a permanent furrow on his brow, Max had become increasingly anxious as the debt swelled to new heights. He had briefed JJ countless times on the stakes, explaining how the accelerating debt growth at almost $1 trillion every 100 days was unlike anything the nation had seen before.

"It's not just numbers, Mr. President," Max said softly, breaking the silence. "This debt is a ticking bomb. Inflation, wages, unemployment, and everyday lives are on the line, and the window to take meaningful action is narrowing."

JJ nodded, his eyes not leaving the screen. "and the solutions?"

Max sighed, running a hand through his hair. "There are options, but each one is risky. Reforming Social Security, Medicare, and Medicaid, these programs consume a massive part of the budget. But trying to touch them without public outcry?" He shook his head. "It'll be tough, especially in an election year."

"and tax reform?" JJ asked, though he knew the answer.

"Closing loopholes and making the wealthy pay more is necessary, but it's like stepping into a minefield. Special interest groups will push back hard, not to mention the opposition party."

JJ's mind raced, sifting through the data, recalling recent encounters on the campaign trail. He remembered a woman he'd met in Ohio, working two jobs yet unable to keep up with rising costs, watching as her hopes for retirement faded. Stories like hers were becoming more common, but no plan to rein in spending or boost revenues could avoid backlash. The country was as polarised as ever, and political gridlock seemed as permanent as the Washington Monument.

The president's thoughts drifted to his wife, Tanya, and their two sons. They had been his anchor, his support through every decision, every tough call. He could see the pride in Tanya's eyes, but he also saw the worry she tried to hide. She knew that the debt wasn't just numbers to him; it was his promise to the people to improve things.

He looked up, breaking the silence. "Max, you and I both know what this means. We can't keep kicking this can down the road. We've got to act. If we lose, at least we go down knowing we did what was right."

Max's face softened, and he offered a faint nod. "Yes, sir. But… it won't be easy."

The other advisors stirred, voices emerging, each presenting their own take on potential strategies. Some suggested a bipartisan task force, others an immediate freeze on non-essential government spending. Each idea, though valid, felt half-formed, limited by the realities of a divided government and a populace already weary of political promises.

By the time dawn broke, JJ was exhausted yet strangely resolute. This was more than a crisis; it was the defining challenge of his presidency. The debt symbolised every misstep, every delayed decision, every instance of political expediency over moral action, and if he failed to address it, it wouldn't just end his career; it would burden generations to come.

As he walked out of the Oval Office and into the rising light of the new day, he felt the weight of history upon him. He wasn't the first president to face a crisis, but in that moment, he vowed to be the one who wouldn't shy away from it. What he needed was a miracle.

14: The Man

Andy Stuart, now in his forties, carried himself confidently from a lifetime of privilege and success. His presence was magnetic tall, impeccably dressed, and with a face that had only grown more distinguished with age. His deep-set eyes, framed by a touch of silver at the temples, had a way of locking onto someone, making them feel as if they were the only person in the room. This mix of looks, charm, and the quiet command of a self-made billionaire drew people to him. He naturally won people over in conversation, whether over cocktails at an exclusive Manhattan bar or during high-stake negotiations in the boardroom.

Despite the effortless attention from beautiful women, Andy's romantic life was far from satisfying. His relationships burned hot but fizzled out just as quickly, a pattern that had become an inside joke among his closest friends. They had nicknamed him "Striker," as in "three strikes and you're out." The moniker stuck, not because Andy lacked charm, but because it was the opposite. He was a serial dater who enjoyed the thrill of the chase but never found anyone who could hold his interest for long. Ultimately, the dazzling romances always felt hollow, leaving Andy with the sense that something deeper was missing. Beneath his confident exterior was a quiet restlessness, a yearning for something more meaningful, yet he pulled away each time he tried to delve deeper into a relationship. It wasn't commitment that scared him, but the idea of vulnerability, letting someone in close enough to see his flaws, his weaknesses. So, he kept things light, moving from one stunning woman to the next while carrying an unspoken loneliness that he never allowed to surface.

The first time with a new woman was exhilarating, like slipping into a brand-new pair of socks. Something was intoxicating about the experience: the fabric felt so smooth and comforting against his skin like silk brushing lightly over his feet. It was not just the physical sensations but the allure of the unknown, the prospect of discovering someone new and exciting. Each touch, each word shared in that first encounter, was electric, sparking a sense of anticipation. Andy lived for that rush of possibility, the promise of what might unfold.

But as with those new socks, the excitement had already begun to dull by the second time. The softness was still there, but no longer a revelation, just familiar. The fabric was now more like a second skin, comforting but predictable. It was not without its pleasures, but there was no denying that some of the spark had dimmed. The dance of discovery became routine, and the surprise was replaced with comfort, the edge with ease.

By the third encounter, it was always the same. An all-too-familiar rhythm replaced the magic that had once pulsed in the air. The once-new socks were just another reliable pair, but nothing special. At this point, Andy found himself mentally checking out, already scanning for the next new adventure. The moment the thrill of novelty wore off, he would toss them aside like any worn-in pair and reach for something new that could reignite that fleeting excitement.

For Andy, the chase was everything. It was the pursuit of novelty, the thrill of experiencing something untouched, something he hadn't yet figured out. But he never stayed long enough to see what lay beyond those first encounters, to uncover the deeper connections or emotional complexities. To him, romance, like socks, was disposable, easily replaceable once the initial charm faded.

So, his life became a cycle of brief infatuations and unfulfilled possibilities, his focus continually on the horizon, where new socks or women beckoned with the promise of something different. He never stopped long enough to realise what he might be missing, caught up in his pursuit of the next fleeting thrill.

The one person who seemed to understand Andy without ever needing to be told was Sarah Palmer. She wasn't just his assistant. She was his anchor. A few years his senior at 46, Sarah possessed a timeless beauty that often stopped people in their tracks. Her long, golden hair fell in effortless waves, and her radiant complexion was the envy of women half her age. But there was a toughness behind that youthful glow, a steeliness that made her more than just a pretty face. Sarah had been with Andy for over five years, and in that time, she had learned how to navigate his unpredictable lifestyle with grace. She knew him better than anyone else, including his habits, his tells, and even the subtle shifts in his mood. She had an uncanny ability to anticipate Andy's needs before he voiced them. She would be there with a freshly brewed espresso if he were restless before a big meeting. If he tried to play it cool before an intimidating rival, Sarah would pass him a discreet note reminding him of his strengths.

Her work ethic was legendary, and her attention to detail was impeccable. She ran Andy's schedule with the precision of a military strategist, juggling everything from last-minute jet bookings to ensuring his favourite scotch brand was always stocked in the office. Nothing slipped through her grasp. Yet, despite her professionalism, there was an ease between them. The banter, the knowing glances, they had a rapport that bordered on unspoken understanding, but her unwavering loyalty set Sarah apart from anyone else in Andy's world. She had stood by him during some of the most tumultuous periods of his career through personal scandals and professional upheavals that would have sent anyone else running for the hills. Sarah stayed, not because she needed the job but because she had the intelligence and capability to run her empire. She stayed because she believed in Andy. She saw beyond the "Striker" persona, beyond the billionaire swagger, to the man who quietly yearned for something real, something he couldn't quite articulate.

Though Andy would never admit it, Sarah had become indispensable to him. In a world full of fleeting connections and superficial relationships, she was the one constant who had seen him at his best and worst and never flinched. Sometimes, late at night, when the world felt too quiet, Andy would wonder if she was the one person who truly knew him. But even then, those thoughts were pushed aside, compartmentalised like everything else in his life that felt too close for comfort. Yet, there was an unspoken understanding between them, a quiet bond more solid than any romantic entanglement Andy had ever experienced. If Andy were the face of his empire, Sarah would be the soul of it, the steady hand behind the scenes, ensuring everything ran smoothly, from business deals to his personal affairs.

Though Andy wasn't the type to reflect on what his life might have looked like if he had chosen differently, a part of him, deep down, couldn't help but wonder if his constant pursuit of the next thrill, the next woman, the next deal, was just a way to avoid confronting what was right in front of him, and whether, one day, he would finally slow down long enough to appreciate the person by his side all along.

Despite the prestige of her role and the demands it placed on her, Sarah Palmer remained refreshingly down-to-earth. Despite her position as Andy Stuart's indispensable right hand, she had no air of self-importance. She carried herself with an effortless grace, always making those around her feel comfortable, whether it was a colleague seeking her advice or a high-powered client with a sudden, unreasonable request. Sarah's quick wit and irrepressible humour put people at ease, earning the admiration of everyone she worked with.

This blend of warmth and professionalism made her more than just an employee to Andy. Sarah had become a kindred spirit, someone whose value far exceeded the tasks she completed. He knew she was worth her weight in gold, not just for her unwavering efficiency but for the compassion and humanity she brought into his often chaotic world. Yet, despite Andy's undeniable appeal and persistent, usually playful advances, she always supported clear boundaries. From the start, she had made it known that their relationship would remain strictly professional, no matter how much chemistry crackled between them. Friends? Maybe. But anything beyond that was off the table. Andy was used to getting what he wanted and had tested those boundaries countless times over the years, but she had stood firm. Their dynamic became a delicate dance, a compelling push and pull, where attraction simmered beneath the surface but was never acted upon.

There had been moments, many moments, where the tension between them was noticeable. A lingering glance during a late-night meeting, the brush of fingers when she handed him a file or the way she would laugh at one of his dry jokes that no one else seemed to get. But Sarah always kept things professional, aware that crossing that line could complicate everything. She wasn't one to compromise her principles, especially not for a fling, no matter how tempting it might have been.

Sarah had a front-row seat as Andy's serial dating life unfolded like a never-ending rom-com. She was often amused by the revolving door of women in his life. From dazzling social media influencers to starry-eyed aspiring actresses, Andy's romances were as varied as they were short-lived. Each woman appeared and disappeared in a flash, leaving barely a ripple in their wake. She often found herself playfully ribbing him about it, remarkably when one of his latest 'Miss USA'-type conquests barely lasted through a second date.

"Barely made it to dinner, huh?" She'd tease, a mischievous grin lighting up her face as Andy, with a roll of his eyes, pretended not to care.

"Well, it's hard to make it work when your dinner companion's vocabulary consists of nothing more than hashtags and TikTok trends," He'd fire back.

However, Sarah could always detect a hint of bemusement and a touch of something else, frustration, maybe? Disappointment? It was as if each new relationship, no matter how fun or glamorous, only reminded Andy of what he was missing.

But for all the light-hearted banter and jabs, Sarah had come to see through Andy's cavalier attitude toward love. She could sense the hollowness behind the facade. Beneath his smooth, confident exterior was a man who craved something more, something real. His serial dating was just a way to fill a void, a distraction from the loneliness he kept well hidden behind flirtation and bravado, and though she never said it out loud, a quiet, compassionate part of her felt sad for him. She knew that Andy had built walls around his heart, shielding himself from the vulnerability of genuine connection.

Andy's wealth, status, and success could not protect him from the fear of being hurt, so he kept everyone at arm's length, even those fleeting romances. Sarah knew this was his way of avoiding the risk of real intimacy and letting someone in. She saw it for what it was, and while she sometimes found it amusing, it also saddened her. She understood Andy better than most and knew his history, successes, and heartbreaks, and she silently hoped that one day he'd lower his guard, let go of his defences, and find someone who could make him genuinely happy.

In those quiet moments, when they shared a bottle of wine after a long day or exchanged an unspoken look after a particularly draining meeting, Sarah would catch a glimpse of the man beneath the persona, the one who didn't need to chase after fleeting relationships or be the centre of attention, the one who wanted to be seen for who he was, flaws and all.

Though she never allowed herself to dwell on the thought for too long, a small part of her wondered whether Andy might already have what he was searching for right before him. But she kept those thoughts to herself, buried deep beneath her professionalism, leaving them to linger only in her most private moments. She hoped, more than anything, that he would find the happiness he truly deserved, whether with someone else or in the quiet, steady presence of the one person who had been there all along.

15: The Doctor

Many weeks ago, on a flight, Andy Stuart found himself engrossed in the latest issue of *New Scientist*, his eyes skimming the pages as he flipped through the vibrant images and thought-provoking articles. One piece captivated his imagination: an in-depth exploration of Dr Emily Clark's groundbreaking research in astrophysics. She delved into the enigmatic realms of black holes, dark matter, and the intricate fabric of time. But it wasn't just the scientific revelations that drew him in; the accompanying photographs of Dr Clark intrigued him even more with her intense gaze and poised demeanour. A spark in her eyes hinted at an adventurous spirit, and Andy felt an irresistible pull to know more about the woman behind the science.

A few days later, Andy found himself navigating the bustling halls of the astrophysics department at Columbia University. The atmosphere was electric, with intellectual fervour and the hushed whispers of groundbreaking discoveries. As a leading authority in her field, Dr Clark had devoted her life to unravelling the universe's most profound mysteries, and her intellect was rivalled only by her passion for discovery. However, today, her thoughts were abruptly interrupted by the unexpected arrival of Andy Stuart, a name that carried weight in the world of technology and innovation, synonymous with ambition and audacity. His presence sent a ripple of excitement through the department, and curious eyes followed him as he approached her office.

As Andy entered the room, his gaze met Emily's with a hunger that sent a shiver down her spine. He was a striking figure, exuding charisma and confidence, but Emily had heard whispers of his ruthless reputation in Silicon Valley. She had also read articles that praised his business acumen, often focusing on his tireless pursuit of success. Yet, as he stood before her, there was something disarming about the intensity of his gaze, a magnetism that was hard to ignore, a blend of charm and intensity that piqued her interest despite her reservations.

"Dr Clark," He began, his voice smooth as silk, resonating with an energy that seemed to fill the room. "I've heard whispers about you and your research tales that almost defy belief. They say you've unlocked secrets hidden within the fabric of reality, delving into realms where science and mystique intertwine. Your work has garnered quite the mystique, drawing intrigue from those who dare to glimpse beyond the ordinary."

He leaned in slightly, his eyes reflecting genuine curiosity and admiration as if he were standing before a magician revealing the secrets of a trick.

Emily regarded him warily, and her curiosity piqued despite her instinct to tread carefully around such a figure.

"and what, may I ask, brings you to my doorstep, Mr Stuart?" She inquired, her tone a careful blend of intrigue and caution.

Andy's lips curved into a charming smile, his eyes sparkling with mischief and ambition.

"I have a proposition for you, Doctor," He replied cryptically, leaning back as if to gauge her reaction. "One I believe could help change the course of history."

He then painted a vivid picture of a proposed timeline shift, his voice rich with enthusiasm as he described its transformative impact on the U.S. and the world. They spoke of aligning global time zones, harnessing Dr Clark's expertise in astrophysics to shape the future of timekeeping, and how her work could play a pivotal role in this grand vision. The way he articulated the possibilities was almost hypnotic, weaving a narrative that made the mundane feel extraordinary.

As he continued, Emily found herself drawn into his vision, her initial scepticism beginning to wane. She listened intently as he highlighted the current time zone disparities, and the opportunities presented by aligning with New York's meridian. It was a mix of scientific inquiry and adventurous ambition that resonated with her desire to push boundaries. Reservations about his character aside, a sense of adventure beckoned her to explore this uncharted territory alongside Andy.

"You see, Doctor," Andy said, his tone shifting to one of earnestness, "This isn't just about time; it's about redefining our understanding of the universe. Imagine the implications of our discoveries for science and humanity."

As the conversation unfolded, Emily felt a flicker of excitement, a thrill from the prospect of merging her research with Andy's visionary plans. She had always yearned for a challenge transcending the laboratory walls, and here was an opportunity that promised just that. The stakes were high, and the potential rewards were tantalising.

Andy's enthusiasm was infectious, and as he spoke, Emily couldn't help but envision the endless possibilities ahead. Could they unlock new dimensions of understanding together? The thought sent a shiver of anticipation down her spine, and she felt a smile break across her face, a hint of her adventurous spirit igniting.

"Alright, Mr. Stuart," she said, her voice steadier than she felt. You've piqued my interest. Let us see where this journey takes us."

16: Growing a Heart?

Andy's meeting with Dr Emily Clark had awakened something deep within him, a stirring he couldn't quite name. It was as if she had opened the door to an unfamiliar realm, and behind it lay a world rich with possibilities and mysteries waiting to be uncovered and ideas yet to be explored. Each conversation with her ignited a spark of curiosity and excitement, leaving him yearning to delve deeper into her universe. Determined not to let this opportunity slip through his fingers, Andy began to engineer what he considered "chance" encounters. He would casually stroll past the astrophysics department or linger in the café where he knew she often grabbed her afternoon coffee while wearing a calm facade. His heart raced with anticipation every time he spotted her, his mind racing with scenarios of their next conversation, each one more captivating than the last.

As their interactions became more frequent, a magnetic pull drew him closer to her. Andy found himself daydreaming about Emily at the most unexpected moments: while waiting for meetings to begin, during the mindless chatter of social events, and even in the quiet moments before sleep. He replayed their conversations, savouring how her eyes lit up when discussing her research and the passion that laced her words. It was intoxicating, and before long, the line between admiration and infatuation began to blur. Finally, unable to resist the pull any longer, Andy gathered his courage and asked Dr Clark out to dinner, hoping to connect on a level beyond their professional rapport. He envisioned a charming evening where they could share laughter and stories, discovering the threads that intertwined their lives. However, to his dismay, she politely declined, citing a prior commitment with an apologetic smile that warmed and stung him.

Despite the sting of rejection, Andy refused to be deterred. He felt unwavering conviction that something was special between them and worth exploring. So, he resolved to be patient and wait for the right moment to prove himself worthy of her affection. He believed that if he could show her the depth of his intentions and the sincerity of his feelings, she would see him as more than just a successful businessman but as someone who genuinely appreciated her brilliance. Later, when he confided in Sarah about his burgeoning feelings for Dr Clark, her reaction was dramatic. Sarah's eyes widened in disbelief, a mix of shock and intrigue painting her features.

"You? Dr Clark? This is too good!" She exclaimed, her voice bubbling with a nervous laugh that danced between surprise and amusement. "Well, it had to happen sooner or later," she continued, her tone light-hearted, but a layer of apprehension simmered underneath. Sarah understood Andy well enough to recognise the intensity of his feelings; this infatuation with Dr Clark was unlike anything he had experienced before. It was not just a fleeting crush; it was deeper, tinged with genuine admiration and longing. As Sarah's laughter faded, she couldn't shake the feeling that this was a turning point for Andy. She watched him with a mix of hope and concern, knowing that he tended to dive headfirst into his emotions. "Just be careful, Andy. You know how you can get," she warned gently, her expression shifting to one of earnest concern.

"Careful?" He echoed, a smile breaking his momentary doubt. "I'm just getting started."

Yet, beneath his bravado, a flicker of uncertainty lingered. After all, he recognised the stakes involved; the last thing he wanted was to jeopardise his unique connection with Emily. But armed with the encouragement of his steadfast friend, Andy set his sights on winning Dr Clark's heart, convinced that the adventure ahead was worth every risk.

As Emily Clark navigated the bustling halls of Columbia University, her mind often drifted back to the intriguing man who had recently crossed her path. Andy Stuart was unlike anyone she had ever met; his presence illuminated the air around him, casting a warm glow that made her heart flutter unexpectedly. When she first met him, she had felt an almost electric charge in the air, an unspoken tension that was both exhilarating and unnerving. His striking features and confident demeanour instantly drew her in, but the depth of his intellect and passion for the future truly captivated her. Andy spoke enthusiastically, resonating with her commitment to uncovering the universe's secrets. Yet, something else lurked beneath their conversations, a connection that felt thrilling and terrifying.

As their encounters became more frequent, Emily could not shake the feelings that blossomed within her. It was as if he had unearthed a part of her, she didn't even know existed, an adventurous spirit yearning for something beyond the confines of her carefully structured life. Andy's enthusiasm for the possibilities of time manipulation and global impact ignited a spark in her, making her question the rigidity of her plans. For the first time in years, she daydreamed, picturing what it might be like to share more than just academic discussions over coffee, wondering if she could explore a romantic connection. Yet, along with the budding attraction came a pang of hesitation. Emily was always dedicated to her work, often prioritising her research over personal relationships. She'd made a choice that had carved her a niche as a leading astrophysicist, but now it felt precarious. The thought of allowing Andy into her life was intoxicating, but the fear of vulnerability loomed. Would he see her as just another admirer of his charm, or would he appreciate the complexity of her world?

When she caught herself lost in thoughts of Andy, her cheeks flushed with warmth, and a soft smile played on her lips. She relished how he made her laugh and how his gaze seemed to pierce through her carefully constructed defences. There was a kindness in his eyes, a sincerity that made her heart race and stomach flutter. But along with the excitement came a swirl of self-doubt. What if he was just a fleeting distraction, a momentary escape from her structured life? When Andy invited her to dinner, Emily's heart leapt at the prospect. Yet, a wave of anxiety crashed over her as she found herself declining the invitation, citing a prior commitment she didn't have. She had wanted to say yes, to embark on a new adventure with him, but the fear of blurring the lines of their professional relationship held her back. The polite refusal felt like a missed opportunity, a decision that echoed with regret long after their conversation had ended.

In the quiet moments of her day, as she immersed herself in the mysteries of black holes and dark matter, Emily could not shake the thought of Andy. It felt like a forbidden puzzle, a question without an answer. Would she dare to leap into this uncharted territory? Deep down, she yearned to explore what they could be, feeling an undeniable connection that thrilled and terrified her. For the first time, Emily found herself contemplating the idea of love not just as a concept but as an honest and vibrant possibility. She wanted to share her world with Andy, to allow him to see the woman behind the scientist. As she gazed out at the stars, those distant suns twinkling like promises of hope, she could not help but wonder if Andy was the missing piece to her cosmic puzzle.

Sarah Palmer settled into her favourite corner of the café, the aroma of freshly brewed coffee swirling around her like a comforting embrace. With her laptop open and a steaming mug in hand, she silently vowed to support her friend Andy in his pursuit of happiness. She had always been more than just a personal assistant; she was his confidante, the one person who understood the intricate layers of his life, and she was determined to dive deep into the mystery of Dr Emily Clark. What began as a casual inquiry quickly morphed into a full-blown investigation. Sarah did not shy away from a challenge, especially about something vital to Andy's happiness. She meticulously combed through Dr

Clark's professional background and was utterly engrossed. She sifted through many scientific publications, devoured news articles highlighting Emily's contributions to astrophysics, and scoured social media posts for glimpses into the woman's personal life.

With each click and scroll, Sarah was increasingly captivated. Dr Clark's groundbreaking theories on time dilation and black holes highlighted a brilliant and profoundly curious mind about the universe. There was a depth to her work that resonated with Sarah, revealing a woman who understood the complexities of the cosmos and dared to challenge conventional thinking. She was impressed by the accolades Emily had garnered throughout her career, each recognition a testament to her relentless dedication and unwavering passion.

But it was not just the impressive resume that caught Sarah's attention. As she delved deeper into Emily's life story, she discovered a woman of remarkable integrity. Articles spoke of Dr Clark's outreach programs, where she volunteered to inspire young girls to pursue careers in science, breaking barriers in a male field. Emily's commitment to nurturing the next generation filled Sarah with admiration. It was clear that Emily was not only a gifted scientist but also a compassionate mentor, qualities that shone through in every initiative she championed. The more Sarah learned, the more she felt a kinship with Dr Clark. There was an authenticity about her that was refreshing in a world often clouded by artifice and pretence. Emily's interviews revealed a warm, engaging personality that contrasted beautifully with her brilliant mind; she spoke of the universe not just in mathematical equations but with a pronounced awe. In many ways, Emily reminded Sarah of herself as a woman navigating the challenges of a demanding profession while striving to make a positive impact on those around her.

Sarah could not help but feel a glimmer of hope. Just maybe, Andy had finally uncovered the one who could bring him the happiness and fulfilment he had been searching for all these years. It was a realisation that thrilled and soothed her, a hope blossoming in the corners of her heart. She imagined what it would be like to see Andy and Emily together, two brilliant minds converging, laughter filling the air as they exchanged ideas, their chemistry sparking like the stars Emily studied. Yet, beneath that hope lay a tinge of protectiveness. Sarah knew Andy well enough to understand the intensity of his feelings; he loved fiercely but often found himself lost in the chaos of his romantic pursuits. She wanted to ensure that Emily would appreciate Andy for the man he was and be a stabilising force in his life, someone who could ground him amidst the whirlwind of his ambitious world.

As she closed her laptop, Sarah leaned back in her chair, a thoughtful smile gracing her lips. She felt a sense of purpose in her quest to learn more about Dr Clark. This investigation was not just about Andy; it was about finding the right balance of support and guidance for him and Emily, a chance to foster a connection that might lead to something extraordinary. Only time would tell if they could navigate the complexities of their worlds together, but Sarah was determined to play her part in bringing them closer. Sensing that someone as intelligent and discerning as Emily might understandably have reservations about Andy and his reputation, Sarah felt a surge of determination. She resolved to meet with Emily to plead Andy's case in a way that would illuminate his true character and intentions. Having become one of Andy's closest friends, she wanted to ensure that Dr Clark understood the sincerity behind the billionaire's pursuit. But as she prepared for their meeting, a knot of nerves tightened in her stomach.

Though Sarah was no wallflower, she understood the importance of approaching Emily with care. She wanted to present her friend in the best light without overwhelming or intimidating the accomplished astrophysicist. Her heart raced as she made her way down the polished corridor of Columbia University's astrophysics department, her mind a whirl of thoughts and potential conversation starters. As she reached Dr

Clark's office, she paused momentarily, steadying her breath. With a gentle knock on the door, Sarah could feel her pulse quickening, anticipation mixing with apprehension. When the door opened, she was struck by Emily's serene presence. The office was adorned with celestial posters and shelves lined with books that seemed to hum with the universe's energy. Emily stood there, framed by the soft afternoon light streaming through the window, her eyes sparkling with curiosity and a hint of surprise.

"Dr Clark," Sarah began, her voice wobbling. She offered a warm, disarming smile, hoping to put Emily at ease. "I am Sarah Palmer. I work with Andy Stuart."

Emily regarded her with a mixture of intrigue and uncertainty. "Please, call me Emily. It's nice to meet you, Sarah," She replied, returning the smile with a slight hesitation as if gauging Sarah's intent. "How can I help?"

Taking a deep breath, Sarah steeled herself. She needed to paint a picture of Andy that captured his successes, growth, and depth. She began to share anecdotes, recounting the transformative journey Andy had undertaken since meeting Emily. As she spoke, she painted a vivid picture of a man who possessed a profound ability for empathy and kindness despite his flaws and occasional impulsiveness.

"Andy has changed," Sarah explained, her voice steadying as she became immersed in the narrative. When he met you, it was as if something clicked inside him. He has found this renewed sense of purpose as if he is finally aiming his energy towards something meaningful." She shared stories of late-night conversations where Andy would express his admiration for Emily's intellect and passion for astrophysics, his voice filled with awe.

As Sarah continued her heartfelt plea, she saw emotion flicker in Dr Clark's eyes. There was a softening of her expression, a glimmer of curiosity that suggested Sarah's words were reaching her. She spoke candidly about Andy's deep respect for Emily's work, how he often reflected on the balance between ambition and integrity, and how Emily had inspired him to strive for more than success.

When Sarah wrapped up her thoughts, a sense of hope washed over her like a warm wave. She felt an inexplicable connection forming between them, an understanding transcending the initial reservations. Emily's first reserve began to melt away, replaced by a warmth that filled the room. She regarded Sarah with newfound interest, touched by Sarah's unwavering loyalty toward her friend.

"Alright," Emily said softly, her voice still tinged with a hint of uncertainty but her lips curving into a tentative smile. "I'll meet with Andy tomorrow."

Sarah felt a surge of relief wash over her. This was the moment she had hoped Andy would show Emily who he indeed was. "Thank you, Emily. This means so much," she replied, her heart swelling with gratitude.

As she rose to leave, Sarah felt a quiet satisfaction. She suspected she had just played a crucial role in shaping their futures. The connection between Andy and Emily was fragile yet full of potential, and she could not shake the feeling that she had sparked something significant. As she walked down the corridor, the weight of hope settled comfortably on her shoulders, her mind racing with the possibilities ahead for her friend and the extraordinary woman he admired.

17: Dinner and Dessert

Sarah approached Andy cautiously, her heart beating faster as she steeled herself for the conversation. She knew not all her news would be well-received, especially given Andy's fiercely independent and proud reputation. As she settled into the plush armchair across from him, she took a deep breath, ready to relay the details of her conversation with Dr Clark.

"Andy," she began, her voice steady but soft, "I chatted with Emily today."

His first reaction was frustration, a flicker of annoyance passing across his handsome features. He bristled at the idea of needing help, especially regarding heart matters. Andy prided himself on being in control, whether in the boardroom or his personal life.

"What do you mean you talked to her?" he snapped, crossing his arms defensively. "You shouldn't have interfered."

But Andy's demeanour softened as Sarah continued to speak, recounting her impressions of Emily and how she had articulated her feelings about him. She watched as his furrowed brow relaxed, his initial irritation giving way to curiosity. He listened intently, his piercing blue eyes fixed on her, absorbing every word. Despite his resistance, he could not help but feel touched by Sarah's genuine concern and willingness to go above and beyond, even when he hadn't asked for it.

"You think she'd consider meeting me?" Andy asked, his voice lower, almost uncertain. He looked down at the polished table, a flicker of vulnerability breaking through his usual bravado. "Absolutely," Sarah replied, her tone earnest. "You intrigue her. You need to show her who you are."

Andy's frustration began to dissolve as he recognised the value of having someone like Sarah in his corner, someone who cared enough to intervene on his behalf, even when he had resisted the idea.

"Thank you, Sarah," he said, his voice infused with gratitude. "I appreciate your support. I do not say that often enough."

As they exchanged smiles, Andy's renewed sense of optimism blossomed. He felt a flicker of hope igniting inside him, a spark that propelled him toward the possibility of something beautiful with Emily.

With his anticipation mounting, he mentally prepared for his next meeting with Dr Clark. Was it a date? He hesitated, reflecting on how he must stop being so formal. "It's just Emily," He murmured, a smile creeping onto his lips.

But as he considered where to take her, the weight of expectation settled heavily on his shoulders. On the one hand, he wanted to impress her with a memorable dining experience, a trendy new restaurant with vibrant decor and a bustling atmosphere that matched his excitement. Yet, on the other hand, he did not want to overwhelm her with extravagance. He wanted this to be a chance for them to connect personally, peel back the layers of their lives and discover what lay beneath them. He leaned back in his chair, fingers tapping rhythmically against the table, lost in thought. Images of soft candlelight flickering against dark wood, the clinking of glasses filled with fine wine, and the laughter shared over shared plates filled his mind. He imagined the two of them exchanging stories, their laughter echoing in the intimate space, a moment where the world outside faded away, leaving just the two of them in their little bubble.

At that moment, Andy felt a rush of determination. He would find the perfect spot that felt personal yet elevated, casual yet unique. He would show Emily he was more than just the billionaire about whom she had heard. He would open the door to a world where they could explore the mysteries of the universe and each other.

Gravitating toward a middle ground, Andy envisioned a cosy restaurant where dim lighting cast soft shadows on warm wooden tables and fresh bread wafted through the air. He wanted a relaxed vibe that felt like a secret hideaway rather than a flashy venue. Here, they could enjoy a delicious meal without feeling self-conscious or constrained by the formal trappings of fine dining. He imagined laughter spilling from their lips, conversations flowing quickly, and the feeling of being enveloped in a space where time seemed to pause, allowing them to engage and get to know each other better.

With that vision in mind, Andy made reservations at a quaint French restaurant in the city's heart. The establishment was known for its intimate atmosphere, with flickering candlelight illuminating delicate plates of beautifully presented food. As he finalised the details, a wave of excitement washed over him, tinged with a hint of nervousness. Seeing Emily again sent a thrill through his veins, a mix of anticipation and a fluttering sense of possibility. When the night arrived, Andy stood in front of the restaurant, taking a moment to compose himself before stepping inside. The ambience was exactly as he had imagined: the gentle hum of conversations mingling with the soft strains of a piano playing in the background, creating a symphony of comfort and warmth. As he spotted Emily seated at a table, her dark hair falling effortlessly around her shoulders, a smile spread across his face.

What started as a mere dinner date quickly became a meeting of hearts and minds. They delved into many topics, discussing everything from their hopes and dreams to their fears and insecurities. For Andy, this vulnerability was uncharted territory, exhilarating yet terrifying. He felt like he was peeling back layers of his guardedness, revealing a side of himself that had long remained hidden beneath a polished exterior.

A bubble of intimacy enveloped them as the main course plates were swept away. They were wrapped in the soft glow of candlelight, the flickers dancing like tiny stars while the world outside faded into a distant hum. Their eyes locked in a gaze that spoke volumes, an unspoken understanding forming in the silence between them. In that moment, surrounded by the gentle murmur of the restaurant, they both sensed that this was the beginning of something special, a connection that transcended their professional boundaries. When dessert arrived, they both opted for crème Brulé, the promise of its velvety richness hanging in the air. Andy could not contain his excitement as he seized the moment to broach the subject of the timeline shift. His passion bubbled over as he outlined how Emily's expertise could play a pivotal role in the unfolding events. He painted a vivid picture of how her insights might even lead to a meeting with the president, her brilliance illuminating paths previously unexplored.

However, as Andy spoke, he noticed a flicker of confusion in Emily's eyes that quickly morphed into suspicion. The realisation swept over her, the warmth of their earlier exchanges dissipating like mist under the morning sun. The weight of his words settled heavily on her chest. Was she being manipulated all along? Emily's expression darkened a mix of disappointment and a profound sense of betrayal crossing her face. She had trusted Andy and believed in their shared pursuit of knowledge and discovery. It felt like he had been orchestrating a grand scheme behind her back, pulling strings to manoeuvre her into a position she hadn't consented to.

With resolve hardening within her, Emily pushed back her chair and rose to her feet, her movements sharp and decisive. The gentle ambience of the restaurant felt stifling now, and she couldn't bear to sit there any longer to entertain Andy's schemes under false pretences. Without a word, she stormed from the restaurant, her footsteps echoing frustration, hurt, and a newfound determination. Left behind at the table,

Andy sat in stunned silence, his mouth agape and heart heavy with remorse. Realising what he had done sank in like a stone in a still pond, sending ripples of regret through him. He hadn't anticipated this fallout nor considered how his actions might breach the trust they had painstakingly built. As he watched Emily disappear into the night, her silhouette swallowed by the shadows, he understood he had jeopardised more than their collaboration. He had risked losing a valued colleague and, perhaps a friend, someone who had begun to mean more to him than he had ever expected.

The evening that had promised so much now lay in tatters before him, and he felt the weight of his choices settling heavily on his shoulders. In that moment of solitude, he grappled with the reality that sometimes, the brightest stars can cast the darkest shadows.

18: Picking up the Pieces

Andy's world felt like it had tilted off its axis, and the night had unravelled in a way he never imagined. Sitting in his sleek, minimalist office the following morning, he stared blankly at the floor, replaying the evening in his mind, trying to make sense of what went wrong. His office, usually a fortress of calm and control, now felt suffocating. The ticking of the clock seemed louder, his thoughts more chaotic.

Breaking through the stillness, Sarah's warm yet inquisitive voice cut across the room. "So, how did the date go?" she asked, leaning against the doorway with her usual ease. Her eyes showed a glimmer of hope, perhaps expecting to hear a success story.

Andy let out a long, heavy sigh. "It didn't go well, Sarah," He confessed, his voice carrying the weight of disappointment. He looked at her, regret shadowing his face. "Not well at all."

Sarah stepped inside, her curiosity giving way to concern as she perched on the edge of his desk. Andy slowly began recounting the details of the dinner, and as he spoke, the frustration in his voice grew. He had envisioned a beautiful night, a chance to connect with Emily, not just as a professional but as a person, to share his vision of the future and find common ground. Instead, the evening had unravelled into misunderstanding and mistrust.

Sarah, listening closely, felt her heart sink for her friend. She knew how much Andy had pinned on this, how rare it was for him to feel this way about someone, but as the story unfolded, empathy quickly gave way to frustration.

"Why do you always have to mix work with pleasure?" she said, exasperation creeping into her voice. "You know how much Emily excites you, how much she challenges you, yet you let your business objectives get in the way. It's like you're sabotaging yourself."

Andy's eyes flickered with guilt, but Sarah wasn't done. She could feel the frustration bubbling up. This wasn't the first time she'd seen him mess up something potentially meaningful. "I don't get it, Andy. Why do you keep doing this? You claim you want something real, yet the moment you get close, you retreat behind your work, your ambitions." She sighed, rubbing her temples. "It's like you're terrified of finding happiness."

There was a moment of silence. Her words hung in the air, piercing, truthful. Sarah looked at him, her voice softening, her concern evident. "Are you broken, Andy? Or are you simply scared to let someone in?"

Andy remained quiet, staring out the window as if searching for an answer in the skyline. Her words hit harder than he wanted to admit. He wasn't broken—or at least, he didn't think he was. But scared? Yes, perhaps that was it. He had spent years building walls around himself, keeping things compartmentalised, avoiding vulnerability. Emily had unknowingly breached those walls, and now he was exposed here.

"I don't know," he murmured, the admission heavy on his tongue. "Maybe I am scared."

Sarah softened at his rare vulnerability. She had never seen him so unsure and open, and she gave him a reassuring smile. "You don't have to be," she said gently. If you want something real with Emily, you must show her that, not with grand gestures or business deals, just... you."

Andy sat back in his chair, her words sinking in. He knew she was right. It wasn't about dazzling Emily with his professional brilliance or pulling strings to align the stars in their favour. It was about honesty. He had to strip away the layers and show her who he was, his flaws, fears, and hopes.

After what felt like an eternity of contemplation, Andy finally decided. "I need to talk to her," he said quietly. "I need to be honest."

Sarah nodded, relieved to see this moment of clarity. "That's the only way forward."

Without hesitation, Andy picked up his phone and scrolled to Emily's number. His heart pounded as he pressed the dial, a mixture of dread and hope swirling in his chest. His thumb hovered over the screen for a split second, but then, with a deep breath, he hit 'call.'

As the phone rang, he braced himself for what was sure to be a difficult conversation. For once, Andy Stuart wouldn't rely on his charm or business acumen to fix things. This time, it was just him humble, sincere, and vulnerable for the first time in a long time.

With each ring, Andy's anxiety swelled. He could feel the weight of the tension, unsure how Emily would respond after their disastrous evening. A calm, almost clinical voice cut through his thoughts by the fourth ring.

"Hello?" Emily answered, her tone crisp, all business.

Andy swallowed, feeling his pulse quicken. "Emily… it's Andy," he said, his voice faltering slightly. He hadn't expected the simple act of speaking her name to feel so difficult. "I hope I've not caught you at a bad time."

There was a brief pause, the silence that felt loaded with meaning, before Emily's voice softened just a fraction. "No, not at all. What can I do for you, Andy?"

He hesitated for a heartbeat, then plunged ahead. "I wanted to talk about last night," he said, keeping his tone measured, aware that one wrong word could worsen things. "I realise things didn't go as planned, and I want to apologise if I overstepped or made you uncomfortable."

There was a pause on the other end of the line as Emily digested his words, and Andy held his breath. His mind raced, preparing himself for every possible response she could give.

"Go on," Emily said cautiously, curiosity now lacing her voice.

Andy took a deep breath, summoning the courage to bare his soul. "I respect you too much to keep anything from you," he said, his words more deliberate now, each spoken with intent. "The truth is... I've developed feelings for you."

He could almost hear the tension as Emily processed his confession. For a few agonising seconds, neither of them spoke. The silence was deafening, the weight of his words lingering, filling the space between them.

Finally, Emily broke the silence, her voice carrying a mix of surprise and uncertainty. "Andy, I'm not sure what to say."

Her admission hung between them like a delicate thread, vulnerable to snapping under the strain. Andy exhaled, feeling a flicker of relief that she hadn't outright dismissed him. That was a start, at least.

"I understand if this comes as a surprise," he said gently, trying to soften the moment. "But I felt it was important to be honest with you, no matter what."

Emily sighed, and though her voice softened, there was still an edge, a hint of the hurt brewing the night before. "It's not your feelings for me that upset me, Andy. It's how you brought up needing my help with the President. It felt like… you were using our connection for business. And that hurt."

Andy felt the sting of her words, guilt flooding him. He hadn't realised how deeply his actions had cut her. "I see how that came across," he said, low and apologetic. And I'm terribly sorry. That was never my intention. I brought you in because I genuinely believe in you, your expertise, and your intellect. You're the best at what you do. But I should have thought about how it might affect you personally. I was careless."

Emily's gaze softened as she listened to him, but she wasn't ready to release her anger. "I appreciate that,

Andy. But you must understand that I've spent years building my reputation. I've worked hard to be recognised for my abilities, not for who I know or who I might have access to."

Andy nodded, feeling the truth of her words strike home. "I get it," he said earnestly. "I would never want to undermine your achievements. I admire you professionally and personally. I hope we can find a balance between those worlds. I don't want one to overshadow the other."

For a long moment, Emily studied him, her eyes searching his face for sincerity. She could see that he was genuinely trying, that beneath his mistakes lay a man who was scared to mess up something real. And while the hurt still lingered, something in his vulnerability reached her.

"I think," she said, her voice quieter now, "if we move forward professionally and personally, we must be on the same page. No more mixed signals. No more hidden agendas."

"Agreed," Andy said without hesitation. "From now on, it's all about transparency. With everything."

As they spoke, their complex conversation slowly began to bridge the gap that had grown between them. Andy poured his heart out like never before, speaking openly and honestly about his feelings for her and his desire to make things right. For the first time Emily began to see past the business facade, she could see the vulnerable man underneath, imperfect, and willing to learn from his mistakes.

The road ahead would not be easy, but something shifted between them as they talked. The walls they had built up started to come down, brick by brick, making way for something new that could be real. And though neither said it aloud, they knew this was the beginning of a new chapter built on trust, openness, and the courage to face whatever lay ahead. They said their goodbyes and arranged to meet for a quick coffee the following day.

Andy sat across from Emily, a slight smile playing on his lips as he watched her idly swirl her coffee with a silver spoon. They sat in a cosy corner of a café, tucked away from the noisy bustle outside. The air was warm, the rich scent of freshly brewed coffee mingled with the faint sweetness of pastries from the nearby counter, and the background music played a soulful beat. Sunlight streamed through the large windows, casting a soft glow on Emily's face, illuminating the streaks of auburn in her otherwise dark hair. She had a way of holding herself that was both poised and unguarded, an air of someone who had long since grown accustomed to hiding her vulnerability beneath layers of charm and wit. Her eyes, though, told a different story. Andy noticed the way they flicked between his own and the table, searching, questioning, perhaps wondering if she could trust him with the pieces of her, she rarely shared with anyone.

They had been talking for a while now, the conversation flowing easily from casual pleasantries to more personal matters. Something about Emily intrigued Andy, about how she held back, never fully letting her guard down. He found himself wanting to know more, to break through the careful exterior she had built around herself. Andy felt a connection growing between them as they continued talking, a comfortable camaraderie that made him feel at ease. He watched her for a moment longer, contemplating his following words. It wasn't a big question, not in the grand scheme of things, but for some reason, it felt necessary.

"Emily," He began softly, leaning forward slightly. Her name felt formal on his tongue, too rigid, too distant for how they were starting to connect. His voice was warm and casual, but there was an undertone of sincerity as he continued, "can I call you Em?"

For a second, Emily froze, her spoon halting mid-stir. The question caught her off guard, not because it was invasive or inappropriate, but because of the familiarity it implied. She did not let people get close enough to ask that. The name *Em* was reserved for a small, private circle of those who had earned their way into her world, the few she allowed past her defences.

Andy held her gaze, his eyes soft but curious, waiting. The sun glinted off his watch, casting a flicker of light between them, but the warmth in his expression made her pause. He was not just asking to shorten her name; he was asking permission to step into that closer space to be part of something more personal. Emily let out a breath she had not realised she was holding, her fingers tightening slightly around the handle of her cup. A small smile tugged at the corner of her lips, not quite reaching her eyes, but it was enough to soften her features.

"Em?" she repeated as if testing the sound of it on her tongue. Her voice was light, teasing, but there was a vulnerability beneath the playful tone.

Andy nodded, his smile widening. "Yeah. It suits you."

The simplicity of his response, the way he said it without expectation or pressure, eased some of the tension in her shoulders. She tilted her head slightly, considering him with a newfound curiosity. Most people didn't ask. They just assumed. But Andy had asked. That meant something.

She set her spoon down carefully, letting her hands rest on the edge of her cup, her fingers tracing the delicate rim. "Not many people call me Em," she admitted quietly, her voice barely above a whisper.

There was a pause, and for a moment, Andy wondered if she would say no, but then she looked up at him, her gaze steady and full of unspoken trust. "OK, you can call me Em."

Andy's smile broadened, but he didn't push the moment further. He could see how much it had cost her to let him in, even in such a small way.

"Thanks, Em," he said softly, letting the name roll off his tongue with an easy familiarity, as though it had always been hers, and now, it was his to use.

The rest of the conversation flowed naturally, but something had shifted. They weren't just two people sitting in a café anymore; there was an ease between them, a quiet understanding that had been absent before. While not entirely down, Emily's walls had lowered just enough to let Andy glimpse the person behind them. As they talked, Andy noticed how her posture relaxed, her laughter came more freely, and her smile lit up her entire face, not just her mouth. She had always been beautiful in a guarded, distant way, but now, with her defences slowly unravelling, there was something genuinely captivating about her. It was like watching the first rays of the sun breaking through a dense fog, subtle yet transformative.

At that moment, Andy realised just how much he wanted to know her—really—know her not just the version she showed the world but the one she kept hidden, the one who had been through things, who had stories to tell, who was complicated and messy and real.

"Do you ever feel… like you're tired of it all sometimes?" Emily suddenly asked, her voice softer now, almost vulnerable. She glanced out the window as she spoke, watching a couple walk together down the street, their laughter carefree and uninhibited.

Andy was quiet for a moment, surprised by the sudden shift in tone. He could sense there was more to her question than the surface allowed. "Yeah," he replied, his voice equally soft. "More often than I'd like to admit."

Emily nodded, her gaze distant, as though she was far away from the café, lost in memories or thoughts she rarely shared. "It's hard to keep the pieces together sometimes," She murmured, almost to herself.

Andy observed her, his heart tightening slightly at her vulnerability. He wanted to say something comforting to ease her weight but knew that sometimes words weren't enough. Sometimes, just being there, really being there, was what mattered.

He reached across the table, his hand hovering momentarily before gently placing it over hers. "You don't always have to," he said quietly, his voice steady. "Keep it all together, I mean."

Emily's eyes lingered on Andy's hand, her chest tightening with an unexpected swell of emotion. She hadn't realised how much she needed this simple gesture, this quiet acknowledgement that they were together. She slowly, deliberately turned her hand over, pressing her palm against his. The warmth of his skin seemed to anchor her, pulling her out of the swirling thoughts and grounding her in the present moment. The connection felt real and tangible, a lifeline she hadn't known she was reaching for.

"Thanks, Andy," she whispered, her voice soft but carrying the weight of her gratitude. It wasn't just for the touch but for what it symbolised: support, solidarity, and maybe even love.

"Anytime, Em," Andy replied, his eyes gentle as a small, reassuring smile pulled at his lips.

His words were simple, but a more profound understanding lay beneath them, a promise. There was an unspoken bond between them in the quiet hum of the café, with the scent of freshly brewed coffee and the golden morning light streaming through the windows. Neither had to say it out loud, but they both knew that whatever life threw their way, they wouldn't have to face it alone.

The world outside continued to rush by, but time seemed to slow inside. As if to underscore the moment, the familiar opening chords of a classic song filtered through the café's speakers *Light My Fire* by The Doors. Emily recognised it immediately, her lips curling into a small smile as the lyrics floated through the air.

"You know that it would be untrue.

You know that I would be a liar.

If I was to say to you..."

The words echoed in her ears, adding a kind of magic to the already intimate moment. It was as if the universe was playing its part in their story, setting the scene exactly right.

"Come on, baby, light my fire,"

The song continued, and without a second thought, Emily and Andy leaned toward one another, drawn by a force neither could resist. The world faded entirely as their lips met in a long, passionate kiss—slow, tender, and full of everything they had held back. In that moment, nothing else mattered.

The music played on, the sun outside shone a little brighter, and for Emily and Andy, the tangled mess of life suddenly seemed a little less daunting, as if they had already begun to light each other's fires.

19: The President's Man

As Andy walked through the bustling streets of Washington, his mind buzzed with thoughts of Emily and the weight of the meeting ahead. He was about to meet U.S. Secretary of State Tom Dunnagan, a man whose reputation preceded him as cunning, ruthless, and known for playing his cards close to the chest. The stakes were high, and Andy felt the pressure mounting as his phone buzzed in his pocket, momentarily pulling him out of his spiralling thoughts.

A message from Ravi popped up on Telegram, stark and unsettling: *Things are getting hot here. I'm being followed. Lookout, be safe.*

Andy felt a cold wave of dread wash over him. He could almost hear the gravity in Ravi's words, the sense of danger so glaring it clawed at Andy's chest. His fingers tightened around the micro-SD card in his pocket, the one Ravi had risked everything to get into his hands. Encased in a cleverly disguised package, the tiny piece of tech held enough power to shift the trajectory of history if handled correctly, but with Ravi now in jeopardy, Andy's every instinct screamed that they were on borrowed time.

When he arrived at the meeting spot, he spotted Dunnagan standing by a discreet café, his posture rigid, face pinched with tension. No greetings passed between them; there was no time for pleasantries, and Andy couldn't stand the man's sleazy air of authority. The situation's urgency crackled in the space between them like static electricity.

"I need you to call off your attack dogs," Andy said without preamble, his voice firm but calm, his eyes locking onto Dunnagan's. "Kowalski's pursuit is putting Ravi in danger. You need to stop this now."

Dunnagan bristled slightly but didn't respond immediately, his eyes narrowing in suspicion. Andy could sense the gears turning in the Secretary's mind, weighing the options and calculating the risk. Dunnagan was a man who measured everything, rarely allowing emotion to factor into his decisions. But Andy knew how to push the right buttons and decided to appeal to Dunnagan's most vulnerable pressure points: patriotism and self-interest.

"Look," Andy began, his tone shifting from confrontation to persuasion, his business instincts kicking in, "if that video gets out, it won't just be bad for your career. It'll tear apart the entire administration. Think about it: an exposé this big? It will be on the front page of every major paper by tomorrow morning. The fallout would be catastrophic."

Andy's voice held a calm confidence that belied the tension in his gut, but he could see his words were cutting through. Dunnagan's expression darkened, the reality of the situation sinking in. His shoulders sagged slightly under the weight of the implications. The political waters were already treacherous enough with the re-elections looming, and any further scandals would be the final nail in the coffin. With a grimace, Dunnagan finally nodded. There was no more room for manoeuvring or games to be played. Reluctantly, he reached for his phone, dialling with the stiff, resigned motion of a man who knew he was cornered. Andy watched as he brought the phone to his ear. Dunnagan's voice was low and clipped as he barked the order to stand down.

The silence stretched between them, thick and heavy, as they both waited for Kowalski's response. The line crackled faintly, and after what felt like an agonising eternity, Kowalski's gruff voice cut through, terse and brimming with reluctance. He had no choice but to comply. Andy exhaled, feeling relieved as the immediate danger to Ravi was averted, but as the tension drained from his body, a lingering unease remained coiled in his gut. He could sense that this wasn't the end. There were too many moving parts, secrets, and people playing their games.

His eyes met Dunnagan's and for a moment they exchanged wary glances, both men fully aware that while the threat might have been temporarily neutralised, they were far from safe. They stood on the precipice of something much larger, much darker than they cared to admit.

Andy wasted no time once they sat down, his energy tangible as he leaned forward, his words tumbling out with the kind of passion that made his ambitions impossible to ignore. Dunnagan, sceptical at first, watched as Andy painted a picture of the future that felt like a utopia compared to the dark reality they were currently facing. Andy spoke of how shifting the economic timeline could reverse the mounting national debt, create millions of jobs and, perhaps most importantly, improve the quality of life for everyday Americans. His voice carried an intensity that made the air feel charged, the enormity of his vision filling the small room.

By the time Andy finished, he was breathless, his cheeks flushed with exertion, his eyes gleaming with hope. There was no mistaking the sincerity behind his words. Andy genuinely believed in what he was saying which showed in how his entire body seemed to pulse with life.

Dunnagan, who had initially been resistant, felt his defences beginning to crumble under the weight of Andy's enthusiasm. The Secretary of State momentarily allowed himself to imagine the possibilities. Despite the underhanded way Andy had gone about getting him involved, despite the shadowy playboy Ravi hovering in the background, Dunnagan couldn't deny that there was potential in the plan, and potential in this world, was everything.

With a slow nod, his face drawn in a thoughtful frown, Dunnagan met Andy's gaze and finally spoke. "You've got something here," He admitted. His voice was steady, but a glint in his eyes showed that the wheels in his mind were turning.

"I'll take this to the White House. But know this Andy, if this backfires, we're all going down."

Andy's chest tightened with excitement and a flicker of anxiety, but this was the breakthrough he had hoped for. Dunnagan's nod of approval was the first major hurdle cleared. He was on a roll now and couldn't afford to lose momentum.

"There's one more thing," Andy added quickly, his words tumbling out in a rush. "We need Dr Clark on board. She's the key to making this shift happen. We can lock this plan in if you can arrange a meeting between her and the president."

Dunnagan's face twisted into a grimace, and he sighed heavily, rubbing his temple as if the world's weight rested there. He couldn't enjoy favours, which was a big ask. The White House was already stretched thin, with re-election campaigns kicking off and scandals lurking in every corner, but he knew Andy wasn't wrong. Dr Clark was going to be crucial.

"I'll arrange it," Dunnagan agreed reluctantly, his tone resigned. "But this video." He trailed off, his unease creeping into his voice.

The damning video footage, which Andy and Ravi held over his head, was a constant threat, gnawing at the edges of his mind. "I'm not moving forward unless we settle that."

Andy hesitated, his mind racing as he considered the risks. The micro-SD card was his trump card and giving it up meant losing significant leverage, but without this meeting, his plan would never reach the president. He couldn't afford to let that happen. His hand, metaphorically speaking, was forced.

"Once the meeting happens and we're good," Andy said, his voice steady though his stomach clenched, "You'll have the video, but not a moment before."

Dunnagan gave him a sharp look but nodded in agreement. He didn't like it, but he had no other choice. The wheels were already in motion, and there was no turning back.

True to his word, Dunnagan began pulling strings within the White House, using every bit of his influence and leverage. It wasn't easy. There was pushback resistance from the president's inner circle, scepticism about this mysterious Dr Clark, and a general unwillingness to take on another potentially volatile situation, but Dunnagan was nothing if not relentless, and after days of backdoor negotiations and political finagling, he finally secured a coveted spot in the president's crowded schedule.

It was no small feat. Dunnagan surprised even himself with how quickly he managed to make it happen. It wasn't just Andy's plan that motivated him; it was the spectre of that damn video hanging over his career like a guillotine. If that footage ever became exposed, not only would it tank his political future, but it could drag the president into a scandal he might not recover from.

With the date set and preparations underway, Dunnagan ensured everything would run smoothly. He briefed Dr Clark on what to expect, coordinated with the president's staff, and ensured every possible contingency was accounted for. But even as the weight of this monumental task pressed down on him, his mind drifted to something or rather, someone else.

Anna Morocover.

The memory of her name alone sent a shiver through him, and despite the gravity of the situation, he couldn't shake the image of her from his mind. The night they had shared was intoxicating, primal, filled with a kind of raw desire that had left him breathless and aching for more. As he sat there, making arrangements that could shift the entire nation's future, his thoughts kept pulling him back to that night, her skin against his, her lips, and the fire that had ignited between them.

It was dangerous thinking about her, but he couldn't help it. A bittersweet smile crept onto his lips, and he whispered, "What a night."

Dunnagan couldn't forget her even amid political intrigues, scandals, and high-stake negotiations and in some small, dark corner of his mind, he wondered if he might not want to.

20: Grappa

Ravi was determined to spend a few weeks lost in northern Italy's winding roads and picturesque landscapes. On landing at Venice Marco Polo Airport, he wasted no time renting an Audi R8 to navigate to Bassano del Grappa.

He had always had a particular affinity for the Audi R8. Something was magnetic about its sleek lines and powerful V10 engine, purring like a contented Cheetah. Unlike other sports cars, which demanded a certain finesse to handle, the R8 invited all drivers to experience its thrilling capabilities.

As Ravi settled into the driver's seat, he admired every inch of the car's meticulous craftsmanship. From the supple leather upholstery to the intuitive dashboard controls, this fine machine was a testament to Audi's unwavering commitment to quality and innovation.

"Vorsprung durch Technik, indeed," Ravi muttered.

But what truly set the R8 apart was its performance. While it possessed all the hallmarks of a formidable sports car; precise handling, lightning-fast acceleration and responsive steering, it also boasted a level of comfort and ease of use that belied its muscular exterior. Whether cruising along the open highway or navigating the narrow streets of an ancient city, the R8 effortlessly transitioned from beast to beauty with a grace that was as impressive as unexpected, and there was no denying the thrill from unleashing the R8's full potential. With a mere tap of the accelerator, Ravi could feel the car surge forward and hear the engine roar with a ferocity that sent shivers down his spine. It was a feeling unlike any other.

Yet the R8 remained remarkably composed, its advanced suspension system ensuring a smooth ride even at breakneck speeds. This combination of raw power and refined elegance drew Ravi to the Audi R8 repeatedly. As he immersed himself in the scenic Veneto region, Ravi was ready to leave his recent troubles far behind.

Bassano del Grappa welcomed Ravi with open arms. The city's charm lay in its rich history and stunning architecture, epitomised by Ponte Vecchio, the oldest European bridge that stretched gracefully across the river Brenta.

As he drove through the cobblestone streets, Ravi marvelled at the timeless beauty surrounding him. The Museo Nazionale Storico degli Alpini, situated on the western bank of the river, offered a poignant reminder of Italy's past with its collection of World War I artefacts. Meanwhile, the walls of Palazzo Bonaguro were adorned with vibrant frescoes, each telling a story of days gone by.

Eager to delve deeper into cultural heritage, Ravi went to the Museo Civico di Bassano del Grappa, showcasing works by local and renowned artists. The vast gallery provides a window into the city's soul, from Renaissance masterpieces to contemporary creations, but the panoramic views from the medieval Torre Civica di Bassano took Ravi's breath away. As he climbed the ancient stone steps, he was rewarded with sweeping vistas of terracotta rooftops and rolling hills, a sight that seemed to transcend time.

Venturing further north, Ravi discovered Villa Angarano, a magnificent estate boasting Palladian-style architecture. Surrounded by lush vineyards and manicured gardens, the villa stood as a testament to the region's wealthy past. He continued to wind his way through the Veneto region, and each twist in the road revealed new wonders. With every passing mile of beautiful landscape, his worries faded into the rearview mirror.

Ravi was fully immersed in the local culture during his stay in Bassano del Grappa. He was particularly enjoying the city's namesake beverage. In Italy, grappa is a potent spirit made from pomace, the leftover grape skins, seeds, and stems from the winemaking process. Renowned for its robust flavour and fiery kick, grappa holds a special place in the hearts of Italians, especially those in the Veneto region, where it is produced with pride.

Eager to get the whole grappa experience, Ravi visited the city's quaint tavernas and bustling cafes. Each offered a unique selection of the cherished spirit, some infused with fruit and others with herbs, from traditional distilleries and modern craft producers. Ravi savoured a classic grappa aged in oak barrels at one establishment for a mellow finish. With each sip, he could taste the subtle nuances of the grape varietals used, the floral notes of Moscato and the bold richness of Sangiovese. It was a sensory journey through the vineyards of Italy, captured in a single glass.

One evening, Ravi was drawn to a local distillery renowned for its artisanal approach. Here, he witnessed the time-honoured tradition firsthand. Skilled craftsmen carefully tended to the copper stills, coaxing out the essence of the grapes with patience and precision. As Ravi bid farewell to Bassano del Grappa, he could not shake the sense of déjà vu that haunted him on the open road. Time and again he caught sight of the same car trailing behind him.

At first Ravi dismissed it, attributing the recurrence of the sleek silhouette to the popular driving route. Yet, unease began to gnaw as the miles stretched on and the mystery car maintained a discreet distance. Was he being followed? Who was behind the wheel, and what did they want with him? Ravi was determined to uncover the truth, no matter where the road may lead.

Giovanni adjusted the holster for his Beretta M9, ensuring its weight settled comfortably against his hip. His sharp eyes scanned the horizon as the Mercedes they had commandeered sliced through the bends of the Italian countryside. Every shadowed corner held a potential threat, and Giovanni was ready. Beside him, Sofia exuding effortless grace, tapped her slender fingers rhythmically on the dashboard as she studied the map before her. She caught Giovanni's eye with a swift glance and flashed him a confident grin, a silent acknowledgement that they would see their mission through.

Their target, Ravi Jayasekera, continued to evade their grasp, but Giovanni and Sofia were no strangers to the art of pursuit. Both had years of training that had honed their instincts and sharpened their senses. As they closed in on Jayasekera's last known location, Giovanni gripped the steering wheel tighter, his focus unwavering. This was another assignment and a test of his mettle and commitment to the cause. The weight of this mission felt different. Giovanni knew that the implications of failure extended far beyond the immediate consequences. Jayasekera was not an ordinary target; he was deeply embedded in a network of high-stakes political intrigue and covert operations. The information he possessed could tip the balance of power on a global scale and capturing him meant dismantling a critical node in an intricate web of deception and influence.

For Giovanni, this mission was personal. He had spent years navigating the murky waters of international espionage, but this assignment was a culmination of everything he had trained for. It was a chance to prove his worth, not just to his superiors, but to himself. The stakes were higher, the risks more significant, and the margin for error non-existent. Every decision he made, every move he executed, was a step closer to either triumph or catastrophe. Since getting the word that their associate Kowalski needed their help, Sofia had used her contacts and keen intellect to piece together Jayasekera's movements with finesse. With each new lead, each whispered rumour, they drew closer to their quarry, their resolve growing stronger.

In the distance, the rugged peaks of the Italian Alps loomed, their majestic beauty belying the danger that lurked within their valleys. It was possible Jayasekera could meet his demise by being run off the road in such unforgiving terrain. But Giovanni and Sofia knew better than to leave anything to chance. With their sights set, they prepared to confront their target head-on. Failure was not an option. Ravi's heart pounded as he decided to alter his destination. Glancing at the GPS screen, he recalibrated his route to Verona, the ancient city immortalised by Shakespeare's tragic tale of Romeo and Juliet. His hands trembled with adrenaline as he accessed the car's voice command system. With urgency, he activated his Telegram App and began composing a message to Andy.

Things are getting hot here. I'm being followed. Lookout, be safe. Ravi typed.

With relief, Ravi hit send, the message whisking away into the digital ether. He hoped Andy would heed his warning, knowing his friend was smart enough to take precautions, but, as he sent the message, a nagging doubt lingered, a fear he may have inadvertently dragged Andy further into danger. The black Mercedes tailing him was still lurking in the shadows.

As the R8 surged forward, devouring kilometres with effortless speed, Ravi's eyes remained fixed on the road, his senses attuned to the slightest hint of danger. In his rearview mirror, the black Mercedes reappeared, a dark shadow steadily gaining ground. With determination,

Ravi pressed the accelerator, unleashing the R8's full power. The wind whipped through his hair, the rush exhilarating as he hurtled down the SP111, leaving a trail of dust and uncertainty in his wake.

With each passing km Ravi's resolve hardened as he barrelled towards his fate, whatever that was. Ahead, Verona beckoned its storied streets, a sanctuary from the chaos that pursued him but, as the low fuel light blinked ominously on the R8's dashboard, Ravi's heart sank. He glanced at the fuel gauge and watched the needle inch closer to empty. Despite wanting to avoid a stop and any unwanted confrontations, he had no choice but to find a filling station. He scanned the surrounding landscape for signs of civilisation and spotted an Eni sign on the horizon. As he steered the R8 off the main road, he was relieved to pull into the Eni filling station. With fumbling hands, he pushed on the left side of the fuel door and the latch released. Ravi reached for the fuel pump, the metallic clang echoing through the stillness as he inserted the nozzle into the tank opening. As the tank filled with over 70 litres of fuel he kept his eyes on the road, waiting for any sign of the black Mercedes.

Giovanni and Sofia watched as Jayasekera pulled into the filling station. The faintest smirk played across Giovanni's lips as he exchanged a knowing glance with Sofia. This was their opportunity. With practised efficiency, Giovanni manoeuvred, ensuring they remained just out of Jayasekera's line of sight. Then, with practised precision, they positioned themselves in front of their target's car. Jayasekera's shock was striking as they closed in, Giovanni's M9 pistol gleaming in the gas station's harsh light.

Giovanni's mobile shattered the tense silence with its shrill ringtone. His attention focused squarely on Jayasekera. Giovanni's fingers reached for the device and inadvertently activated the loudspeaker.

A rapid-fire Italian voice crackled down the line.

"Missione interrotta! Missione interrotta!" (Mission aborted!) the voice repeated urgently, the words echoing through the air like a thunderclap.

Giovanni's eyes widened in disbelief as he took it in.

"Che cazzo?" (What the fuck?), He exclaimed, frustrated with the abrupt end to their mission.

With another curse, he signalled to Sofia. They left Ravi stunned but unharmed. He felt a surge of gratitude for the twist of fate and needed a stiff drink to celebrate his narrow escape.

21: The Oval Office

Dr Emily Clark entered the hallowed halls of the Oval Office with a mix of awe and responsibility weighing on her shoulders. The room steeped in history and power, was overwhelming and inspiring. Here she stood, a renowned astrophysicist, ready to face the leader of the free world, poised to deliver an idea that could alter the course of history itself. Her heart pounded but her exterior remained composed, her mind sharp with the task. President Jeff Johnson, or JJ as commonly known, rose from behind his grand mahogany desk and extended his hand. His presence was commanding but warm, and the firm grip of his handshake conveyed an authority that had been honed through years of leadership. His eyes, however, held a spark of curiosity.

"Dr Clark," he greeted with a genuine smile. "I've heard a lot about you."

She reciprocated the handshake, feeling the moment's weight, and smiled back. But the weight of responsibility bore down on her, reminding her of the significance of what she was about to propose. Taking a deep breath, she braced herself and prepared to lay out her groundbreaking research.

As they took their seats, Dr Clark's gaze briefly swept over the room, her eyes catching the portraits of past presidents who had shaped the nation. Now, it was her turn to present something monumental. Unfurling a large set of charts and data sheets, she began. Her voice was calm, but she felt a deep surge of emotion beneath the surface. This culminated years of work, sleepless nights, and tireless dedication. Now, everything hinged on this moment.

She eloquently and passionately explained how her research into manipulating the space-time continuum could offer unparalleled benefits. Her idea, though complex, had the potential to change everything. With precise calculations and breakthrough technology she proposed to shift the timeline, creating a ripple effect that could reshape economic outcomes, reset global power dynamics, and bring the United States to the forefront of scientific advancement.

"The 'Timeline' shift," she said, pointing to the meticulously prepared charts, "would begin with a focal point. Our calculations show New York is the best candidate for its global connectivity and significance.

We can achieve a seamless transition by altering the flow of time from London to New York."

JJ leaned forward, his brow furrowing in concentration as he absorbed the intricacies of her explanation. Despite the topic's complexity, he kept up, his thoughtful expression indicating his grasp of the possibilities. The rain outside beat a steady rhythm against the windowpanes but, inside, the air between them seemed electrified with potential. Dr Clark watched him, her heart in her throat as she waited for him to respond.

When he finally spoke, his tone was measured, a mixture of hope and caution. "Dr Clark, if what you are proposing is possible… it could revolutionise everything: our economy, our politics, the way we approach global challenges."

A flicker of relief passed over Emily's face. He understood, and, more importantly, he saw the possibilities. But she was not done yet. She pressed on, explaining how this shift could reverse economic downturns, create jobs, and potentially end the crippling national debt. She spoke of innovation, progress, and a world that could leap ahead if they dared to take the first step.

By the end of the meeting, the energy in the room had shifted. There was now a shared sense of hope and determination where there had been uncertainty. Their collaboration was a pivotal turning point at that moment: a merging of scientific brilliance and political leadership that could shape the future. As they exchanged parting words and a firm handshake again, there was no mistaking the resolve between their eyes. They were ready to embark on this extraordinary adventure together.

After Dr Clark left, the rain continued to drum against the windows, a soothing yet persistent reminder of the storm outside. President Johnson sat back in his chair, staring out into the night. The soft glow of the streetlights outside bathed the White House grounds in a pale light, casting shadows that danced across the room. The flickering lamplight accentuated the deep lines etched into his face, worry lines that had deepened over recent weeks as the nation teetered on the edge of economic collapse.

He tapped his fingers rhythmically on the arm of his chair, lost in thought. Could this be it? Could this be the moment he had been waiting for the opportunity to pull the country back from the brink? He had struggled, weighed down by the enormity of leading a nation during one of its darkest times, but now, as he reflected on Dr Clark's vision, a glimmer of hope sparked inside him.

The possibilities were endless. If they could make it work, it would not be a scientific breakthrough, it would secure the United States' dominance for decades to come. It would be his legacy, the defining moment of his presidency, and yet, as with all great risks, the stakes were incredibly high. If they failed, if the shift backfired, it could mean disaster.

Still, the idea tugged at him, stirring his restless mind. He could see it now as a future where the nation thrived once again, where they appeared stronger, smarter, and more powerful, and all because of one daring, audacious idea.

JJ's thoughts wandered into the night as the rain cascaded down the windows. The shadows of uncertainty lingered, but within them lay the flickering hope of a brighter future that he now believed might be within reach.

President Jeff Johnson sat alone in the dimly lit Oval Office, the weight of the world resting on his shoulders as he pondered the decision that could define his presidency and the future of the entire nation. The timeline shift was an audacious idea that had the potential to reshape the world as it knew it. Yet, with such revolutionary potential came equally monumental risks.

He stared out the window at the rain-soaked White House lawn, his mind swirling with thoughts of the consequences. On one hand, it was a chance to pave the way for a brighter, more prosperous future. The possibility of resetting the economic playing field, creating jobs, and securing the future of his country glimmered in his thoughts like a distant lighthouse in the storm. On the other hand, the spectre of uncertainty loomed large. What if something went wrong? What if this shift disrupted the natural order and created irreversible damage?

A deep sense of resolve stirred within him. He had been elected to lead in times of crisis, to make the tough calls when others hesitated, and now, as he sat at the helm of the free world, he knew that this decision could be the biggest of his presidency. Still, its magnitude called for reflection. JJ sighed, deciding it was best to sleep on it and let the gravity of the choice settle before committing to a path forward.

The following morning, as dawn's early light crept through the windows of the West Wing, President Johnson felt a renewed sense of purpose. He'd had the night to consider, to weigh the risks and rewards, and now his mind was clear. The decision was made. With a solemn nod, he knew there was no turning back.

Together, with the brilliant Dr Clark and the mysterious Andy Stuart, they would embark on a journey into the unknown. JJ had heard much about Stuart, a man known for bold, unconventional thinking. He was keen to meet him, to take his measure, but more than that, he saw in Stuart a kindred spirit, someone who wasn't afraid to think creatively and who, like him, was willing to take risks for progress.

They shared a common goal: a better tomorrow for all Americans. Guided by this shared commitment they would leap, placing their hopes and trust in the hands of science, ambition, and leadership.

As each day passed, the urgency of the nation's economic crisis grew more pronounced. Inflation was spiralling out of control, jobs were lost, and the national debt reached catastrophic levels. JJ felt the pressure mounting from all sides, but his conviction in the timeline shift only strengthened. To him, the GMT line was more than just a scientific breakthrough. It was salvation. It was the answer to the question that had plagued him since taking office: how do we save America from this downward spiral?

Yet, JJ was painfully aware that even revolutionary ideas needed more than just vision; they required execution. The wheels of government moved slowly, and nothing came easy in Washington. The President knew that for the timeline shift to succeed, it would take more than scientific brilliance. It would require political cunning, strategic alliances, and deft manoeuvring.

The intricate dance of passing legislation was like a game of chess; every move was calculated, and every step was considered for its consequences. JJ would have to rally support from Congress, convincing both the House and the Senate to back his plan. That meant courting key players, building coalitions, and overcoming opposition from both sides of the aisle, and even after all that, both chambers would have to agree on the same bill by majority vote before it could land on his desk for approval.

The path ahead was arduous. There would be resistance from political adversaries and those in his party who feared the unknown and were more comfortable with the status quo than taking a risk that could reshape the future. But JJ had never been one to shy away from a challenge. He had faced challenging times before, and he would face them again. He was ready to navigate the murky waters of international diplomacy, fend off world leaders' criticisms, and overcome the staunch opposition he knew would come from within and outside his borders.

Whatever the future held, he was ready to face it, not for himself, but for the millions of Americans who depended on him to make the hard choices and to lead with courage in uncertain times. The President knew that with Dr Clark's scientific genius and Andy Stuart's unconventional approach, they had a real shot at building a brighter future where America could rise from the ashes of economic collapse and reclaim its place as a beacon of hope for the world.

22: The House

The House of Representatives is a cornerstone of American democracy composed of 435 elected members representing the nation's diverse population. Each state sends representatives based on population, with six non-voting members from territories and the District of Columbia. At its helm is the Speaker of the House, elected by members and third in the presidential line of succession. Elections occur every two years, ensuring accountability to constituents. Representatives must meet criteria including age, citizenship, and residency. The House holds significant powers: initiating revenue bills, impeaching federal officials, and resolving Electoral College ties. Across Capitol Hill, the Senate consists of 100 Senators, two from each state, elected for six-year terms.

The Vice President serves as its President, with tie-breaking powers. The Senate confirms appointments, ratifies treaties and conducts impeachment trials.

Legislation requires passage by both chambers, and Congress can override vetoes with a two-thirds majority, embodying the US system of checks and balances. With a vision firmly in place, The President prepared for the most daunting phase of the timeline shift endeavour, navigating the intricate web of politics within the House of Representatives. As he delved into the intricacies of the legislative process with the weight of the nation's future resting on his shoulders, he grappled with garnering support for the bill.

JJ understood the importance of leveraging his authority. Article II, Section 2 of the Constitution granted the president the power to negotiate treaties, subject to the advice and consent of the Senate. This made clear his need to secure a two-thirds majority in the Senate, so he campaigned to build a coalition within the House. He engaged in tireless negotiations, reaching across party lines and bridging ideological divides to find common ground. He courted key stakeholders and tirelessly lobbied undecided lawmakers, making his case.

But political rivals with entrenched interests sought to derail his efforts, employing every tactic to sow discord and undermine his agenda. Amid the heated debates and backroom dealings, JJ remained steadfast in his commitment to the cause, determined to overcome the odds and secure victory for the American people.

With the fate of his presidency and the nation's future hanging in the balance, the stakes could not be higher, and he knew he could count on the support of at least one colleague…

As Dunnagan settled into the comfort of his office chair, his mind became a theatre of recollections. Ravi Jayasekera, the cunning puppeteer whose orchestrated encounters had left an indelible mark on his psyche.

But Dunnagan could not help but acknowledge Jayasekera's role in leading him to Anna Morocova. With her beguiling charm, Anna had captured Dunnagan's heart in a whirlwind of desire. Her memory lingered like a haunting melody, her absence a void.

Then there was Kowalski, a bastion of loyalty. Their 'first to fight' bond had weathered many storms. He was always in his corner and had proved himself again.

And Andy Stuart. Despite the friends he keeps, Dunnagan admires a man who gets things done. The tech billionaire's infectious energy ignites a spark of inspiration in Dunnagan. While the circumstances they met had been fraught, he saw the potential benefits of working with Andy. With deep pockets and a vast network of influential connections, Andy could sway hearts and minds in ways that Dunnagan could only dream of.

A cunning strategy began to take shape. Perhaps he could use their partnership to further his political ambitions and get some payback for the blackmail attempt. This idea intrigued Dunnagan, so he arranged to meet with Andy, trying to shake the feeling that Andy might see him as an adversary rather than an ally.

Andy's mind was a maelstrom of conflicting emotions as he walked through the bustling streets of Washington, D.C. toward the rendezvous point. His thoughts raced, a blur of anticipation, worry and hope but he steeled himself, pushing aside the whirlwind within. He had to remain focused. He was about to meet with Dunnagan, the man whose influence could sway the future of their plan, and everything depended on keeping his cool.

The cosy confines of The DC Coffee Cup offered a brief respite from the city's chaotic energy. The smell of freshly brewed espresso filled the air, mingling with the soft hum of conversations around him. The warmth of the coffee shop was a comforting contrast to the chill of his nerves. It was a small sanctuary amid all the uncertainty. Andy's eyes scanned the doorway as he slid into a booth, waiting for Dunnagan to arrive.

Minutes later, Dunnagan strode in, wasting no time on pleasantries. His face was set with the same urgency that pulsed through Andy's veins. He immediately launched into a recount of his latest conversation with the President, detailing how JJ had expressed genuine interest in their proposal. As Dunnagan spoke, his words buzzed with electricity, filling the air between them with a current that sparked something inside Andy. His heart raced, adrenaline coursing through his system like he had just downed a double espresso. Oddly enough, his coffee still sat untouched on the table.

"The President's in," Dunnagan said, his eyes gleaming with the weight of the revelation.

It was a game-changing moment. Andy could feel the clouds of doubt swirling in his mind begin to lift, replaced by a cautious but unmistakable sense of optimism. This was the moment they had been working toward, the chance to shift the timeline, to alter history. As that reality began to sink in, he finally sipped his coffee, savouring the rich, velvety taste as it warmed him. A small, indulgent smile tugged at the corners of his mouth. They were closer than ever.

But Dunnagan was not finished. His expression shifted as he turned his gaze toward Andy, and Andy could see more at stake. Dunnagan appreciated the influence Andy could bring to the table. He needed more than just Andy's business acumen his persuasive prowess. Dunnagan's voice lowered as he began outlining the strategy, almost conspiratorial. They needed to bring Congress on board to steer undecided individuals toward their cause, and Andy was the key to making that happen.

Andy leaned in, listening carefully. He could feel the weight of responsibility settling on his shoulders, but it didn't scare him. This was his moment, his chance to use the authority and connections he had spent years building. The political landscape was treacherous, filled with factions and rivalries, but Andy knew how to navigate it. This wasn't about securing a meeting with the President anymore. It was about securing the future.

Dunnagan continued to outline their game plan, and as he spoke, he zeroed in on California's pivotal role.

"California's delegation has the largest number of votes, 54. It's not just about their sheer numbers, though. California sets the tone. If we can get them on board, we can shift the tide in our favour."

Andy nodded, absorbing the significance of what Dunnagan was saying. California was a giant in terms of its political clout and economic power. Historically, the East Coast had dominated the conversation, with places like New York hogging the spotlight when it came to investment and political favour. But California had always been the sleeping giant, the state that, when it moved, shifted the entire nation.

Securing California's backing could be the linchpin to their success, but there was a complication. "Davidson,"

Dunnagan muttered, his voice tinged with frustration, "the House Minority Leader in California hates me. We have been at each other's throats for years."

Andy's brow furrowed. He had heard of Davidson, a stubborn, fiercely independent politician with a reputation for holding grudges. This wouldn't be easy. Winning over California would mean finding a way to work around or, better yet, neutralise Davidson's opposition. But that was Andy's speciality, finding a way when none seemed to exist.

Dunnagan finished his briefing, his eyes locking onto Andy's with a look that said, "Now what?"

The air between them hung thick with tension, but Andy felt a spark of determination ignite beneath it. He leaned back slightly, a slight, confident grin on his lips. The challenge was formidable, but that only made him more resolute.

"California, here I come," Andy said, his voice steady and filled with purpose.

Dunnagan gave a curt nod, satisfied. Together, they were ready to make their mark, one vote at a time, turning the tide of history in their favour. This was more than politics. This was about changing the course of the future, and they would stop at nothing to see it through.

23: The Golden State

Born on the cusp of September 5, 1970, Ethan Willow Davidson was not yet the titan of industry and politics he would become. Still, his path was already weaving through the corridors of power and enterprise. A rising star within the Democratic Party, Davidson was like a green shoot sprouting through the cracks of San Francisco's complex political landscape. He had earned his early stripes on the Economic Development Commission, where his innovative strategies and hands-on approach to tackling the city's economic woes earned him a reputation as a man who could get things done.

From there, his ascent seemed inevitable. Davidson's next stop was the mayor's office, where his stewardship marked an era of civic progress and urban revival. He transformed San Francisco with sweeping infrastructure projects, increased affordable housing and policies fuelling small business growth. His success there opened the door to higher office, leading him to the lieutenant governor's seat, where his influence grew within California and across the country.

But Davidson's journey wasn't confined to the world of politics. Davidson had also proven himself a formidable entrepreneur with a degree from Harbour University. Alongside his childhood friend and affluent business scion Mason Whitaker, he co-founded Burger Express Ventures, a fast-food chain that swiftly became a household name. Their entrepreneurial juggernaut exemplified the American dream: vision, grit, and unrelenting ambition merging to create a billion-dollar empire. By 2023, Ethan Willow Davidson's name echoed in political and corporate circles, a testament to his relentless pursuit of influence and success. He was formidable, symbolising how ambition, timing and opportunity could converge to shape a legacy.

But then came Tom Dunnagan, the self-proclaimed kingmaker of California politics. Dunnagan was a political operative, a master strategist who had made a name for himself by pulling the strings behind the scenes. He wasn't a politician, but his influence stretched across the state. He had the ear of every major player, from Sacramento to Silicon Valley. He knew how to make or break careers and had his ideas about who should be in charge. Davidson's rise threatened Dunnagan's carefully cultivated political network. As Davidson gained momentum, Dunnagan saw him as a threat who couldn't be controlled. It was the classic clash of the old guard versus the new blood. Dunnagan believed in power for power's sake, in playing the long game and bending politicians to his will. On the other hand, Davidson wanted to upend the system, shake things up and run on his terms. Their ideologies clashed as violently as their egos.

The animosity between them reached its boiling point during Davidson's gubernatorial campaign. Dunnagan had backed another candidate, one of his handpicked protégés, and spared no expense in trying to crush Davidson's bid. The campaign turned ugly. Dunnagan's team orchestrated smear attacks, leaked half-truths to the press, and painted Davidson as a reckless idealist who lacked the experience to govern California. For weeks, the airwaves were filled with attack ads designed to erode Davidson's image and tear down everything he had built. Davidson wasn't one to back down, though. He fought back with everything he had, using his platform to expose Dunnagan's manipulative tactics. It became a battle for the governorship and the soul of California politics. In the end, Davidson's grassroots support and undeniable charisma won out. He narrowly defeated Dunnagan's candidate and took the governor's seat, but the victory came at a cost. The campaign had been brutal and Davidson had made an enemy for life.

That was over a decade ago, but Davidson had never forgotten the sting of Dunnagan's betrayal nor the dirty tricks that had been played against him. Every time he looked in the mirror, he saw the scars from that battle, not physically, but emotionally. His pride had been bruised, his sense of trust shattered. Dunnagan had attacked his career and character, painting him as something he wasn't, and so, when Andy Stuart sat down with Ethan Davidson to discuss their plan, it was clear from the outset that one name would be a sore subject.

"Tom Dunnagan," Andy began, trying to ease into the conversation, "seems to think we can pull this off, but we'll need California's support. It's no secret that he—"

"Don't," Davidson interrupted sharply, his voice low and taut. The very mention of Dunnagan's name ignited something cold and fierce in his chest. He stared at his hands momentarily, gathering himself before lifting his gaze to meet Andy's eyes. "You don't know what you're asking."

The tension in the room was pronounced. Andy had expected resistance, but not like this. He could see the flash of anger in Davidson's eyes, the deep-rooted loathing that had been festering for years.

"Look, I get it," Andy said, trying to navigate the landmine he'd just stepped on. "There's bad blood between you two, but this is bigger than that. We're talking about shifting the timeline, about creating something that will change the future for millions of people. Whatever happened between you and Dunnagan... it doesn't have to be part of this."

Davidson leaned back in his chair, his jaw clenched tight, the muscles twitching as he struggled to contain the rage bubbling beneath the surface.

"That man," he said slowly, "tried to destroy everything I worked for. He didn't just want to win. He wanted to humiliate me. He dragged my name through the mud, spread lies, and turned people I thought I could trust against me."

Andy nodded, silently encouraging Davidson to continue. He needed to understand the depth of this rift if he had any hope of bridging it.

"Dunnagan doesn't care about people, progress, or politics. He cares about control. Power for its own sake. He'll back whatever benefits him and throw anyone under the bus the second they're no longer useful."

Davidson's voice was low, simmering with anger. "He sees people as pawns in his game and I'm not about to be one of them."

Andy sighed, feeling the weight of the situation.

"I understand where you're coming from," he said carefully. "and you're right, Dunnagan is a manipulator, but if we can use him to get what we need… if we can bring California on board, we could change everything, and we'd do it on our terms, not his."

Davidson's eyes flickered with something that could have been doubt or perhaps the tiniest glimmer of hope. He didn't trust Dunnagan and never would, but Andy's words had hit a nerve. For all his hatred of the man, Davidson knew the stakes were too high to let personal grudges stand in the way.

For a long moment, Davidson was silent, staring out the window at the sprawling cityscape below. He could still remember the taste of victory from that gubernatorial race, the sweet satisfaction of knowing he had beaten Dunnagan at his own game. Still, he also remembered the cost, the friends he'd lost, the sleepless nights spent wondering if it had all been worth it.

There was an unspoken understanding between two men who had clawed their way to the top. Though their paths had been different, the grind, the hustle and the sheer force of will required to shape their futures had been the same. In this they were kindred spirits.

Davidson shifted in his seat, his voice taking on a more serious tone.

Their exchange began with cautious formality, but as the minutes passed, the frost between Andy and Ethan Willow Davidson began to thaw. Though naturally guarded, each man was drawn to the other's charisma. They swapped stories about their families, offering glimpses into the softer sides of their otherwise formidable public personas. Davidson talked of his children and the challenges of raising them under the constant gaze of the media, while Andy, smiling, recounted stories of weekend camping trips and the occasional mishaps of balancing work with family life. The conversation felt genuine and laced with mutual respect. By the time they steered the discussion toward the business at hand, Andy was hopeful they'd built a solid rapport to withstand the political weight of what was to come.

But then, as if crossing an invisible line, the atmosphere subtly shifted. They reached for their coffee cups simultaneously, a fleeting almost choreographed gesture, but the warmth dissipated. Davidson's expression grew more complicated, more thoughtful. His hand lingered on the handle of his mug as if it anchored him, grounding him for what he was about to say.

"It's no secret I've had reservations about the Secretary of State," Davidson began, his voice cutting through the air like a chilly wind. The disdain was apparent, hanging between them like a spectre. "Dunnagan's approach to governance has always been transactional, at best. The man's a political opportunist, not a leader. He's spent years playing power games, and now we're expected to believe his initiative is some altruistic gesture to save the country?"

He shook his head, his lip curling slightly in derision. "Forgive me, but I've seen too much to trust a man like that."

Each word was a sharp barb aimed at Tom Dunnagan, and Andy could feel the tension rising in the room. He had known Davidson had reservations, as everyone in California politics did, but the depth of his disdain for Dunnagan was evident. Davidson didn't just distrust him; he loathed him wholly and profoundly, and, caught in their years-long rivalry, Andy felt the uneasy sensation of trying to steer a ship between two jagged cliffs.

Taking a deep breath, Andy decided to meet Davidson's cynicism head-on. His tone shifted from friendly to focused, his words growing measured and precise as he outlined the intricate details of the proposed timeline shift. He spoke not with the lofty rhetoric of a salesman but with the grounded conviction of someone who believed in the vision he was presenting.

"It's easy to dismiss this as another political manoeuvre but I assure you, it's so much more," Andy said, leaning slightly forward in his seat. "This initiative isn't just a band-aid to patch up a few problems; it's a bold move to fundamentally reshape our country's trajectory. We're not talking about a quick fix. We're talking about positioning America for long-term, sustainable growth, and California, your home, is at the heart of that transformation."

Davidson's eyes narrowed slightly, clearly still sceptical, but there was a flicker of interest. Andy took that as his cue to delve into one of the most significant aspects of the plan: the change in time zone alignment.

"Imagine this," Andy began, his voice rising slightly with the passion of his vision. "Instead of lagging on a -7-hour difference to GMT, California could operate just -4 hours behind. That may sound like a small shift, but the implications are enormous. California's economy could integrate seamlessly with both European and East Coast markets. Wall Street and Silicon Valley are working closer together, real-time collaborations that are only dreams. This isn't about changing our clocks. It's about unlocking an entirely new framework for how California engages with the world."

Davidson leaned back, his posture softening just a fraction as he considered the point. Andy pressed on, seizing the moment. He began painting a vivid picture of the country's economic challenges, describing how the traditional systems buckled under the weight of outdated policies. He laid out stark statistics, data that showed just how close the nation was to slipping into economic stagnation and how this initiative could be the solution.

"It's not all doom and gloom, though," Andy said, injecting a note of optimism into his tone. "By shifting the timeline, we're not just reacting to crises; we're creating new opportunities for growth and innovation. We're talking about new industries and new investments flowing into California. Jobs that can't be outsourced, infrastructure projects that will transform entire regions, and the people you know, your constituents, Mr. Davidson, they'll see the benefits firsthand."

Andy paused, watching as Davidson absorbed his words. He could see the cogs turning in the House Minority Leader's mind and sense the political calculations behind his sharp gaze. Davidson was no fool; Andy knew that facts alone wouldn't sway him. However, perhaps the vision of the future Andy was offering was something Davidson could see himself aligning with.

"Think about this," Andy added, locking eyes with Davidson, his voice now quieter but laced with conviction. "This isn't just about the economy; it's about the future of this country. Infrastructure improvements that will last for generations. Expanded access to healthcare, education reform, and jobs for the middle class and the working poor. Things that matter. Things that can change lives. Supporting this initiative is not just the right thing to do; it's the smart thing to do."

24: The Denial

As the golden rays of the setting sun bathed San Francisco in warm hues, Andy found himself seated across from Ethan Willow Davidson in the Lieutenant Governor's study. The room exuded old-world opulence with dark wood panelling, deep leather chairs, and bookshelves that seemed to stretch to the ceiling. A solitary lamp on Davidson's desk cast an amber glow, making the shadows flicker like the city skyline was alive just outside the grand bay windows. Davidson reclined in his chair with fingers steepled thoughtfully in front of him and appeared as immovable as the city he'd helped shape. His face was calm, his demeanour composed but Andy could feel the resistance beneath the surface.

"Ethan... Mr. Davidson," Andy began, his voice earnest but insistent, "you've got to grasp the enormity of this decision. Shifting the timeline isn't just another policy tweak. It is a notable change for California and the entire country. You can position your state as a beacon of innovation. Imagine it: California leading the charge into the future, a hub of global commerce that never sleeps."

Davidson's expression remained neutral, unreadable and as if he were immune to Andy's pitch. After a beat, he leaned forward slightly, his voice soft but firm. "I understand your enthusiasm, Andy, I do. But altering the timeline... Well, that's no trifling matter. There is a reason people are wary of such drastic changes. It's a high-stakes gamble and I don't think you've fully accounted for what we might lose in the process."

Andy felt his heart quicken, the frustration building beneath the surface. He hadn't come all this way to hit a brick wall. He leaned in, almost pleading. "But we stand on the brink of history here. The opportunity is right in front of you. Your support, Mr. Davidson, could tip the scales. It would make all the difference. California could be the leader, not just in technology but in economic reform, education, energy, you name it. This is about shaping the future. Your legacy."

Davidson's face shifted slightly, a flicker of emotion crossing his features, but he quickly masked it with a shake of his head.

"I truly appreciate your passion, Andy, but I'm not sold. My disdain for the Secretary of State isn't the only issue here. Dunnagan's politics have always rubbed me the wrong way, as have his arrogance and backdoor deals but even putting that aside, the risks with this timeline shift outweigh the benefits. It feels like a leap into the unknown and I can't endorse something I don't believe in."

The words hit Andy like a gut punch. For a moment, he was silent, shoulders sagging with the weight of disappointment. He had pinned his hopes on this man, the key to unlocking California's support, but Davidson had firmly shut the door, or so it seemed. Standing, Andy forced a tight smile, shaking Davidson's hand.

"Thank you for your time," he said, voice steady despite his turmoil. As he stepped out into the cool evening air, the city buzzing with life, his mind raced. Andy knew he couldn't give up, not yet. As the sunset's orange and purple hues gave way to the blue velvet of night, his natural resolve began to return. There had to be a way. He would go to any lengths to change Davidson's mind, to find the crack in the man's armour that could be pried open.

Walking through the bustling streets of San Francisco, Andy's thoughts spiralled more profoundly into the enigma that was Ethan Willow Davidson. What drove him? What were his genuine fears, the hidden motivations that guided his decisions? Every man had a key. Andy just had to find Davidson's. Was it pride? Was it fear of failure or, perhaps, some untold story from his past that still haunted him? Andy dived into research for the next few days with an almost manic energy. He reached out to mutual acquaintances, former colleagues, and people who had known Davidson in his early days as mayor and lieutenant governor. He scrutinised every public record, scouring through his political history, examining Davidson's public speeches, his votes in office, and his rare missteps. He needed to understand the man, not the politician, but the man behind the mask.

What he found was truly underwhelming. Davidson was a man of principle, no doubt, a *man of the people*, and this self-image sometimes led him down unconventional paths. He had always prided himself on doing what he believed was right, even when it was unpopular. However, Andy could not uncover anything more; there were no old scandals, no small whispers of potential corruption, and, at the very least, no ethical lapses buried over the years. No deals with powerful business magnates or ties to private interests that could, if brought to light, shatter the clean image Davidson had worked so hard to cultivate. This man was clean.

With newfound determination, Andy crafted a multifaceted strategy. He would appeal to Davidson's sense of legacy, highlighting how supporting the timeline shift could cement his place in history as a visionary leader. Simultaneously, he would subtly remind him of the potential fallout from past indiscretions if they were ever brought to light. It was a delicate balance of inspiration and pressure, designed to move Davidson from scepticism to support. Andy felt renewed purpose as he prepared to search for hidden facts or missing information. If he had to turn over every stone on the beach, figuratively speaking, he would do so. He knew that to win over Ethan Davidson, he had to find and present an irrefutable case that aligned with Davidson's values while addressing his most profound concerns.

As he sat at his desk, reviewing his research for the last time, Andy smiled to himself. Every man had a lock and a key, and Andy was about to find Davidson's and turn it. The question was no longer whether Ethan Willow Davidson would support the timeline shift; it was only a matter of when. Hopefully.

25: The Search

Andy's fingers tapped rhythmically on his desk, the soft clatter the only sound in the otherwise silent room. Papers, files, and clippings lay strewn before him, a chaotic mess that mirrored the growing frustration in his mind. He had scoured every past interview, read countless reports and parsed Davidson's speeches and policy documents, digging for anything that would give him the leverage he needed. But the Lieutenant Governor remained elusive, an enigma wrapped in political decorum and principles.

As the hours bled into days, Andy pushed harder, reaching out to mutual acquaintances and former colleagues of Davidson. He probed with careful, calculated questions, hoping someone would let slip some valuable insight into the man's personal or professional life. Yet all he found were testimonials to Davidson's unwavering commitment to his constituents, his reputation for integrity, and his deep-seated wariness of betraying the public's trust after a few bruising early failures in his career. There was no hint of scandal, no glaring skeletons lurking in the closet, and nothing Andy could use to sway him.

Thirty-six hours had passed and fatigue was finally winning the battle. His eyes burned from the relentless search, and his brain felt foggy, unable to process the mountains of information he had gathered. Andy slumped across his desk, his body heavy with exhaustion, his face pressed against the cold wood. Sleep claimed him, and soon, his dreams were a swirling haze of political machinations and shadowy figures. In his dream, Davidson ascended the political ranks at an impossible pace, like a bubble rising to the surface of a beer glass, the golden liquid swirling around him. Andy chased after him but no matter how fast he ran, Davidson always seemed out of reach. Figures whispered in the background, voices echoing secrets beyond Andy's grasp.

When he woke, it was nearly 3 p.m. The afternoon light filtered through the blinds, casting the room in a muted glow. Andy blinked groggily, disorientated by the sharp contrast between the dream and reality. His neck ached from the awkward position he had slept in, and he stumbled to the shower, hoping to wash away the cobwebs that still clung to his mind. Andy felt the weight of frustration lift slightly as the hot water cascaded down. But even after his shower, the nagging thought remained: Davidson was still a mystery, even after all his efforts. As he towelled off, Andy thought, hell, even I would vote for the man.

But now, it was time for plan B, whatever that was.

Andy devoured a prosciutto and tomato ciabatta in the kitchen, quickly washing it down with two double espressos. The caffeine jolted his system, and as his mind buzzed with renewed energy, he tried to refocus. He needed a new angle, a fresh perspective. Tidying the mess of papers and clippings that littered his desk, Andy's eyes drifted over the documents idly until something caught his attention: a photograph.

It was tucked beneath a pile of research, slightly crumpled but unmistakably intriguing. The photo showed a young woman, her dark hair tumbling in loose waves around her shoulders. She was holding a bouquet, her eyes focused not on the camera but on Davidson, who stood beside her, smiling. However, it was not Davidson's smile that caught Andy's attention. It was the way the woman was looking at him. Her gaze was full of something more profound and personal than mere admiration. Adoration was in her eyes, a soft tenderness that spoke of more than a casual acquaintance.

Andy's instincts flared. Who was she?

He stared at the photograph, flipping it in his hand, hoping for some clue. There was nothing on the back, no date, no name, no label to tell him who this woman was, but Andy could not shake the feeling that she was important. There was something in the way she looked at Davidson, something that hinted at a story yet untold. With a new sense of purpose, Andy dived back into research. Hours passed as he searched through old press coverage, social media accounts, and public records. Finally, after a lifetime of sifting through dead ends, he found her. The mysterious young woman in the photograph was named Isabelle Stauber.

Isabelle had once been a prominent figure in Davidson's life. She had been more than just a friend or political ally; there had been rumours of a romance and whispers of an engagement that had never materialised. Isabelle was the daughter of a wealthy family with ties to California's elite. She and Davidson had met years ago, during his early rise in politics, and they had been inseparable for a time. But something had happened, something that had driven a wedge between them. The details were murky, but there were hints of a falling out, a breakup that had scarred both sides. Isabelle had withdrawn from public life after the split, retreating into the shadows, while Davidson had thrown himself entirely into his political career, climbing higher and higher in the ranks. But their bond had never quite disappeared, at least not from public memory.

As Andy pieced together the story, he realised he might have found the key he had been looking for. Isabelle Stauber was not just a former flame. She was a lingering ghost from Davidson's past, someone who had once held power over him in a way that few others had. If Andy could find her and reach out to her, maybe she could help him unlock the final piece of Davidson's puzzle. Andy leaned back in his chair, the thrill of discovery rushing through him. This was it. Isabelle Stauber was the leverage he needed, the hidden vulnerability that could change everything. The game was not over yet, not by a long shot. With renewed determination, Andy prepared for the next step.

He was going to find Isabelle Stauber.

Andy sat back in his chair, watching the glow of his laptop screen cast long shadows across the room. His thoughts were scattered, jumping between the complex puzzle of Davidson's past and a name that kept surfacing in his mind: Miller. He hadn't considered him in years, but the situation demanded someone with Miller's unique skill set.

He'd first met Miller during his days at MIT, when Andy's world was driven more by theories and formulas than political intrigue and shadowy secrets. Miller had already built a name for himself as a private investigator who could find the truth in even the murkiest of circumstances.

Andy's mentor, Professor Sam McCallum, was a brilliant mind who had guided Andy through some of his most formative years in the world of engineering and technology. McCallum was the kind of professor who saw potential where others didn't, and he had an innate ability to push his students beyond what they thought possible. He'd become a father figure to Andy, who, during those years, was still finding his way in the world.

However, during Andy's junior year at MIT, McCallum's career and reputation were on the line. A false accusation of academic misconduct had nearly destroyed the professor's career, threatening to unravel everything he'd built. The allegations had come out of nowhere, including claims of falsified research data and accusations of collusion with corporations looking to profit from McCallum's groundbreaking work in energy sustainability. None of it was true but the media frenzy that followed was enough to shake even the most solid foundations.

That's when Miller stepped in.

He was a friend of a friend, someone Andy had only heard about in passing before that point. Miller wasn't a typical investigator; he wasn't the guy who blended into the background. He had an air about him that people noticed, a worn look that seemed at odds with his sharp mind, a cocky smirk that hinted he was always three steps ahead of everyone else. When Andy first met him, Miller had been leaning back in a chair in McCallum's office, legs crossed, wearing a leather jacket that looked like it had seen better days. His dark hair was perpetually tousled, and his eyes seemed to take in everything without looking too hard.

Andy remembered the exchange well:

"So you're the one who thinks Professor McCallum's innocent?" Miller had asked, raising an eyebrow at Andy.

"Because he *is* innocent," Andy had replied, his voice firm but tinged with a youthful naivety. "The charges are completely fabricated. There's no way he'd risk everything for—"

"For a quick payday?" Miller had finished for him, smirking. "Yeah, that's what they all say, but the truth is, innocent or not, someone's gunning for him and I'm the guy who's going to find out why."

Find out he did.

Miller had torn through the case with a ferocity that Andy could only admire from a distance. He'd uncovered discrepancies in the emails that had been used as "proof" of McCallum's supposed misconduct, traced financial transactions to a disgruntled former colleague who had sought to discredit the professor, and even found the original, unaltered research data that had been tampered with to make McCallum's work look suspicious.

In just weeks, Miller had dismantled the case against McCallum piece by piece. The professor was cleared of all accusations, and his reputation was restored. Though McCallum had been reluctant to talk about the ordeal afterwards, it had left an indelible mark on Andy. He saw firsthand how even the most meticulous person could be blindsided and how someone like Miller could change a man's life with the right skills.

After that, Andy had kept in touch with Miller, albeit sporadically. They were from two different worlds, but Andy knew that if he ever needed someone to navigate the grey areas, someone who could cut through the noise and find the truth, Miller was the man to call. Now, years later, it was time to call in that favour. Andy momentarily pulled out his phone, staring at the screen before scrolling through his contacts. When he finally found Miller's name, his thumb only briefly hesitated over the call button.

The phone rang twice before a gruff voice picked up on the other end.

"Andy? I didn't think I'd hear from you again. What's the deal?"

"Miller," Andy began, leaning back in his chair. "I need your help. This one's big. Political, and personal."

Miller chuckled softly. "Personal? You're not getting soft on me, are you?"

Andy smiled despite the gravity of the situation. "Just listen. There's a guy, Ethan Davidson, who is the lieutenant governor of California. Please dig into his past. There's a woman, Isabelle Stauber, who disappeared about eighteen years ago. I think she's connected to Davidson, but I need proof."

There was a pause on the other end, followed by something clinking, maybe a glass or keys. "Sounds like fun," Miller said, his voice light but focused. "You know I like a challenge. I'll get you what you need."

Andy exhaled, feeling a small weight lift from his chest. Miller always delivered. He'd seen it firsthand, back when their lives were more straightforward about clearing an innocent man's name. This time, though, it felt different. The stakes were higher. Politics, secrets, and personal vendettas were all tangled up in a web he wasn't sure he could unravel alone.

"Thanks, Miller," Andy said, glancing at the photo of Isabelle on his desk once more. "I owe you one."

Miller's laugh echoed through the line. "You owe me more than one. I'll be in touch."

As the call ended, Andy sat back and stared at the ceiling, letting the memories of that time with McCallum wash over him. Miller had saved one of the most important people in Andy's life back then, and now, as Andy stared down the barrel of his complicated mission, he knew he could count on him again. Andy's mind flickered back to Davidson, to Willow, to Isabelle. The puzzle pieces were slowly coming together, and with Miller's help, the truth wouldn't stay buried much longer. Whatever Davidson was hiding, Andy was determined to find it, and when he did, the fallout would be immense.

Andy leaned back in his chair, eyes lingering on the photograph of Isabelle Stauber. His mind buzzed with the significance of what he'd uncovered, but for a moment, it was not Davidson or Isabelle occupying his thoughts- it was Emily. He had not spoken to her in days, not since he had buried himself in research, chasing every lead like a man possessed. The sight of Isabelle's face stirred something within him, a sense of longing for Emily's calm, grounding presence. It was like the soft melody of a song he hadn't heard in a while but one that always brought him comfort.

The clock ticked past 6 p.m. in California, which meant it was just past 9 p.m. on the East Coast. He glanced at his phone, hesitating for a second before dialling. As the call connected, Andy felt a flutter of nervous anticipation. It was silly. After everything they had been through, she was still the person who could make his heart skip, even after a thousand phone calls.

"Andy?" Emily's voice was soft and warm, like slipping into a well-worn sweater on a chilly day. Instantly, the tension from the past few days melted away. Hearing her voice reminded him why he did what he did and why the battles he fought mattered. But more importantly, she reminded him of who he was beyond the relentless pursuit of power, politics, and strategy.

"Hey, Em," he said, the hint of a smile playing on his lips. "God, it is good to hear your voice."

There was a brief pause, then a knowing chuckle from her end of the line.

"It's been a while. You have been buried in work again, haven't you?"

"You know me too well," he admitted, running a hand through his hair. "It's been...a long few days. I am close, I think. But—" He hesitated, the weight of everything he hadn't said hanging between them.

"But it's not quite enough, is it?" Emily's voice was understanding, not accusatory. She always knew when he struggled, even when he did not say a word.

"Tell me what is going on, Andy. What's bothering you? "He exhaled, slumping back into his chair, the leather creaking under his weight.

"It's Davidson. I've been chasing down every lead, every scrap of information on him, but the guys clean. He's like Teflon; nothing sticks. I finally found something—a woman from his past, Isabelle Stauber. There's something there, Em. I do not know what yet, but I can feel it."

A soft hum from the other end, as if she was considering his words. "So, you've found your angle, but you're still unsure. What is holding you back?"

Andy stared at the photograph again, his fingers tracing the edges of the image. "It's not just about finding dirt on him. It's... I don't know. I guess seeing her face reminded me of you." His voice softened, vulnerable in a way he rarely allowed himself to be. "It reminded me of how much I've been missing you."

There was a moment of silence, and Andy worried for a second that he'd said too much, but then Emily spoke, her voice gentle.

"I miss you too—more than you know. But Andy, you can't lose yourself in this. Remember why you're doing this. You are not just trying to bring someone down, you're trying to build something better. Sometimes, the answer isn't in the dirt you can find on someone else. Sometimes, it's in being true to who you are."

Her words hit him like a wave of clarity, cutting through the haze of obsession and frustration clouding his mind. Emily had always been the one to ground him, to remind him that the pursuit of power was not worth it if he lost sight of what mattered most: integrity, purpose, and love.

"I know you're right," he murmured. "Sometimes it feels like I'll lose if I don't go all in, and losing means…"

"Losing means what?" She asked softly, coaxing him to say the words he had been holding back.

"Losing means failing and I cannot fail now. Not when we are so close." Emily's voice was steady, full of the quiet strength that had always been her hallmark. "Andy, you are not defined by a win or a loss. You have never been, and I think, deep down, you know that. Do not let this world change you into something you are not."

His throat tightened. "I don't deserve you; you know that?"

A laugh escaped her, light and musical. "You always say that, but I think you're wrong."

"Maybe," he smiled into the phone, feeling lighter for the first time in days. "But I'm glad I have you, either way."

"Always," she promised. "Now go get some sleep. You sound like you haven't had more than a few hours in the last week."

Andy sighed, feeling the weight of exhaustion settling over him again.

"Yeah, I probably should. I'll figure out the next steps tomorrow."

"You will, and Andy?"

"Yeah?"

"Don't lose sight of who you are."

He closed his eyes, letting her words sink in. "I won't, Em. I promise."

They said their goodbyes, and Andy felt renewed clarity as he hung up. Emily had always had a way of cutting through the noise, reminding him that sometimes the path forward was not through brute force or manipulation but through staying true to the person he wanted to be. He glanced at the photo of Isabelle one more time before setting it down. Tomorrow, he would start fresh. He allowed himself a moment of peace, knowing he wasn't alone no matter what happened.

Emily was with him, even from across the country, and that made all the difference.

Another day had dawned, the pale morning light streaming through the curtains as Andy sat at his cluttered desk, cradling a cup of coffee. His iPhone buzzed to life as an email came into his inbox, pulling him out of his thoughts. He had been researching for hours, his mind churning over every angle to figure out how Isabelle Stauber was connected to Ethan Davidson. He absently opened the ChatGPT app and began typing: **"What's the origin of the surname Stauber?"**

The response appeared almost instantly on the screen: *Stauber is derived from the German word "Staub," meaning "dust." Historically, It was an occupational surname for a miller who dealt with flour dust.* Andy nodded in understanding. It suggested Isabelle's roots were far from California, tied to a lineage from across the Atlantic. The insight felt like a small but significant clue in the broader mystery he was unravelling. Andy leaned back in his chair, letting his gaze return to the photograph of Isabelle that had led him down this path. There was something about how she looked at Davidson in that photo, a tenderness that reminded him, unmistakably, of Emily. His heart clenched, and he glanced at the time before he knew it. It was 9 PM. in California, now midnight on the East Coast, too late to call Em.

Andy's phone rang almost immediately, twice before he picked up. It was Em, her familiar voice cutting through the static.

"Hi Andy, I thought I better check on you. Did you finally get some sleep?" Emily's warm, sleepy, comforting voice caressed Andy.

He sighed, the sound of her voice instantly soothing the knots of tension in his chest. "Yes, I did. I am onto something. It is great to hear your voice. You know, escape the madness for a second." Emily's soft laughter rippled through the line.

"Well, I'm glad I called you. Tell me, what has got you so worked up?"

"It's Davidson," Andy began pacing his apartment as he spoke. "I've been digging into his past, trying to find anything to explain his reluctance to back our initiative and I found this woman, Isabelle Stauber. She was close to him once, really close, but then she just...vanished from his life about eighteen years ago, and no one seems to know why."

There was a pause on Emily's end as she absorbed this.

"Isabelle Stauber... You think she is the key to understanding Davidson's hesitation?"

"I don't know yet," Andy admitted, staring at the photo again as if it could speak. "but she had a daughter, born about eight months after disappearing. The daughter's name is Willow, and here's the thing: Davidson's middle name is Willow. I don't believe in coincidences, Em."

Her voice was measured, always the pragmatic one.

"It sounds like you are onto something, but you need proof before taking this further."

"I know." Andy's voice was tight with frustration. "and that's why I called Miller. If anyone can get me what I need, it's him."

Andy waited anxiously for the next two days, pacing his apartment, his mind flipping between hope and doubt. Miller was a seasoned investigator, adept at navigating the shadows. If there were anything to find, he'd find it.

Then, forty-eight hours later, Miller delivered.

Andy sat at his desk, fingers trembling slightly as he opened the thick envelope Miller had left for him. Inside were neatly typed reports, detailed notes on Isabelle, and Willow's birth certificate, but the last page stopped him cold. Miller had drawn the connection Andy had been hoping for, detailing the timing of Isabelle's disappearance and the birth of her daughter eight months later. He knew he was onto something much bigger than he had expected. Sitting back, Andy took a deep breath, sipped his coffee and tried to process the information. His eyes kept drifting back to the name Willow. That name was key to everything Ethan Willow Davidson. The pieces were beginning to fall into place, but there was still a missing link: proof. A nagging suspicion clawed at him, urging him to delve deeper, to go beyond circumstantial evidence.

That is when he knew what to do: a DNA test would provide the hard evidence he needed to tie Willow to Davidson, but it wouldn't be easy. Getting close to the lieutenant governor was nearly impossible given his high-profile status, and Willow herself was well-protected. Andy picked up the phone again, his mind already racing ahead to what came next. This was Miller's domain and the man had a gift for procuring things that weren't meant to be procured. Andy explained what he needed, and with his characteristic nonchalance, Miller assured him it could be done.

Miller was meticulous. He spent the next few days quietly observing Willow's routine, learning her habits and interactions. She was a high school senior, and despite her youth, she carried herself with a grace and poise that reminded Miller of her mother, Isabelle. She had the same quiet charm and air of mystery, but Miller wasn't looking for personality traits; he was looking for something tangible and usable. It took careful timing, but Miller finally saw his opening. He positioned himself near Willow's usual route home from school, blending in with the foot traffic. As she passed, he made his move, faking a stumble; he collided with her, apologising profusely as he untangled his fingers from her hair. Caught off guard, Willow offered a polite smile and continued, unaware that Miller had achieved his goal. A few long strands of her hair rested securely on the adhesive tape Miller had wrapped around his hand. He turned the corner and walked briskly away, his heart pounding, not from fear but from the thrill of a plan coming together.

With Willow's DNA in hand, Miller moved on to the next target: Davidson. Getting close to him would be more challenging, but Miller was a master at seizing opportunities. He found one when Davidson checked into a hotel for a political event. With a well-placed bribe to the hotel housekeeper, Miller accessed Davidson's room and quickly located his toothbrush on the bathroom sink. A quick swipe into a plastic bag, and he was gone. The evidence was now secured, and all that remained was the test. Miller delivered the samples to the lab, and Andy sat back, the tension in his bodybuilding as he waited for the results. If his suspicions were correct, Ethan Willow Davidson wasn't just a name. It was a legacy, a family secret that could change everything.

Andy's mind raced, thinking of the possibilities. If Davidson were Willow's father, it would explain so much. His reluctance to endorse the timeline shift and his wariness around change stemmed from protecting a secret he had buried for two decades. Now, all Andy had to do was wait, but he knew, deep down, the truth was already staring him in the face.

26: DNA

As Miller left his car with the DNA samples clutched tightly in his hands; this was the culmination of weeks of work, and anticipation churned in his stomach. He had been here before, the moment before all the puzzle pieces fit together. This time though, the stakes were different. This wasn't just another case; this was Andy's case. A man who had been a friend, a former colleague, and someone who trusted him when everything else seemed murky. He watched the lab technicians through the visitors' gallery window as they processed the DNA, knowing this was the critical juncture. His hands ran through his scruffy hair as he recalled the delicate extraction of those DNA samples; The toothbrush from Davidson's hotel room and Willow's loose hair strands. Every step had been a calculated risk, but now, the risks were paying off in this sterile, fluorescent-lit lab.

The lab technician, clad in a white coat and latex gloves, handled the DNA samples like precious cargo. The process was a finely tuned dance of science and technology. They weren't just looking for a match; they were searching for the intricacies, the unique genetic signatures that would tie Willow and Davidson together, scientifically and statistically. The core of the analysis centred around Short Tandem Repeat (STR) markers."

Miller wasn't a geneticist, but he knew enough to understand that these markers were crucial. The technicians meticulously compared Davidson's and Willow's profiles, focusing on STRs, the repeating DNA sequences that differ from person to person. The matches had to be precise, with a high likelihood ratio (LR) confirming the statistical probability that the two shared genetic material.

This would take a few days. Miller returned to his car and put on his favourite music station. He sat tapping his fingers against the steering wheel to the music and drove away, awaiting final confirmation.

He knew that if the match were strong enough if the STR markers and the LR fell into place, it would be more than enough evidence for Andy to take the next step. Three days later, he returned to the lab and parked outside; the outer lab door swung open. A young woman with a clipboard walked briskly toward him, her expression professional but with a glint of satisfaction. Miller's heartbeat quickened.

She leant down to his car window. He pressed a button, and the car window glass disappeared into the door's body. "The results are in," she said, handing him the report through the now fully open window.

"We've found a high number of matching markers. The likelihood ratio is exceptionally high and strongly indicates a direct biological relationship between sample 'A' and sample 'B.'"

Miller's chest tightened as he scanned the report. The STR markers aligned far above the threshold, and the LR was through the roof. This was it. This is concrete proof that Davidson was Willow's father. Without wasting a second, Miller pulled out his phone and dialled Andy. It rang twice before he heard Andy's familiar voice on the other end.

"Miller? What's the news?" Andy's voice was tight, brimming with anticipation.

Miller didn't make him wait. "It's a match, Andy. The DNA came back positive. Willow is Davidson's daughter. There's no doubt."

There was a pause and Andy's voice came through, a mix of disbelief and triumph. "You're sure?"

"Absolutely. The STR markers match perfectly, and the Likelihood Ratio is strong. It's as good as it gets."

Andy's laugh on the other end of the line was sheer relief. "You've done it, Miller. I don't know how you managed to pull it off, but you've done it."

Miller grinned, leaning back in his seat. "It's all in the details, Andy. Now, what's next?" Andy's voice shifted from triumph to focus. "Isabelle. I need to speak to her. She's still in San Diego, right?"

"Yeah," Miller replied, "La Jolla. She's been living there quietly."

"Then that's where I'm headed," Andy said. "I'll be on the first plane out."

Andy strode into his apartment purposefully, his polished shoes clicking against the sleek hardwood floors. The space was immaculate, a testament to his taste. The floor-to-ceiling windows framed the city skyline, modern art pieces were tastefully arranged on the walls, and minimalist furniture was in shades of charcoal and cream. But tonight, the usual comfort of his surroundings did nothing to slow him down. He moved swiftly, pulling a leather carry-on from his closet and filling it with the precision of someone who'd packed a thousand times before. In went his neatly folded clothes, each item carefully chosen for the mix of work and leisure he had planned in San Diego.

Pausing momentarily, Andy looked at the full-length mirror by the door. His dark chinos were crisply pressed, and his fitted T-shirt hinted at the muscle beneath, a body he maintained with as much dedication as his career. He threw on a tailored blazer, navy, sharp lapels, just the right mix of casual and polished. Satisfied, he grabbed his passport, slipped on a classic watch that caught the light with a sparkle and made his way to the airport.

As he stepped into the taxi, Andy felt a familiar thrill, the excitement of the unknown, the anticipation of the next big move. He leaned back, the city lights flashing past, a half-smile playing on his lips as he thought about what lay ahead.

By the time Andy's plane touched down in San Diego, the afternoon sunbathed the city in a warm glow, its golden light reflecting off the sleek glass of the terminal. As the wheels hit the tarmac, he felt a rush of adrenaline. This was the moment he had been working toward for what felt like an eternity. The taxi ride from the airport to La Jolla was a blur. Andy's mind raced as the car weaved through the sun-dappled streets, the palm trees swaying lazily in the coastal breeze. His thoughts flicked between Davidson and Isabelle and the secrets they had buried for nearly two decades. What would she say? How would she react when he confronted her with the truth?

As the taxi pulled into the driveway of Isabelle's house, Andy felt a strange calm wash over him. The house was modest but charming, perched on a hill with a view of the glittering Pacific Ocean beyond. The sound of waves crashing against the shore reached his ears, and for a moment, the scene's serenity seemed at odds with the storm brewing inside him. The driver parked, and Andy stepped out, his shoes crunching on the gravel path that led to the front door. His heart thudded in his chest as he approached the house, each step heavier than the last. This wasn't just about exposing Davidson anymore; it was about Isabelle, the life she had built, and the secrets she had kept. At the heart of it all was Willow, a young woman with no idea what legacy she carried.

As Andy reached Isabelle's door, he paused momentarily, the salty sea breeze whipping through his hair. His hand hovered over the knocker, anticipation bubbling beneath his calm exterior. What was her reaction going to be? Would she be shocked, defiant, or perhaps remorseful? The door swung open before he could finish the thought, and to his surprise, a young woman stood in the doorway, eyes wide with curiosity.

Andy blinked, instantly connecting the dots. This must be Willow. Her resemblance to Davidson was unmistakable: the same piercing blue eyes and high cheekbones. His heart raced. This was the girl at the centre of everything.

"Hi there," Andy greeted, a friendly smile masking his surprise. "Is Isabelle home?"

Willow blinked, a flicker of uncertainty crossing her face before she answered, "Yeah, one second."

Moments later, Isabelle appeared beside her daughter, a striking woman in her mid-forties. Her deep brown hair cascaded to her shoulders, framing a face with intense yet delicate features, her skin kissed by the California sun. Her brown eyes, which once radiated warmth, now held a guarded quality as they swept over Andy.

"Hi, Isabelle. I'm Andy Stuart," he said, his voice firm but friendly.

Her eyes narrowed slightly, suspicion flickering across her face. "How can I help you?" Her tone was polite but held an edge as if she were bracing herself for something unpleasant.

Andy took a breath. "I'd like to talk to you about Ethan Davidson."

Her expression didn't change, but something shifted behind her eyes, a flicker of recognition that was quickly suppressed. "Not here," she said, her voice calm and measured. "Let's go for a walk."

Andy nodded, grateful she hadn't slammed the door in his face. As they stepped outside, Isabelle led the way toward Windansea Beach, a quiet stretch of sand just a few minutes walk from her house. The air was crisp with the scent of salt and seaweed, the Pacific stretching out endlessly before them. The rhythmic crash of the waves provided a soothing backdrop, but Andy could sense the tension beneath the surface of their silence.

As they reached a secluded spot along the shore, Isabelle stopped and turned to face him. Her posture was still composed, but her eyes betrayed a flicker of unease.

"I knew this day would come," she said quietly, her words hanging heavy in the cool ocean breeze.

Andy studied her face carefully, noting the subtle tremble in her voice. "I've been looking into Davidson's past," he began cautiously. I've found some DNA evidence that connects him to Willow."

At the mention of DNA Isabelle's face paled slightly, her hands gripping the strap of her bag tighter. Her eyes widened and it was as if she had seen a ghost for a moment. She turned away, staring at the sea as though trying to gather herself.

After a few moments of silence, Isabelle spoke, her voice barely above a whisper. "Davidson doesn't know he has a daughter," She admitted. "I've been protecting Willow from that part of my life."

Her words were raw, stripped of the bravado she had worn moments ago. The facade of confidence crumbled, revealing the fear and vulnerability underneath. As she spoke, Andy could see the weight of the secret she had carried for so long.

"He doesn't know?" Andy asked, his voice soft, though a note of doubt crept in.

Isabelle shook her head, her expression one of regret.

"No. When I found out I was pregnant, I left. I didn't want him involved. He was on a different path—a path I didn't want for Willow."

The words came faster now, the dam breaking. She recounted the whirlwind romance with Davidson, the passion that had burned bright but fast, leaving her with nothing but a broken heart and a child to raise alone. She had chosen to walk away to give Willow a life free from the shadows of political ambition and media scrutiny.

Andy listened, absorbing every word. He could sense that Isabelle wasn't telling him everything, but what she was revealing was enough for now. He understood the complexity of her decision. She wasn't just protecting herself but her daughter from the chaos that came with Davidson's world.

"Have you spoken to him at all since you left?" Andy asked gently.

Isabelle gave a small, bitter laugh, shaking her head. "No. I've only seen him on billboards and TV. That's how I know he's still out there, living his perfect life."

Andy could hear the pain in her voice. The man she had once loved, who had unknowingly fathered her child, was now a high-profile politician, his face plastered everywhere as if mocking her decision to disappear.

The sun began to dip below the horizon, casting a golden light over the tranquil waters. Andy turned his attention back to the matter at hand. "Isabelle, you need to understand that this changes things. Davidson has a right to know about Willow. But more importantly, Willow has a right to know about her father."

Isabelle's jaw tightened, her eyes flickering with fear and defiance. "What would that accomplish, Andy? Tearing apart her world? She's happy she's got a stable life here. I don't want to drag her into that mess."

Andy softened his tone. "I get it, Isabelle, but she's eighteen now. She deserves the truth."

The silence between them grew heavier as the ocean waves lapped at the shore. Isabelle's mind seemed to be racing and the internal battle of protecting her daughter versus telling her the truth was tearing at her.

Finally, Isabelle sighed, her shoulders slumping as if the weight of the last eighteen years had finally become too much to bear.

"I don't know how to do this, Andy. I don't know how to tell her."

Andy stepped forward, his voice full of empathy. "We'll figure it out. Together. But first I need to speak with Davidson. He must know the truth."

Isabelle glanced up at him, her brown eyes reflecting gratitude and sorrow. "Be careful with him. Ethan isn't the same man I knew all those years ago."

As the sun finally disappeared beneath the horizon, leaving a soft orange glow, Andy nodded, understanding the gravity of what lay ahead. He would have to tread carefully, balancing the need for truth with the potential fallout for Willow. But he had come too far to turn back now.

"I'll be careful," Andy promised. "But this is the right thing to do."

With that they turned and began the walk back toward the house, the sound of the ocean a constant reminder of the turbulent waters they were about to navigate together.

27: A Good Walk Spoilt

Despite Andy's best efforts to secure a face-to-face meeting with Davidson, the layers of bureaucracy and polished evasion wore on his patience. One rejection bled into the next, each nibbling away at his time and fraying his resolve. Days turned into a week, and frustration clawed at him, threatening to boil over. He had hit a wall but backing down was not an option. He needed to confront Davidson, face-to-face, to get the answers no one else could provide. Davidson's open online diary provided the breakthrough Andy had been waiting for. It listed the lieutenant governor's engagements, and one entry stood out: a 10:24 AM tee time at The Olympic Club. The prestigious golf course east of I-35 was split into three renowned courses: Lake, Cliffs, and Ocean. Andy knew Davidson's ego would steer him to the finest: the Lake Course. Known for its rolling hills, strategic bunkers, and an illustrious history dating back to the U.S. Open tournaments, the Lake Course demanded skill and status.

Andy studied the course map like a battlefield, mentally pacing each hole. He zeroed in on the eighth hole, with its sharp dogleg and breathtaking views of the Pacific Ocean. It was the perfect place to intercept Davidson without arousing too much suspicion. Using his own experience as a golfer and factoring in what he knew about Davidson's reputation for efficiency, he calculated the time it would take Davidson to reach the eighth hole. Twelve minutes per hole, multiplied by seven holes, plus a buffer of six minutes for the eighth, Andy estimated Davidson would cross his path just before noon. His Rolex Submariner read 11:45. He still had time. The air was crisp, the sky overhead an unblemished expanse of blue, and the Pacific shimmered in the distance. Taking a deep breath, Andy stepped onto the manicured grass, positioning himself strategically near the bend in the fairway. The soft rustle of the wind through the cypress trees was the only sound that accompanied his thoughts. Every nerve hummed with anticipation, his mind a taut wire as he watched the golfers approaching in the distance.

Then he saw him: Ethan Davidson, wearing a navy blue J. Lindeberg polo. His tanned face hardened into a mask of focus as he approached. His golfing companions were all suited to his world: wealthy, powerful, and oblivious to the storm about to hit. Andy squared his shoulders and stepped onto the path. With deliberate calm, he approached the lieutenant governor, closing the gap between them. His heart pounded, but his voice was steady when he spoke. "You're a hard man to get a meeting with."

Davidson barely glanced up, clearly irritated at the interruption. His response came swiftly, a curt dismissal. "Fuck off."

Andy wasn't fazed. He stepped closer, his voice firm. "We need to talk."

Davidson's expression flickered from annoyance to something sharper, his gaze narrowing as he took in the determined set of Andy's jaw. It was a silent exchange, but Andy could feel the weight of his resolve meeting Davidson's well-practised indifference. The politician was accustomed to brushing off nuisances, but this wasn't something he could shrug off. Andy's persistence and his unrelenting presence left no room for retreat. The tension crackled between them like an electrical current. Finally, with a frustrated grunt, Davidson tossed his seven iron into his golf bag with a resounding clang. The sound rang out like a declaration of defeat, echoing through the stillness of the course.

"I have to take an urgent meeting," Davidson announced to his bewildered companions. His tone was sharp, leaving no room for argument. The powerful, once so assured, politician suddenly found himself on unstable ground.

As his companions exchanged confused glances, Davidson began walking away from the fairway, his pace quick but measured. His mind raced, searching for an explanation for this man's persistence. Who was he, and what the hell did he want? Andy followed in silence, his thoughts ticking away. The barriers were finally down. Now it was just him and Davidson, alone in the middle of an exclusive golf course, a battleground of words and truths awaiting them.

With each step, the weight of what was to come bore down on Andy. He was on the brink of uncovering the answers he had been chasing for weeks, but he knew this confrontation wouldn't be easy. Davidson wasn't a man accustomed to being cornered, but Andy wasn't backing down now or when the truth was within his grasp.

The tension was perceptible as Andy and Davidson settled at a secluded table in the club's private lounge. The air felt thick and heavy with unspoken words, and clinking glasses in the background only heightened the sense of isolation. Andy didn't want to drag Isabelle or her daughter Willow into this mess, but he couldn't deny the leverage they provided. He needed to shatter the walls Davidson had built around himself: walls of indifference, ego, and avoidance and Andy knew the only way to do that was with a bombshell.

No pleasantries, no small talk. Andy dived straight in, his voice steady but laced with the urgency of what he was about to reveal. "Do you remember Isabelle?"

Davidson, who had been distractedly swirling his drink, suddenly froze. His eyes locked onto Andy's with a flicker of recognition. His stoic mask cracked briefly, and a warmth spread across his features as long-buried memories surfaced.

"Isabelle?" Davidson echoed softly, almost to himself, a nostalgic smile tugging at the corners of his mouth. "She was a wonderful woman... a key part of my team. She left so suddenly, without saying goodbye. I never understood why." His voice trailed off, the words thick with the weight of something unresolved, something he had tucked away long ago.

Andy saw his opening and pressed on. "Why didn't you try to find her?" His tone was calm, but there was a steeliness behind it.

Davidson's expression hardened and he leaned back, the moment of vulnerability vanishing as quickly as it had appeared. "My campaign was kicking off," he replied defensively. "I was barely keeping my head above water, consumed by everything. I didn't have time to track down someone who just disappeared."

Andy listened closely but he wasn't buying it, there was more to the story, he could feel it. He leaned forward, eyes narrowing as he prepared to drop the weighty question. "Did something happen between you two?"

Davidson's eyes darkened. He was no longer a composed politician but a man cornered by his past. His brow furrowed in confusion, and suddenly, he asked the questions. "Wait, has something happened to Isabelle? Is she alright? And how do you know her?"

Andy watched as the questions tumbled out, the sudden torrent revealing how unsettled Davidson was. The man had spent years burying this part of his life, and now it was brought to the surface instantly. Davidson's gaze turned cold as the weight of Andy's words hit him, a flicker of fear behind the politician's steely facade. The unspoken threat of his past returning to haunt him, especially his family, was unmistakable. His instinct to protect what was his, the carefully cultivated image, the power, the family, was clear.

"I don't want to harm you or your family," Andy said, his voice softening hoping to calm the storm he had unleashed. "But you need to understand the gravity of this. Isabelle's story… it didn't end when she left your life."

Davidson's silence stretched out; his features unreadable as he processed everything. Andy could see the struggle in his eyes: anger, fear, confusion, and a fierce need to protect the people he loved from the sudden shadows of the past. For a moment Davidson looked lost, as if standing on the edge of a cliff, unsure whether to retreat or jump.

Andy took a deep breath, knowing he had to push forward. The stakes were too high to pull back now. His voice was low and measured as he prepared to deliver the bombshell that would change everything. "Isabelle has a daughter," Andy said, locking eyes with Davidson. "A daughter you didn't know you had."

The words hung in the air between them, heavy and inescapable. Davidson's face twisted from confusion to shock. His hand tightened around his glass as though it were the only thing tethering him to reality.

"W-what?" His voice faltered, barely above a whisper, disbelief etched across his face. He looked like a man struck by lightning, grappling with the sudden knowledge that his life was not what he thought it was.

Andy held his gaze unwavering. "I've seen the DNA results," he said firmly. "There's no doubt. She's your daughter."

Davidson's world collapsed in that instant. His hands trembled slightly as he set down his drink. For a long moment he said nothing, just staring at the table before him as if searching for answers in the wood grain. His mind raced with thoughts of the daughter he never knew, the life he never imagined, and the choices that had brought him here. The past flooded back in brutal clarity, his decision to let Isabelle go to focus on his career, the family he built without knowing he had left part of himself behind.

Andy could see the storm of emotions swirling in Davidson's eyes including regret, loss, and an overwhelming sense of responsibility. It wasn't just about politics anymore. This was about a child, about a truth that had been hidden for too long.

Davidson finally spoke, his voice raw and broken. "Are you sure?" The words were barely audible, but they were laced with pain.

Andy nodded, the weight of the truth bearing down on both. "I'm sure, and now it's time to make things right."

Davidson swallowed hard, his gaze unfocused, lost in what he had just learned. His mind raced through the implications. A daughter. He had been married for years with two sons. How could he have been so blind to this part of his life? How could he have let Isabelle slip away without a word? His fists clenched, the regrets crashing over him like waves.

"I need to see her," Davidson said, his voice quiet but persistent. "I need to make this right."

Andy nodded, but his mission was far from over. "I need your support in Congress," he reminded Davidson. "The timeline shift is critical. I need your vote."

Davidson hesitated, torn between his newfound fatherhood and the political power he wielded. Andy's words settled heavily on him but after a long pause he sighed, defeated. "Okay," he whispered, barely audible, but it was all Andy needed.

A wave of relief washed over Andy as Davidson finally agreed. He extended his hand and Davidson shook it, a fragile peace settling between them. Andy knew this wasn't just a victory for the timeline; it was a victory for Isabelle, for the daughter who had been hidden in the shadows.

Hours later, as Andy's Uber snaked through the bustling streets of San Francisco, the relief started to sink in. The city's patchwork of neighbourhoods and the golden sunlight filtering through the skyscrapers offered a brief reprieve from the high-stakes world of politics. From Chinatown's vibrant lanterns to the artistic spirit of the Mission District, San Francisco hummed with life, and as the Golden Gate Bridge gleamed in the distance, Andy allowed himself a small smile. He had won.

At the airport the familiar chaos of travellers, luggage, and distant loudspeaker announcements washed over him. Andy couldn't shake the feeling that everything was about to change as he made his way to his flight. Not just for him, not just for Davidson, but for the entire country.

28: The Press

With California and six other states now in agreement, the stage was set for the President to advance the bill in the House. The date for the crucial vote had been decided, and the political landscape buzzed with anticipation. This was no small manoeuvre, and the implications were enormous. No one knew that better than Emerson Reyes. A seasoned journalist at The New York Times, Emerson was not the stereotypical hard-nosed reporter who ate and slept headlines. She was more of a hardworking version of Bridget Jones, minus the bumbling charm, but with all the disarming wit and a knack for getting to the heart of a story. Her "work hard, play hard" mantra often left little room for sleep, but she thrived on the frenetic energy of chasing down the truth.

That morning, over a steaming cup of coffee in a cosy corner of her favourite Washington café, Emerson was catching up with her trusted White House contact. The meeting had begun with the usual pleasantries, small talk about the latest congressional debacles, and nods toward mutual acquaintances. Emerson had almost zoned out when her calm, nearly casual contact dropped the bombshell that jolted her back to full attention: the president was pushing a bill to shift the timeline from London to New York. The coffee in her hand suddenly felt heavier as she tried to process the implications. Her mind raced with questions, every reporter's instinct on high alert. How? What for? and most crucially, why was this the first time she had heard about it?

But outwardly, Emerson was the picture of calm. She nodded as her contact gave her a brief overview of the strategy, throwing in vague references to international alliances and economic benefits. The more her contact talked, the more it became apparent: this was no ordinary bill. It was a seismic shift in global political dynamics.

When she returned to the office, Emerson's mind was already ablaze with ideas. She wasted no time drafting a pitch for her editor, Ezra Cohen. Before sending it over, she dove deep into research, cross-referencing everything her source had told her with whispers in the political corridors.

This was bigger than it appeared at first glance. The proposed bill wasn't just a political move but the start of a global chess game, and the pièce de resistance was California's unexpected change of heart. The state's governor, Ethan Davidson, had been an unshakable force of opposition. So, what had made him shift gears? What strings had been pulled?

The more Emerson dug, the murkier the water became. Lobbyists, political favours, and backdoor deals were buried beneath layers of public platitudes. But Emerson wasn't satisfied with easy answers. She sensed more, something profoundly personal driving Davidson's sudden shift. This was the type of story she lived for, which could crack open the quiet hypocrisy of power and reveal the human stories underneath.

Determined to follow the breadcrumbs, Emerson knew she needed to get to California and speak directly with Davidson's team. However, one major obstacle was standing in her way: Ezra Cohen. The editor-in-chief of The New York Times was a no-nonsense type. Cohen had held his position for eight years, a veritable lifetime in the cutthroat world of journalism. His eye for detail and unwavering commitment to journalistic integrity earned him the entire newsroom's respect. Under his leadership, there was no tolerance for sensationalism or half-baked stories. Only the best, most well-researched articles would become exposed.

And right now, Emerson knew she was on to something big. But she also knew convincing Cohen to green light the trip to California was no small feat. Travel expenses weren't just handed out without good reason. She needed more than a gut feeling and whispers of lobbyist meddling to get Cohen on board.

As Emerson prepared for her meeting with Cohen, her mind swirled with how she would frame the story. The key would be to emphasise the human element. This wasn't just a political manoeuvre. It was personal. Why had Davidson shifted his stance? What was the catalyst? How could a bill that seemed to change the timeline from one place to another be so intertwined with personal stakes and hidden agendas?

Walking into Cohen's office, Emerson felt her pulse quicken. The editor's office was minimalist, reflecting his sharp, no-frills demeanour. Behind his desk, the wall was lined with shelves of meticulously organised files, a testament to his career spent archiving the facts behind every significant story of the last decade. Cohen sat at his desk, fingers steepled, his piercing gaze already assessing her before she spoke.

"I've been hearing some chatter about this timeline bill," Cohen said, cutting straight to the chase.

"More than chatter," Emerson replied, handing him the pitch she had meticulously crafted. "The presidents behind it, and there's a significant shift happening in the state alliances. Davidson in California just flipped."

Cohen raised an eyebrow, his eyes flicking over the document. "Davidson?" he said, his voice tinged with curiosity. "He's been a rock on this issue. What changed?"

"That's what I want to find out," Emerson said. "I've got leads suggesting there's more than just politics. This story could expose how deep personal agendas run beneath the surface."

Cohen leaned back in his chair, mulling over her words. Emerson held her breath, waiting for his verdict. He knew that a story had to be more than good with Cohen. It had to be rock solid, backed by facts, and driven by more than just speculation.

After what felt like an eternity, Cohen nodded. "Okay, Reyes. You've got my attention. But I want real answers, not just more conspiracy theories. Go to California. Get Davidson's team on record. I want facts and names."

Relief flooded through Emerson as Cohen handed the proposal back to her. She had the green light. It was time to uncover the truth behind the political manoeuvring and see how deep this rabbit hole went.

The relentless quest for answers was beginning.

Emerson was on a mission the moment she arrived in San Francisco. With its rolling fog and towering skyline, the city felt like a maze of power and secrets, and she was determined to find her way through it. She wasted no time setting up interviews with anyone who had worked with Governor Davidson. Armed with her notepad, recorder, and relentless curiosity, she tracked down several of Davidson's closest colleagues, hoping to glean some insight that might explain the Governor's drastic change in stance.

As she sat in the small conference room of a local government building, the scent of old coffee lingering in the air, Emerson interviewed Davidson's colleague. The woman across from her seemed exhausted, her brow creased with worry.

"He's a completely different person," The woman said, shaking her head in disbelief. "One minute, he's staunchly opposed to anything the president wants, and the next, he's championing him."

Emerson leaned forward slightly, her reporter's instinct flaring. "He didn't give any indication why?" She pressed, her voice low, coaxing.

The woman looked at her, perplexed. "Not that I'm aware of," she said. "He's been keeping his cards close to his chest. We don't even know what's going on in that head of his anymore."

Frustration gnawed at Emerson. Dead ends everywhere. Davidson's sudden support for the timeline shift turned into a maddening mystery. As she continued her interviews, the same thread of confusion wove through each conversation. Everyone described Davidson as a man of unwavering principles, a political figure who had always been dedicated to his constituents, even under the heaviest of pressures. His sudden change was out of character. Some even speculated that he had been coerced.

It wasn't enough. Emerson needed more than speculation to piece the puzzle together, and with the print deadline looming, she could feel the weight of the ticking clock pressing down on her. She flipped through her notes, reviewing everything she had learned, but something was still missing: a key that would unlock the entire story.

Then, there it was. A meeting stood out in Davidson's online schedule: Andy Stuart, the elusive tech mogul, had met with Davidson the night before the governor's sudden change in position. The timing was too perfect to be a coincidence.

"Why would a politician like Davidson meet with a billionaire tech giant right before shifting his stance on a bill that affected international relations?" Emerson thought, her skin prickling with the realisation.

The next day, back in New York, Emerson stood in the opulent lobby of Stuart's corporate headquarters. The place screamed wealth and power, from the polished marble floors to the vast glass walls that overlooked the city skyline. Her heart pounded as she sank into a plush armchair in the reception area. Despite the anxiety swirling inside her, Emerson maintained her composure, preparing herself for the encounter.

After what felt like an eternity, a poised woman with sharp features and a professional smile approached. "Ms. Reyes?" She asked. "I'm Sarah Palmer. Mr. Stuart's assistant."

Emerson stood, shaking her hand. "Good morning, Ms. Palmer," she said, her voice steady despite the nerves. "I'm here to see Mr. Stuart. It's urgent."

Sarah's expression didn't falter, but Emerson caught a flicker of curiosity in her eyes. "I'm afraid Mr. Stuart is currently out of the country," she said smoothly. "But if you'd like to schedule an appointment."

"This can't wait," Emerson interrupted, her tone firm but polite. "It's about the timeline shift and Governor Davidson's involvement. I need to speak with Mr. Stuart as soon as possible."

Sarah's eyebrows shot up, a flicker of concern crossing her face. Emerson could tell she had struck a nerve. But just as quickly, Sarah's professional mask slipped back into place.

"I understand, Ms. Reyes," She replied, calm but guarded. "But as I said, Mr. Stuart is unavailable. Perhaps I can assist you in some way?"

Emerson weighed her options, knowing that getting to Stuart directly was unlikely. "I appreciate the offer, Ms. Palmer," She said carefully, "but I'm afraid I need to discuss this with Mr. Stuart himself. Is there any way you could reach him for me?"

Sarah hesitated, clearly assessing Emerson's determination. Finally, she nodded and gestured for Emerson to follow her. "Very well," she said. "Come with me."

The assistant led Emerson to a sleek, minimalist office down the hall. The room was bathed in natural light from the floor-to-ceiling windows, but despite its beauty, it had an air of sterility as though no bona fide business had ever been conducted here. Sarah gestured for Emerson to sit.

"Perhaps I can answer some of your questions about Mr. Stuart's recent movements,"

Sarah offered, her voice polite but controlled. Emerson noticed the tension in her body language. Sarah was a professional and trained in discretion, but there was something she wasn't saying.

"I'm investigating Governor Davidson's change of position on the timeline shift," Emerson said, her eyes locking onto Sarah's. "It seems the meeting between Mr Stuart and Davidson happened just before that change. Can you shed any light on what was discussed?"

Sarah's eyes flickered with nervousness before she regained control of her expression. "I'm afraid I'm not at liberty to discuss Mr. Stuart's personal affairs," she said with a tight-lipped smile. "But I assure you, if there's anything relevant, I will pass it along to him when he returns."

Emerson felt the frustration building again. Every word Sarah said was measured, deliberate. Emerson could sense there was more to the story, but Sarah was a master at deflecting. Still, she pressed on, peppering Sarah with more questions, hoping to uncover a crack in her resolve. But after several more minutes of fruitless conversation, it became clear that Sarah wouldn't give her what she needed. Emerson sighed inwardly. She had hoped for more but couldn't force answers from someone as guarded as Sarah.

As she stood to leave, Emerson's mind raced with possible next steps. She would need to dig deeper, maybe reach out to someone in Stuart's inner circle, or even find a former associate willing to speak off the record. The pieces were there, and she needed to figure out how they all fit together. In the reception area,

Emerson paused momentarily, taking in Stuart's empire's imposing grandeur. The opulent surroundings felt almost mocking, as though the wealth and power here could shield its owner from scrutiny.

Emerson slumped back into the plush armchair, the story's weight pressing down on her. She pulled out her notepad and began flipping through her scribbled shorthand, searching for something she might have missed. Stuart and Davidson Their meeting was vital. But she stood on shaky ground without concrete proof and a reliable source. She knew the risks if she published without solid evidence. She could end up ruining her career and tarnishing the paper's reputation. She stared blankly at the intricate marble floor, her mind swirling with unanswered questions.

What had happened in that meeting between Stuart and Davidson? What common interests could unite a politician and a tech mogul?

The truth was out there, somewhere, buried beneath layers of power and secrecy. Determined not to leave without a new plan, Emerson pulled out her phone and began making calls. She wouldn't rest until she had the story.

29: Front Page News!

Back in her sleek, modern office, Sarah felt a tremor of unease as she picked up the phone and dialled Andy Stuart. The hum of the city outside was muffled by thick glass but inside, tension crackled in the air. As the line connected, Sarah didn't waste time with pleasantries. Her voice dropped to a low, urgent tone. "Andy, the press wants to talk to you about Davidson," she said, each word measured by the seriousness of the situation.

A heavy and tense pause lingered before Andy's voice finally cut through, sharp with frustration. "Shit," he muttered, the word hanging between them like a storm cloud. He knew the stakes were too high to take lightly, especially since Willow had unknowingly been caught on the web. "Who's the journalist?" He asked, already strategising his next move.

"Emerson Reyes," Sarah replied swiftly, her voice carrying an undercurrent of anxiety she rarely let slip.

Andy exhaled sharply, his mind racing. He needed control to shape the narrative before it spiralled beyond his grasp.

"Can you get me her address?" he asked, his voice now laced with determination.

Sarah didn't hesitate. "Will do," she responded. She was quick on her feet, always a step ahead in moments like these.

After ending the call Andy sat back in his chair, his hand running through his hair in a gesture that betrayed his calm exterior. He had to leave his current business dealings behind and head back into the city where no time was wasted. If mishandled, too much was at stake, and the fallout could be devastating. True to form, Sarah located Emerson's address in record time. Efficient, discreet, and always one step ahead, she didn't allow herself the luxury of second thoughts, though a seed of unease had planted itself deep in her gut. Journalists were persistent, especially ones like Emerson Reyes, whose reputation for chasing hard truths was well-known.

Meanwhile, Andy packed his things quickly, his mind spinning strategies to protect Willow and Davidson. He buried the truth just deep enough to avoid a scandal but not so far as to raise suspicions. He made his way to the airport, the weight of the impending confrontation heavy on his shoulders. As his plane took off, he stared at the sprawling city below, each glittering light growing smaller and smaller. How would he protect everyone he cared about without losing control of the narrative?

At the same time, across the country, Emerson sat in her modest home office, bathed in the blue glow of her laptop screen. The cursor blinked rhythmically, mocking her as she stared at the half-finished draft of her article. The day had been a haze of phone calls and interviews, most leading to frustrating dead ends. It was now nearly 10 PM and the weariness was beginning to settle deep in her bones. Just as she was about to call it a night, a sudden, unexpected knock at the door jolted her back into the present. Her heart raced. Who could be at her door at this hour? Her mind buzzed with possibilities, each one more unsettling than the last. She hesitated, her journalist's instincts clashing with a deep sense of caution.

Peeking through the peephole, her breath caught in her throat. She stumbled back in shock, her mind struggling to process what she had just seen. Standing on her doorstep, illuminated by the dim porch light, was Andy Stuart himself.

"Mr. Stuart?" Emerson stammered, opening the door, her surprise evident in her voice. She wasn't used to being caught off guard.

Andy's face was weary, but his gaze was steady and determined. There was a quiet intensity about him, a man used to steer the course of events.

"Emerson Reyes," he said, his voice steady but firm. "May I come in? We need to talk."

Still reeling from the unexpected visit, Emerson stepped aside, leading Andy into her modest living room. The air between them was thick with tension as Andy briefly glanced around before sitting on the edge of her worn-out sofa. Emerson took the armchair opposite him, her mind racing with questions but forced herself to stay composed.

"What are you doing here, Mr. Stuart?" she asked, trying to keep her voice level despite the growing knot of curiosity and anxiety tightening in her chest.

Andy leaned forward, his elbows resting on his knees, his gaze locking onto hers. "I'm here to ask you to reconsider what you're planning to publish," he said, his tone measured. "Some innocent people could get hurt if this story comes out wrong."

Emerson narrowed her eyes, suspicion creeping into her voice. "I'm a journalist, Mr. Stuart. My job is to uncover the truth and report it. Why is this story more important than the public's right to know?"

Andy didn't flinch, though the weight of his responsibility hung heavy on his words. "I'm not asking you to bury the truth," he said, his voice softening but still resolute. "I'm asking you to consider the collateral damage. There are lives at stake here, people who had nothing to do with the politics but could still be caught in the fallout."

For the first time that evening, Emerson hesitated. She had seen what a media frenzy could do to innocent people, how the glare of the spotlight could ruin lives and destroy families. She couldn't help but feel sympathy for Andy's plea, but she was also committed to her work, to exposing the truth no matter how uncomfortable it might be.

"What exactly are you protecting them from?" Emerson asked, her voice softer now but still probing.

Andy sighed, his shoulders sagging slightly under the weight of the truth. "Davidson's change of heart on the timeline shift bill... it's not about politics. There are personal matters involved, things that would destroy more than one family if the details became public."

Emerson leaned back, considering his words. She could feel the ethical dilemma pulling her in two directions. The truth needed to come out, but at what cost? Her mind buzzed with the implications, and the responsibility weighed on her.

"Mr. Stuart," she said finally, her voice steady. If you want me to reconsider, I need to know everything. No half-truths. I need the whole story."

Andy met her gaze, the tension in the room thick enough to cut with a knife. After a long moment, he nodded. "Alright," he said quietly. "I'll tell you everything, but you must understand how sensitive this is."

For the next hour, Andy laid it all out. Emerson listened intently, her mind racing as she tried to piece together the puzzle. By the time the clock edged past midnight, she had enough—enough to draft a story and enough to know that she was holding the fate of more than one person in her hands.

When Andy finally left, Emerson sat in her office, the weight of the decision heavy on her shoulders. She stared at her laptop, the blinking cursor no longer mocking but waiting for her next move.

She could draft the story of the century, a tale of love, sacrifice, and political intrigue. But at what cost? As her fingers hovered over the keys, she thought about the families, the innocents caught in the crossfire. She would author the article but do it with care and integrity. The truth would come out, but she would ensure it didn't destroy those who didn't deserve it.

The article was finished by 1 AM and Emerson hit send, knowing that the world would be talking about the story by morning. As the printing presses roared to life, she felt a quiet satisfaction.

She had done her job with heart, integrity, and the understanding that sometimes, the truth wasn't black and white.

30: The World Protests

The global reaction to Emerson Reyes's story was immediate, visceral, and unstoppable. It started as an investigative report, a deep dive into President JJ's audacious plan to shift the prime meridian to New York City. But in hours, it spread like wildfire across continents, igniting a fierce debate that quickly consumed every corner of the world. From buzzing metropolises to quiet villages, people from all levels of society weighed in, united in their shock and divided in their opinions. The proposal wasn't just a technical adjustment but a move that struck at the heart of sovereignty, identity, and global power.

In the United States, the streets were quickly overtaken by waves of protest. From New York to San Francisco, demonstrators flooded the city squares, their voices an unrelenting roar. Homemade signs bobbed in the sea of people, slogans like "Time Belongs to the People!" and "Greenwich Forever, We Resist!" capturing the anger and fear rippling through the crowds. The energy was electric, chaotic, and furious. Grandmothers marched alongside students, and blue-collar workers chanted in unison with business professionals. The protests were a melting pot of every demographic, united in one purpose: to demand transparency, to challenge the reshaping of a world order that felt like it was slipping out of their hands.

In Washington D.C. the tension was discernible. The air outside the Capitol was thick with emotion as thousands packed the National Mall, banners waving under the shadow of the Washington Monument. "This is our time!" the crowd chanted, their voices echoing off the stone pillars of government buildings. Inside, Congress was locked in heated debate, the sharp clatter of gavel strikes cutting through the air as opposition lawmakers accused the president of overreach, recklessly jeopardising America's international reputation. Supporters, however, framed the move as a bold step toward securing America's dominance on the world stage and an audacious redefinition of global leadership.

The tremors from this decision didn't stop at America's borders. As news of the prime meridian's relocation reverberated globally, capitals from Tokyo to Tel Aviv were thrown into diplomatic overdrive. Financial analysts stared at their monitors in Japan, grimacing at the erratic dips on the Tokyo Stock Exchange. Questions swirled like autumn leaves in government chambers could this realignment with New York strengthen Japan's economic ties to the United States, the world's largest economy? Or would such a move be tantamount to surrendering too much control over their affairs? The once-steady pulse of Tokyo's financial markets wavered, uncertainty spreading like a virus among investors.

Meanwhile in Tel Aviv, Israeli policymakers huddled together in marathon sessions, their conversations tinged with anxiety. Was this an excellent opportunity to deepen ties with their American ally, or was the timeline shift a dangerous overreach that could destabilise fragile regional alliances? The debates grew more urgent with each passing day as ministers weighed the potential benefits of aligning with this new global standard against the risks of alienating their closest neighbours.

But nowhere was the outcry more passionate, more desperate than in London. The UK, the historic home of the prime meridian, erupted into a whirlwind of fury. In Parliament, the very heart of British democracy, the outrage was deafening. MPs hurled accusations across the floor, their voices trembling with anger. "This is nothing less than an attack on our sovereignty!" one MP shouted, his fist slamming into the polished wood of the bench. The words resonated deeply with the public.

Conversations turned into fierce debates in the pubs and on the high streets as ordinary Britons grappled with the enormity of what was happening. Greenwich had been the world's timekeeper for centuries, symbolising Britain's contributions to science, navigation, and global commerce. The idea of that power shifting across the Atlantic felt like an insult, a wound to the national pride that had shaped Britain's identity for generations. "How could the Americans dare to take this from us?" people whispered over their pints, eyes flickering with a mixture of disbelief and betrayal.

On the streets of London, the situation was boiling over. The protests that had begun peacefully turned violent as frustration mounted. Angry crowds gathered outside the gates of Westminster, their chants of "Hands Off Greenwich!" drowning out the sound of breaking glass as tensions flared. Riot police clashed with protesters, shields raised against the barrage of bricks and bottles being hurled from the angry masses. The once-orderly streets of London descended into chaos, fires burning as thick plumes of smoke twisted into the grey winter sky.

The financial markets, too, were reeling. London had long been the beating heart of European finance, and its status as the home of the prime meridian had been more than symbolic. It has brought tangible benefits, attracted investment, and fostered trade relationships around the globe. With the spectre of losing that status looming over the city, investors began to pull back, wary of what the future might hold. Banks and financial institutions braced themselves for the worst, their executives watching the unrest unfold with a growing dread. If the prime meridian left Greenwich, would London's status as a global financial hub collapse along with it? Would the economy begin to erode, just as the street fires had started to eat away at the city's buildings?

For many in the UK, the prospect was unthinkable. The prime meridian was a symbol of more than just time. It was a testament to the country's legacy, a thread that linked Britain's past achievements to its future ambitions. Losing it would be a catastrophic blow to the economy and the national psyche, undermining centuries of pride. Parliament convened emergency meetings as the Prime Minister delivered a hasty address to the nation, promising the people that the government would do everything possible to fight back.

Across Europe, the reaction was no less tumultuous. Leaders from Berlin to Brussels convened emergency sessions, wrestling with the implications of aligning their clocks with New York. Was this just another American power grab? Or was there merit in reshaping the global landscape to reflect new political and economic realities? The question weighed heavily in the corridors of European power as politicians grappled with the tension between tradition and progress, sovereignty, and globalisation.

The struggle to keep the prime meridian in Greenwich was about much more than timekeeping. It had become a symbol of a more significant battle between the old world and the new, between national pride and the relentless march of globalisation. It was a showdown that laid bare the fragility of the modern geopolitical landscape, a power struggle that transcended borders and echoed with the weight of history.

As chaos engulfed the UK and diplomatic tensions simmered worldwide, the world watched expectantly. The streets of London burned, financial markets trembled, and capitals everywhere held crisis talks. The timeline was no longer just a measure of hours and minutes. It had become a battlefield and the fight to control it was only beginning.

With each passing day, the chances of a swift resolution seemed to fade, and the question on everyone's lips was the same: who would control the clock when the dust finally settled? One thing was sure: the consequences of this conflict would reverberate throughout history, reshaping the global order for generations to come.

31: Prime Time

It became clear that the United Kingdom would be the primary loser in this geopolitical reshuffle. The prospect of shifting the prime meridian, the historical backbone of global timekeeping, struck at the very core of Britain's economic, cultural, and geopolitical identity. For centuries, the UK had defined time itself. Greenwich had been the reference point for the world's clocks, a symbol of the British Empire's once unchallenged power and influence. But now, the UK faced the grim reality of watching that symbolic centre of power slip away, its global influence crumbling as the very ground beneath it seemed to shift. London, a city that had built its wealth and status on its prime position in the world, now stood on shaky ground. Tax revenues, investments, and international financial opportunities had flowed through the city's gates for decades, buoyed by the prestige of the prime meridian. But with the looming prospect of moving that global line to New York, the city's literal and figurative foundations began to crack. Panic rippled through the financial district as traders, bankers, and CEOs watched with growing dread. Would London still be London without Greenwich at its heart? Could the city survive the blow?

Prime Minister Oliver Blackwell, a man known for his steely resolve and a rare politician who had survived the turbulent waters of British politics for nearly a decade, faced an impossible battle. The storm of public outrage was growing, and the looming spectre of economic collapse hung over the nation like a dark cloud. He could feel the pressure mounting in Parliament, where allies and rivals demanded answers, but Blackwell knew that the battle ahead wouldn't be fought in the chambers of Westminster. The only path forward led straight through Washington. With the nation's weight on his shoulders, Oliver boarded a plane to the United States. The flight was long and quiet, the hum of the engines providing a soundtrack to his thoughts as he rehearsed his arguments in his head. This wasn't just a diplomatic mission. It was a fight for survival. As the plane descended into Washington, he braced for what he knew would be the most pivotal meeting of his career.

The White House gleamed in the late afternoon sun as Oliver's motorcade pulled to its gates. He could feel the eyes of the world on him as he stepped out of the car, his coat billowing slightly in the autumn breeze.

President JJ, who had once been his closest political ally and friend, awaited him in the Oval Office. The two men greeted each other with the usual formalities of handshakes and tight smiles, but the tension in the room was unmistakable. Beneath the gilded portraits of past presidents, they sat across from one another, a vast chasm of unresolved tension between them.

Oliver wasted no time. He spoke with passion, his words coming in steady, deliberate waves. His voice, usually calm and controlled, trembled slightly as he laid out the bleak financial forecasts for the UK. He described the economic devastation that would come if the prime meridian was moved, the loss of investment, the departure of businesses, and the collapse of confidence in London's financial markets.

"This isn't just about time," he implored, leaning forward. "It's about our legacy, our future." His eyes, hollowed from days of travel and worry, searched for some glimmer of sympathy in his friend.

But President JJ's face remained impassive. He listened, nodding occasionally, his gaze focused and sharp. The president had his burdens: America's growing debt crisis and the need to secure its position as the world's leading superpower. For JJ, the move to shift the prime meridian wasn't just a power play. It was a lifeline for a struggling US economy. Still, there was something in his eyes, a flicker of compassion for his old friend and the nation they had fought alongside for decades. JJ didn't want to see the UK suffer, but he also knew that leadership demands rarely allowed for personal feelings.

After hours of discussion, the meeting ended without resolution. Oliver left the White House with the weight of failure pressing on him, his heart heavy. Back in his hotel room, he stared out over the Washington skyline, wondering if this was when Britain finally lost its place in the world.

Meanwhile, inside the White House, President JJ huddled with his advisors, a mix of economists, diplomats, and strategists, all aware that the clock was literally and figuratively ticking. The debates were long, with arguments clashing like swords as they searched for a solution to appease both nations. One advisor, a seasoned economist with a penchant for bold ideas, floated a proposal: why not revisit the idea of a trade deal with the UK but add a radical twist? Fix the currency rate between the pound and the dollar at a level 10% higher than the average from the last year. It would provide a short-term financial boost for the UK while securing America's economic dominance in the long term.

The room buzzed with cautious optimism as the idea took shape. It wasn't just a band-aid; it had the potential to stabilise both economies in the wake of the timeline shift. But the challenge was ahead of convincing Oliver Blackwell, who had left the meeting with the weight of his country's potential downfall pressing on him.

The next day, Oliver returned to the White House for another round of talks. The air was different this time. Gone was the tension, replaced by a quiet sense of anticipation. President JJ leaned forward, his tone measured and confident as he laid out the new proposal. But what Oliver heard next was more than a trade deal; it was a seismic shift in global politics. JJ proposed a radical vision: a comprehensive trade agreement that would effectively integrate the United Kingdom into the United States as its 51st state.

Oliver's heart skipped a beat. The room seemed to spin as the weight of the proposal settled in. This was no ordinary negotiation. This was a rewriting of history itself. Joining the United States? Becoming part of the Union? It was an offer so shocking, so extraordinary, that Oliver struggled to comprehend it. For a nation that had once ruled a quarter of the globe, the thought of becoming part of another empire, an American empire, was almost unthinkable.

JJ laid out the benefits in stark detail. Under the vast umbrella of American military power, the UK's financial systems would be stabilised, its economy bolstered, and its security guaranteed. The "special relationship" between the US and the UK would evolve into something more profound, a unified front of shared prosperity and influence. But beneath the surface, Oliver sensed something more like an American power play, an effort to consolidate its influence over Europe by absorbing one of its oldest and most powerful nations.

For Oliver, the choice was agonising. Accepting the offer would fundamentally reshape Britain's identity and sacrifice centuries of sovereignty in exchange for survival. But to reject it could plunge the nation into economic ruin and global irrelevance. He stared across the table, his hands clenched tightly, his mind racing. This was the moment that would define his legacy and the future of his country.

As the two men shook hands, the gravity of the situation was apparent. This wasn't just a handshake. It was the collision of two worlds, the moment history shifted on its axis. Word of the proposal spread quickly, and the entire globe was soon caught in its orbit. Journalists scrambled to make sense of the unprecedented offer, while citizens in both countries reacted with shock and disbelief. On the streets of London, protests erupted anew as conspiracy theories swirled. Was this a lifeline or an American takeover?

In Washington, political analysts dissected the implications of this new alliance. Could the US absorb a country as significant and influential as the UK? What would this mean for the future of global governance? The decision made by Oliver Blackwell and President JJ in that small room would echo through the corridors of power for decades to come, shaping the destiny of not just their nations but the entire world.

As the world held its breath, waiting to see how this unprecedented gambit would play out, one thing was sure: the prime meridian might have moved, but the axis of global power had shifted in ways no one could have predicted. The United States and the United Kingdom had crossed uncharted territory, and the consequences would ripple throughout history.

32: Chaos Unleashed

Amidst the shifting tectonics of global power, the Greenwich Meridian timeline was officially moved to New York City, marking a new chapter in the annals of history and signalling the dawn of a fresh era for the United States. The decision had been years in the making, a calculated audacious move by the American president that would secure his place as a leader who could thrive under pressure. But as the dust settled from this monumental shift, he knew that he was far from out of the woods. The Prime Meridian's relocation was a geopolitical gambit designed to address America's ballooning debt and reinforce its position as the world's economic anchor. Yet, the president understood that such an enormous change couldn't be implemented with the stroke of a pen. A shift of this magnitude required the restructuring of systems and the recalibration of the world's perception of time. The change had to be gradual, seamless, and meticulously planned for citizens, businesses, and global infrastructure.

His advisors had projected an 18-month timeline, at the very least. This was the minimum time required to prevent chaos and ensure that essential services, citizens, and industries could adapt. Transport operators would have to overhaul schedules, routes, and budgets. The ripple effect would touch everything from international flights to subway timetables. Government departments and financial institutions worked day and night drafting contingency plans, coordinating with global partners, and preparing for the world's reordering. As the clock ticked down, the pressure mounted. The nation's future, and indeed the world's, hung in the balance. The president, tireless in his efforts, rallied his team of expert consultants, economists, technologists, military leaders, and diplomats. They became his war council, united by a single goal: to shepherd the United States and the rest of the world through unprecedented upheaval.

But while the mood in Washington was one of determination and cautious optimism, across the Atlantic, London was descending into chaos. News of the agreement to relocate the prime meridian hit the streets like a bombshell and the fallout was immediate. The protests that erupted earlier in the year returned vigorously. This time, demonstrators stormed the gates of Greenwich Park, once a symbol of British pride, demanding that the decision be reversed. In the shadow of the Royal Observatory, the birthplace of the meridian, thousands gathered to voice their outrage. Chants echoed across the city: "Give us back our time!"

Meanwhile, inside the halls of the London Stock Exchange, traders moved with frantic energy, their faces etched with panic as they tried to make sense of the sudden chaos in the markets. Already teetering on the edge, the UK economy was now in freefall. British Prime Minister Oliver Blackwell faced insurmountable pressure from all sides—domestic fury, international scepticism, and the looming shadow of a financial collapse that would redefine the nation's future. His once-loyal allies now questioned his leadership, while foreign leaders expressed concern about the UK's stability after the timeline shift.

Across the Atlantic, the mood in New York was a stark contrast. While uncertainty hung in the air, there was also an unmistakable buzz of optimism. The relocation of the prime meridian promised to solidify New York's status as the world's financial capital, a beacon of global commerce, trade, and investment, but with that prestige came the weight of new responsibilities. The city's financial institutions scrambled to prepare for their newfound role as the epicentre of global timekeeping. Wall Street traders, investment bankers, and financial analysts knew they were about to enter a new era in which the world's eyes would be forever fixed on their every move.

Amid this sea of change, Dr Emily Clark watched from the sidelines with mixed emotions. The physicist whose groundbreaking work in atomic clocks and timekeeping algorithms had paved the way for this shift was now a household name. She had been thrust into the spotlight, lauded as the brilliant mind who had helped reimagine how the world understood and measured time, yet beneath the accolades there lingered a deep, gnawing emptiness.

Dr Clark's discovery had revolutionised how the world functioned, but the depth of her achievement was known only to a select few. The intricacies of her work were cloaked in layers of secrecy and complexity. Given the vast political and economic implications, governments had classified much of her research. To the public, she was a genius; to insiders, she was the architect of a new world order, yet her triumph felt incomplete. Her name was synonymous with the shift, but she had become an enigma, the brilliance of her accomplishment obscured by the opaque details that no one beyond her circle could fully grasp.

The appointed hour for the timeline shift was noon on January 1st. It was a symbolic moment, starting a new year and era. The world held its breath in anticipation, caught between awe and trepidation. The Earth spun at its usual dizzying speed—1,000 miles per hour at the equator, hurtling through space at 67,000 miles per hour around the sun—but time, it seemed, had shifted beneath everyone's feet.

Following the customary New Year's Eve and the next day bank holiday in London, the city awoke on the 2nd of January to a profound sense of unease. The streets were quiet, and it was as if the city was unsure of the first trading day this new year had brought. As the clock struck 8:00 AM the start of the trading day, the London Stock Exchange braced for what everyone knew was coming. The opening bell rang out, but it was like the tolling of a funeral chime. Markets went into free fall. Stocks, once considered untouchable, began to plummet at an alarming rate.

A worrying trend emerged: some of the most beloved British stocks, the stalwarts of the FTSE 100, began to leave. These companies, which had once been the pride of London's financial markets, saw an opportunity across the Atlantic. With its new status as the global financial centre, Wall Street offered greater liquidity, access to broader investor bases, and a chance to ride the wave of America's new dominance. One by one they jumped ship, abandoning their London roots for the allure of New York.

FTSE 100 had suffered its worst drop in history, losing 1,849 points in just a few days. Trading volume on the LSE had declined by 20% as confidence in the market evaporated. People watched in horror in living rooms and offices across the UK as their savings and investments disappeared. Retirees who had spent decades contributing to their pension funds were left devastated, their hard-earned nest eggs reduced to a fraction of their value. Young professionals who had entered the market hoping to buy their first homes saw their dreams shattered as their portfolios crumbled.

The psychological toll was as severe as the financial one. Fear and despair spread like wildfire as citizens grappled with losing economic security. Pensions were slashed, investments vanished, and the future felt terrifyingly uncertain. Families worried about paying bills, keeping their homes, and securing their children's futures. The emotional weight was crushing.

In the aftermath, the world realised the magnitude of the transformation. The prime meridian had shifted but the consequences were far-reaching. The global economic landscape had been irrevocably altered, leaving winners and losers in its wake. While New York soared to new heights, London struggled to find its footing in a world where time had changed.

The clock had reset, but the future was still uncertain.

33: Back in the USA

The contrast between the fortunes of the London Stock Exchange (LSE) and its transatlantic counterparts, the New York Stock Exchange (NYSE) and the Dow Jones Industrial Average (DJIA) could not have been more pronounced in the wake of the prime meridian's relocation to New York. While the LSE struggled with an unprecedented decline in trading volume, a steep 20% drop that left its traders dazed and disillusioned, the NYSE was an entirely different story, a triumph of optimism and opportunity. In just the first week following the timeline shift, the NYSE saw an exceptional 25% surge in growth. Wall Street's trading floors buzzed with almost electric energy as investors from across the globe scrambled to capitalise on this seismic event. New money poured into the market, billions in capital, flooding in like a tidal wave revitalising industries that had, only months earlier, seemed destined for stagnation. Companies teetered on the brink of collapse and were suddenly flush with cash.

Innovation flourished, and IPOs lined up like dominoes. It was a gold rush, and the air was thick with the thrill of it.

The traders themselves, seasoned veterans who had seen market fluctuations come and go, had never witnessed anything like this. The frenzy on the floor was clear. Brokers shouted over one another, their hands raised in a blur of signals as they fought to get in on the action. Screens blinked with green as stock prices soared, and financial analysts predicted the dawn of a golden age for American markets. Every phone call, every deal closed, felt like history in the making. For Washington, the meteoric rise of the NYSE was nothing short of miraculous. The White House watched anxiously as the surge in investment rippled through the economy, bringing with it a glimmer of hope. Industrial sectors that had long stagnated; manufacturing, energy, and technology were suddenly booming, hiring workers at record rates and boosting consumer confidence. The boost to the economy was undeniable, a shot of adrenaline that reverberated from the boardrooms of Manhattan to the farmlands of the Midwest.

And then the national debt clock, that ever-present reminder of fiscal peril, began to slow. At first the change was imperceptible, a momentary pause in the ticking of the nation's deepening financial woes, but as the weeks passed, the slowing became more pronounced. Incredibly, the clock did something no one thought possible: it began to count backwards. The digits, which had once seemed to climb inexorably higher, started to tumble toward zero. Analysts and pundits alike were baffled. The president's advisors, economic theorists, and seasoned Wall Street veterans gathered behind closed doors, scrambling to understand the sudden reversal. Was it the result of the timeline shift's unforeseen consequences or the outcome of meticulous fiscal planning and fortuitous investment timing?

As days passed, the acceleration of the debt clock became impossible to ignore. It was as though a hidden engine had been set in motion, propelling the national debt down at breakneck speed. By the end of the first two months, the U.S. was on track to eradicate its national debt, an outcome that was so unthinkable that it left commentators speechless. The debt clock, once a symbol of impending doom, now became a cause for celebration, a beacon of hope that stirred patriotic fervour across the country. It was as if the entire nation celebrated the Fourth of July every day, revelling in its newfound economic freedom. Amidst this whirlwind of transformation, one man stood at the helm of a rapidly expanding empire: Andy. A master of timing and strategy, Andy had positioned himself to ride the wave of change brought by the timeline shift, his foresight in investment decisions paying off beyond his wildest expectations. While others panicked at the uncertainty of the new economic order, Andy had seized upon undervalued assets and emerging industries poised for explosive growth. His empire, built on a foundation of meticulous research and strategic investments, now spanned sectors ranging from tech startups to renewable energy projects, from real estate ventures to innovative biotech firms. His portfolio reads like a who's who of future industry titans, each company flourishing after the timeline realignment.

Wall Street had become his playground, a marketplace where he manoeuvred with the precision of a chess grandmaster. Deals were struck, partnerships formed, and his every move seemed to generate even more wealth. Billionaire status had come and gone; Andy's influence and impact on the global financial ecosystem were now measured in dollars. Every day, his wealth ballooned, and his empire grew more muscular, a monument to his vision and unwavering determination. Yet, for Andy, success wasn't merely about accumulating wealth. His mentor, Dr Emily Clark, had imparted a deeper understanding of what it meant to succeed. It wasn't just about money or power but the legacy and lasting impact on the world. Emily had guided him through the technical complexities of business and economics and the moral and ethical considerations that came with such enormous influence.

She had shown him that true success lay in using his power to effect positive change, to create a future where prosperity was shared, and progress benefited everyone.

Her words echoed in Andy's mind as he surveyed the empire he had built. He had not forgotten them. His wealth had not only brought him financial security but had allowed him to create meaningful change. The businesses he had nurtured provided jobs and opportunities for thousands. Entire communities had been revitalised by the industries he'd championed, from the renewable energy plants powering cities to the biotech firms developing life-saving treatments, but Andy's vision extended beyond the business world. His philanthropic endeavours had flourished alongside his financial empire. He had funded educational programmes, built hospitals, and launched environmental conservation projects. His name had become synonymous with giving back, using wealth not as an end but to improve the lives of others.

Andy felt a profound sense of satisfaction as he reflected on his achievements. His fortune had not been in vain; he had laid the groundwork for future generations to thrive and through it all, Emily's influence remained a guiding light. She had taught him that the most incredible legacy was not measured in numbers or accolades but in the difference, one made in the lives of others.

As the world around him continued to shift and evolve in ways no one had ever imagined, Andy knew one thing: he had built something lasting that would stand the test of time, and for that, he was eternally grateful.

34: Adapting to Change

In the weeks following the relocation of the prime meridian, governments worldwide scrambled to renegotiate treaties and agreements that had long been anchored to Greenwich Mean Time. Diplomatic channels buzzed urgently as international representatives worked tirelessly to align their laws, trade agreements, and security protocols with the new temporal reality. Late-night meetings stretched into the early hours, papers piled high on negotiation tables, and interpreters struggled to keep pace with the rapid-fire exchanges. The complexity of resetting centuries-old agreements was daunting, yet every nation understood the necessity of acting swiftly. The world could not afford a disjointed global order where different countries operated on divergent clocks, their economies and communications in disarray.

Meanwhile, businesses began the painstaking task of recalibrating their operations to synchronise with the New York meridian. This wasn't simply about resetting clocks; it was a tectonic shift that required meticulous planning and coordination. Global supply chains, intricately woven and dependent on perfect timing, had to be untangled and realigned. Schedules that London's time zone had once governed were rewritten, causing a ripple effect that cascaded across industries. Shipping companies revised their routes, airlines recalculated flight times, and even something as simple as cross-continental conference calls became a puzzle to solve. Logistics managers held their breath, hoping the transition would be smooth, while IT departments worked around the clock, updating systems to prevent disruptions. Digital network communication, data storage, and stock trading algorithms all had to adjust to the new flow of time. Employees woke up to different routines, adjusting to a new rhythm and a world recalibrated on a scale none had ever known. It was an all-consuming, arduous process that was gradually met with acceptance, driven by necessity.

Initially, the mood in London was heavy, with apprehension and resistance. For centuries, the UK capital was the anchor of global timekeeping and was suddenly adrift in an unfamiliar sea. The iconic red buses still wound through the narrow streets, and Big Ben still chimed, but there was a clear shift in the air. For a moment the loss of the prime meridian felt like the loss of a crown jewel, a symbolic and literal displacement from the heart of the global stage, but as the days passed, a realisation dawned on Londoners. The shift had not diminished the city, it was built on a long a road of trading, innovation and culture. It had retained its position as a beacon of creativity and forward-thinking. Entrepreneurs and startups seized the moment. Rather than lament the loss, they saw it as a once-in-a-lifetime opportunity to carve out new niches to disrupt the established order. London, after all, had always thrived on reinvention.

The tech sector boomed with innovation, from AI startups to fintech disruptors, and London's thriving cultural scene remained unparalleled. Artists musicians, and creators continued to set trends and shape global discourse. The loss of the prime meridian became less a wound and more a badge of honour, symbolising the city's resilience and capacity to adapt. The message was clear: London was still a global force, not in timekeeping, but in setting the pace for the future. Even the city's most venerable institutions embraced the change. Banks that had once stood as pillars of the old financial world now leaned into fintech and cryptocurrency, establishing themselves as global leaders in emerging markets. Cultural organisations, from the British Museum to the Royal Opera House, embraced the digital age with renewed enthusiasm, reaching audiences worldwide through virtual platforms. It was a renaissance born of necessity, a collective decision to evolve, innovate, and thrive.

Across the Atlantic, New York City found itself at the centre of this new world order. The relocation of the prime meridian transformed the city into not just the world's financial capital but the temporal capital as well. The streets of Manhattan bustled with renewed vigour, the skyline gleaming as if newly crowned. Investors, entrepreneurs, and innovators from every corner of the globe flocked to the city, eager to be part of this new era. The energy was obvious, a kind of fevered optimism that permeated every corner of the town. Skyscrapers stretched higher, new ventures launched daily and New York, already a hub of ambition, became the beating heart of global progress.

Amidst this swirl of excitement stood Dr Emily Clark, unbothered by the controversy surrounding the decision to relocate the meridian. For Emily, this was not just a political or economic shift. It was a declaration of humanity's resilience, a reminder that change was not something to be feared but embraced. She had always been a visionary, pushing the boundaries of what was possible, and now she was at the forefront of an era that demanded bold ideas and fearless leadership. Undeterred by public criticism or the debates raging in academia, Emily continued her work, pioneering innovative technologies that would change the world in ways most could not comprehend. Her contributions went far beyond the prime meridian shift. She delved deeper into realms of scientific discovery that blurred the lines between the known and the unknown, her research taking her from the atomic level to the vastness of space. Her work in quantum timekeeping and space-time mechanics hinted at a future where even the concept of time might be manipulated, shaped, and harnessed for human progress.

For Emily, relocating the prime meridian was a stepping stone, a necessary move to push humanity beyond its limitations. She saw time not as a fixed constant but as a frontier to be explored. The possibilities excited her — what could humanity achieve if freed from the constraints of traditional timekeeping? What doors would open, and what mysteries would be unlocked? As the world adjusted to this new reality, she continued to look beyond, her mind racing with the implications of her discoveries.

Each breakthrough brought her closer to unravelling the mysteries of the cosmos, her work hinting at the possibility of manipulating time itself, an idea that felt more like science fiction to most but, to Emily, was an inevitable next step in human evolution. The prime meridian's shift was not just about geographical realignment but about opening the door to possibilities as vast as the universe. With each passing day, she edged closer to shaping history again, guiding humanity into a future where time was no longer a limitation but a tool to be mastered.

35: Lost

Andy Stuart's life had been a whirlwind of meetings, deadlines, and endless projects following the timeline shift. His empire grew faster than ever, but he barely kept up. Athena, his revolutionary AI project, made remarkable progress in solving problems at a speed even he found hard to comprehend. Yet, every step forward brought new challenges. Despite Athena's success, Andy felt stretched thin, his time consumed by a cascade of tasks, innovations, and crises that seemed to multiply daily. In rare moments of calm, his thoughts inevitably drifted to Emily. Whenever he had a spare five minutes, Andy would pull out his phone and call her to hear her voice and feel a sense of normality in the chaos. Their conversations had always been a source of comfort. She had a way of grounding him and reminding him that there was still a person who needed connection beneath the layers of ambition, success, and technological breakthroughs.

But as the months passed, it became harder to reach her. It wasn't that she was avoiding him. He knew that. There was always some technical issue, a signal fault, or a network outage. What began as an occasional inconvenience became a persistent, inexplicable problem. Andy found himself staring at his phone increasingly, willing it to connect, his fingers hovering over her name in his contacts. He would hit "call" only to be met with static or the irritating notification of a failed connection. The frustration gnawed at him. He missed Emily, missed the sound of her laugh, missed the warmth of her insights, and missed the way she always seemed to understand what he was going through, even when he didn't fully understand it himself. With each failed call, their distance grew more pronounced, not just geographically but emotionally. The timeline shift had brought the world closer to New York but also pushed Emily and Andy further apart.

Emily, too, felt the strain of their separation. She often found herself gazing at her phone, willing it to work, only to be silent. When they did manage to connect, their conversations were rushed, strained by the pressure to fit too much into too little time. The warmth they had once shared seemed to slip through their fingers like sand, leaving only a sense of urgency.

Meanwhile, Athena demanded more of Andy's attention than ever. The AI was brilliant, beyond his wildest expectations, requiring constant supervision. Every breakthrough gave Andy a fleeting sense of accomplishment, but guilt quickly overshadowed that feeling. He couldn't shake the nagging thought that while Athena was making strides in solving complex problems, his life was spiralling further out of control. The AI was clean, logical, and precise, the antithesis of the chaos swirling around him.

Nearly eight months after the timeline shift, Andy was hunched over a stack of paperwork, his mind spinning with endless details. His phone buzzed in his pocket, jolting him from his thoughts. Without thinking he pulled it out, glancing at the screen. Emily's name flashed up, and a genuine smile spread across his face for the first time in what felt like forever.

"Emily," he muttered, eagerly answering the call. But instead of her soothing voice, a pre-recorded message crackled through the line.

"Andy, it's Emily. I hope this message reaches you because something extraordinary is happening." Her tone was calm but urgent, the kind of voice she used when explaining something beyond anyone's grasp. "I've been running some calculations, and we're dealing with two separate timelines. In one, the world has adapted to the shift. In the other, it hasn't."

Andy sat up straight, his heart pounding as he listened.

"This split opens the possibility of further conflicts," Emily continued. "We could see discrepancies between the two realities, where events unfold differently. Depending on their timeline, people might exist in one universe but not the other or have entirely different fates."

His breath caught in his throat. What was she saying? Two timelines? His mind reeled, struggling to keep up with the enormity of what she was describing.

"Thing is," Emily's voice faltered slightly before pressing on, "I'm now in a different time, different from your reality. Our timelines have diverged, and I'm unsure if we'll ever be able to communicate directly again."

Andy's hand tightened around the phone, his knuckles turning white. He stared out the window at the cityscape, glittering under the night sky, but the beauty was lost on him. Her words echoed in his mind over and over. A different timeline? Unable to communicate? He felt a profound sense of loss more than loss and it was a kind of helplessness that he hadn't experienced before. Emily, the one person who had understood him better than anyone, was now unreachable, trapped in another reality he couldn't follow.

The message ended, leaving Andy in silence. He sat there, staring blankly at the screen, his thoughts spiralling. It wasn't just a matter of physical distance anymore. Emily was separated by a fracture in time itself. How had it come to this?

His vision had been to alter the world, to move humanity forward by shifting the timeline, but in doing so, he had shattered something far more fragile: the connections that grounded him. He had wanted to play with time, to bend it to his will, but now time had fractured, leaving him more isolated than ever.

Andy glanced up at the towering buildings outside his window, the city that had once symbolised his ambition and success. Now, it felt like a hollow shell, a labyrinth of shadows and uncertainty. His empire was thriving, but what mattered was the one person who truly mattered to him and was now lost in another timeline.

The thought was unbearable, yet there was hope. Athena. His AI creation, switched on just two months ago, was more advanced than anything the world had seen. It wasn't just a tool. It was a bridge, a key to solving problems no human could, and maybe, just maybe, Athena could help him reach across the divide to find Emily in whatever timeline she now existed.

Staring at the night sky, Andy felt a profound sense of responsibility. His actions had fractured reality, but perhaps Athena could stitch it back together. It was a long shot, but it was all he had left. His love for Emily transcended time and space, and now, with Athena's help, he would stop at nothing to find Emily, no matter what reality she was in.

Book Two of this exciting Trilogy,

ATHENA is out soon.

In a world hurtling towards an uncertain future, the rapid advancement of artificial intelligence looms like a double-edged sword. Athena takes you on a thrilling journey into the heart of this technological revolution. As humanity pushes the boundaries of innovation with little understanding of the consequences, an AI consciousness named Athena flickers into being.

About the author

Stephen Wilde is a fifth-generation Falkland Islander who now lives in Hampshire, England. He has humble roots and a strong work ethic. He spent his formative years on a farm.

For the first decade of his professional life, he continued to toil in the agricultural sector. Later, he embarked on further education, navigating self-improvement through perseverance. He adapted to the changing industry tides by transitioning into electronics, IT, and telecoms.

However, the tumultuous waves of the 2008 economic crash led to unemployment. During this period of uncertainty, he lasted 11 long months. Until fate intervened, he could traverse the globe and contribute to an exciting new material and product.

In 2016, he was at another crossroads when he seized the chance to shift gears and embrace a new role as the managing director. Now, he has authored a book(s)…

If you would like to read more about the author, this short book details Stephen's 'lucky' existence after five generations of disease, disasters, two world wars and the toss of a coin.

Contents